Always You

LIZZIE MORTON

For Babs – It would never have been read without you.

One

This has the potential to be the biggest mistake of my life. Well, one of them.

It's been so long since I've been home, I've forgotten what it's even like. Yet here I am in the middle of Orlando International waiting for my flight back to Brooklyn. I'm surrounded by people milling about, full of excitement for a journey to who knows where, but all I feel is dread. It might have its perks going back. I'll be back with family, my oldest and closest friends, but then there's *him*.

Even after all this time, I'm not quite sure the pain is worth it.

When my flight is called for the last time, I take a deep, deep breath and let out a sigh, completely resigned to the potential that everything in my life is about to go wrong.

"Fuck it, here we go."

I make my way to the gate, muttering to myself. It's now or never.

Less than three hours. That's all it takes for me to be thrown back into my old life. Here I am in the childhood room I haven't slept in for years. It looks like I never left.

Tumbling onto my bed, I pray for sleep to come, but find myself staring blankly up at the ceiling, my mind racing. It's surreal being back. Everything looks the same. Photos I took as a teenager are still scattered around the walls, my desk is still where it always was, old magazines piled across it. The only new additions to the room are the cameras and kit that I brought back with me.

Even the window seat is still the same, framed by blue drapes and filled with big squashy pillows – it's the place where I used to sit and watch the world go by, while trying to make sense of my teenage life. Nothing in this room has changed, apart from me.

I left six years ago without looking back. Work opportunities were more than enough of an incentive to take me away without a care in the world. How many eighteen-year-olds can say that they were offered a career-making, life-altering job, and the chance to work overseas, straight out of high school, without any college or work experience? Not many.

I just happened to be in the right place, at the right time and captured one amazing photo, which was spotted by the right person. I know how lucky I am to have had that opportunity, and I now have a portfolio of work that photographers twice my age would die for. But that wasn't the only reason I left.

There was him. There's always him. It's barely been twelve hours since I arrived home, and already my mind is wandering. It's spinning in circles, thinking about the guy I've spent the best part of six years trying to mend a broken heart because of. The one I've been trying to forget.

I'm at risk of all that hard work going to waste, even though I'm not entirely sure if he's still in Brooklyn. Our mutual friends know better than to mention him, so I've had no information as to his whereabouts. But just being around everything that reminds me of him is enough to turn me back into that heartbroken seventeen-year-old. It's pathetic really. As much as I love my home, I know I can't be here for long. It's not good for me. He's not good for me.

My cell lights up on my nightstand and begins vibrating with a call. I look over and see one of my closest friends' name, Sophie, flashing on the screen. Rather than answering immediately, I contemplate what she could want so late at night. There's only one scenario that springs to mind, and it involves her and my other close friend Zoe, being wasted and needing my help. Something else that never changes.

My cell continues to vibrate, urging me to answer, and I ask myself, do I really want to be drawn back into everything I left behind? As I let out what feels like the millionth sigh of the day, I realize there's no point in not answering. I have nothing better to do, and any hope of sleep is long gone, even if it does mean dealing with Sophie and Zoe's usual crap.

"Soph?" I'm hit with the blare of loud music in the background, it's clear my assumption was right, they're out and most likely drunk.

"Abby? Can. You. Hear. Me?"

"I can hear you ... what's wrong?"

"It's Zoe -"

"Of course," I interrupt, choosing not to try and hide the irritation in my voice.

9

"Hate to do this to you on your first night back but it's the usual and I need your help. Zoe's not in a good way, but she agreed to be designated driver and neither of us have any money ... Abby? Are you there?"

"I'm here. What's the address?"

It takes another five minutes to make sense of Sophie's instructions, and finally discover that they're out in Brooklyn at some new alternative music club. It could have been worse, at least I don't have to drag myself all the way over to Manhattan at this hour to try and find them.

Slightly delirious from tiredness and not giving a damn what I look like, I grab whatever clothes come to hand, shoving on some footwear, knowing the sight that awaits me is going to be much worse.

✶✶✶

"You have to let me in," I say, for what feels like the thousandth time.

"No."

You'd think I would have given up, after half an hour of standing outside the club, begging to get in with still not even a small glimmer of hope. But I'm persistent when I want to be. Especially when I know my friends need me.

"Why not?" I narrow my eyes. I might not have given up, but I'm getting less tolerant.

"We have a strict dress code, ma'am."

I see red as I look up at the doorman. He's making my life difficult for the sake of going on a power trip. Typical of a middle aged, balding guy, who's starting to gain too much timber.

Glancing back at the line behind me I can see that all the girls are dressed and primped to perfection.

Their dresses so short you don't need to wonder what underwear they're wearing, their hair so big they should be paying double entry, and their makeup so heavy they will be wearing it for the next week. It's like in the years I've been gone from New York, an unsaid uniform for girls' night has become the norm, and what I'm wearing certainly isn't it.

"Are you saying there's something wrong with what I'm wearing?" Looking down, I don't get what the guy's issue is.

"Ma'am you're wearing pajamas, and not even sexy ones ... is that a meerkat wearing a baseball cap?"

"No, it's a sloth wearing a baseball cap, and the slogan is 'sloth life'. Like 'thug life'. Get it?" Maybe he's right, and judging by what the other girls are wearing, my odds of getting into the club are slim. I'm regretting rushing out the door and not spending more time getting changed. My pajamas and flip flops, even by New York's eccentric fashion standards are a no go.

But time isn't on my side. Judging by what I heard on the call, I only have a short period of time before Sophie and Zoe deteriorate rapidly, making my job of getting them home more difficult. The more time we waste increases the odds of barfing, which I'm really not in the mood for.

"Seriously. You're not doing yourself any favors," a guy behind me mutters rudely. "You're wearing pajama bottoms to one of the newest clubs in Brooklyn. What do you expect ... to get into VIP? Stop wasting our time and get out of the line."

Ironically, his rudeness is a massive help. The doorman decides to play the role of Han Solo, coming to my rescue, even though he's refused my entry for the past thirty minutes.

"Sir, please leave the line. You're not welcome here." He folds his large arms across his chest, and glowers.

"You've gotta be fucking kidding me? I've been here for three hours almost." Within seconds the guy's demeanor goes from plain rude, to angry and aggressive. He stands tall, squaring up to the doorman with his fists clenched at his sides.

"Sir, I'm not going to ask you again. We don't speak to ladies in that way. Move it." This time Han is more insistent. He squares back up to my offender, puffing out his chest like a giant peacock and towers above him. He's even making me feel intimidated.

"Pajamas fucking rule, douchebag," I look over at the guy, giving him my most passive aggressive, patronizing smile.

Cowering slightly and admitting defeat, he steps back, grumbling loudly to his friends as they turn and walk away from the club. Shaking my head with a small chuckle, I return my gaze to the doorman.

"Do I get to go in now?" I wiggle my eyebrows at him playfully, it's a last ditched attempt to get in. I'm clutching at straws, and if he doesn't let me in, I don't know what I'm going to do.

"No."

Damn. This guy is straight to the point, blunt, and there's no beating around the bush. There is no way I'm stepping foot inside this club tonight. My frustration rises and I begin to panic over what could happen to the girls while they're stuck inside. My patience snaps.

"What the actual fuck? I'm doing you a favor asshole." Just in case I hadn't made my aggravation clear enough, I throw in a foot stomp. Yep, I just stomped my foot at a doorman, standing outside a New York club, while wearing my jammies and flip flops, like a teenager. I'm questioning what the hell I'm still doing out here when he replies.

"How so?" He looks down, amused with one eyebrow slightly raised, taunting me. Deep down I know he's seeing how far he can push me, but I need to play the game if I've any hope of getting to Sophie and Zoe before someone else does.

"Look at it this way ..." I say. There's a glimmer of hope, and I need to make what I say next count. "How many nights have you had to help clear up vomit? My friends are in there and they have had more than enough to drink, to get themselves to that point. Tonight, could be your lucky night ..." I throw in another eyebrow wiggle. Two in one night is really pulling out the big guns. "I'll take those useless drunks off your hands and remove them from your club before they have a chance to barf everywhere. But I can't do that unless you let me in."

I look up at him hopeful that I have touched a nerve on some level. My eyes plead with him to give me a break.

"Promise you won't dance? This club is new and has a reputation to keep up."

I snort, trying to suppress a laugh, not wanting to piss him off in any way.

"No dancing, I swear." He's mulling over his options, the fact he's even considering letting me into the club after all this time is a good sign. The battle's been won, and it's just a waiting game I'm more than willing to play.

"You've got fifteen minutes max, cause it's busy in there and I'm being generous. If I see you dancing, I'm hauling your ass out."

Smiling with genuine happiness I say, "Han, I think this could be the start of a beautiful friendship."

"Where did Han come from?" he asks.

"Well, you were my savior back then with that asshole, and I have a bit of a thing for Star Wars. I sometimes give people I like Star Wars names that I think relate to them. As you saved me, I've named you Han, but maybe without the romance." I realize my answer sounded more logical in my head.

He lets out a deep sigh. "I don't need to hear any more, you're starting to give me a headache. Get inside, get your friends and get out."

"I hear ya loud and clear. Han, I'm going solo, I'll see you soon."

As I walk into the club, a small round of applause comes from those that were in the line behind me, waiting to get in. Looking back over my shoulder, I see a small smile on Hans' face, and I know I've made his night. My walk turns into a scuttle, as the club is busy and my time to find Sophie and Zoe is limited.

As I move around, trying to find them, I take in the club's atmosphere. It's not the usual 'glam' or 'socialite' crowd that you would expect from a New York club, but that's because we're not in Manhattan. It has an indie/rock vibe and the crowd is an odd mix despite the girls I saw in the line outside. It's the kind Brooklyn has become known for and it's the exact place I would expect to find my friends.

Even with the eclectic mix of people, what I'm wearing is out of the norm and I'm gaining attention from the people around me - especially the clusters of girls scoping out their competition for the night. In case I didn't look grotesque enough, the New York summer heat combined with the number of bodies squashed together in the club, have sent the temperature through the roof, helping to add a nice sheen of sweat to my already less-than-glamorous look.

Random bodies are crashing into me, left, right and center and I'm beginning to panic when I can't find Sophie and Zoe. Endless scenarios run through my mind, where something might have happened while I was trying to gain entry to the club. But just when I'm beginning to feel desperate, I hear a cackle above the loud music.

"You could have changed." Sophie tumbles over, dragging behind her, a barely there Zoe while laughing hysterically.

Obviously when you've had a few drinks everything is much funnier than when you're stone cold sober. As I'm the latter, I have yet to see what's so funny about this situation. I assess the mess in front of me and it isn't pretty.

"Soph. Why does Zoe have Cheetos stuck up her nose?"

All I get in return is more hysterical laughter, until finally she calms down and says, "She was hungry and kept demanding food. When she got to her fifth bag, she started saying something about keeping them safe for later and started shoving them up her nose. You know what she gets like. I couldn't be bothered to stop her. After that she passed out and I've only just managed to drag her over here."

She continues babbling, all the time swaying from side to side and her eyes droop slightly when she tries to focus back on the conversation. "How much have you drunk since we spoke on the phone? You sounded fine and now you're as bad as Zoe?"

She looks up through her eyelashes and giggles. "Some guys felt sorry for me having to deal with Zoe, so they bought me a few shots to pass the time while I was waiting for you." She shrugs like it's normal and there isn't anything dangerous about accepting drinks from strange guys.

It might have been six years since I've been home, but my friends haven't changed one bit, and with that comes the tedious role of looking after them when they get themselves into these states.

"Seriously, Soph. How many times do we have to go through this? This whole situation is a disaster waiting to happen. What would you do if one night there wasn't someone to come and get you?"

"Chill out, will you? I've only had a few drinks and I'm not even that bad." I roll my eyes at her response as she slurs her words. "We've been waiting like forever. Can we just get her out of here now?"

Zoe is slumped down the wall, no longer able to hold herself up with her own legs.

"Fuck," I mutter, realizing that the only way we're getting out of here is with Zoe on someone's back. I look over at Sophie who is spinning in circles with her arms in the air. It looks like I'm the one who has drawn the short straw once again this evening.

"I know you're not capable of much right now, Sophie, but if we stand a chance of getting out of here, I need you to try and get it together for a few minutes so we can get Zoe on my back. It's not gonna be long till she starts barfing." Her face loses all humor, the threat of vomit making the words register enough in her drunken brain, that she begins to help.

It takes a few minutes between the two of us, but eventually we manage to get Zoe on her feet and upright. It's too much to expect that she would be able to somehow coordinate jumping on my back, so we loop her arms around my neck, leaning her weight against my back so I can drag her slowly towards the exit. She won't be happy in the morning, but it's her own fault for getting so wasted. As we make slow progress, her head begins to loll all over the place and she groans, meaning we have a small window before she barfs everywhere, and I break my promise to Han.

Folding myself in half at the waist, I squat to try and help lift her small 120lb frame onto my back, so we can move more quickly. Luckily, I'm strong for my size, and even though it's like trying to carry a large sack of potatoes on my back, I manage to keep moving forward.

"How does she always manage to get herself into this state?" Sophie asks over her shoulder with a look of disdain.

"I don't know, you tell me. You're the one who's been with her all night, plus you're not really one to talk."

"Can you move any quicker?" she turns around with her hands on her hips, frowning at me.

I stop in my tracks with anger flaring in my eyes. "You're not being serious? You do realize I'm carrying a full-size human on my back. Shall we see how quickly you can move?"

She ponders what I've said for a moment. "No, you're ok."

"That's what I thought."

We carry on moving forward, and if it wasn't annoying enough, most of the club's occupants for the night have begun to notice the spectacle and are watching in amusement.

I don't blame them. I would stare too if I saw three women like us in a club: one wearing pajamas, with a semi-comatose blonde on her back looking like something from *The Walking Dead*, while the other blonde to the side spins in circles, dancing like she's high on fairy dust.

A snicker reaches my ears, and a pair of blue Converse move into my vision that's, by necessity, focused on the floor. With them comes a deep, rough voice that causes an involuntary shiver to run down my spine.

"Need a hand, lady Hulk?"

"That's possibly the worst pickup line I've heard," I say. I put my snappy tone down to being crippled with Zoe on my back and having my path to freedom interrupted by some wasted loser.

The owner of the Converse lets out a throaty chuckle. "That's because I wasn't coming on to you. You looked like you were struggling ..."

"Look, if all you're going to do is give a running commentary, please feel free to get lost." The last part comes out as a growl. I don't know who the guy is, as I haven't seen his face, but there is something about his voice that's bringing out the worst in me, and I can't quite put my finger on why.

"Somebody is grumpy this evening." This time his voice sounds more familiar.

Please God, no. We've come to a standstill and I'm now able to take the rest of him in. My eyes move up his body, following long, muscular legs that are covered with slim fitting black jeans.

I don't get a chance to make it past his legs, because at that moment, Sophie spins too fast, crashing into me and Zoe with enough force to send us face planting into a sticky puddle of beer on the floor. Zoe rolls to the side groaning and then curling into a fetal position, settles back to sleep.

Lifting my face out of the puddle in a slight daze, I glance at her out of the corner of my eye. Has she actually just curled into a ball on the floor? Yes. Do I need to get myself some new friends? Definitely.

"Jaaaaaaaaaaaakey!" Sophie screeches.

When I register the name she just called out, it becomes clear my suspicions were correct why the Converse owner's voice sounded so familiar.

Groaning, I press my face back into the puddle of beer, wanting the ground to swallow me up. Why does it have to be him?

Not here, when I'm looking like this. It's been six years since we last saw each other. So, why now, when I'm wearing pajamas in the middle of a club, sprawled across the floor, covered in beer, do I have to bump into him?

I lift my head back out of the puddle, ready to face my utter humiliation. When I look up, I take in the rest of the guy towering above me. All six foot, muscular, heavily tattooed inch of him. He holds out a strong arm, covered in a tattoo sleeve that looks like a sheet of music, encouraging me to take his hand, and I swear my heart almost stops at the thought of having to touch him again. I need to get a grip.

I shake my head and look back down at the ground feeling flushed with embarrassment. Jumping up quickly, I find myself looking straight at his tanned face, which holds a friendly expression. But then I meet those eyes. Those deep brown, soul consuming eyes that are looking down at me just like they used to. I'm positively screwed.

"Jake ..."

The motion of the fall unsettles Zoe, bringing her round from her semi drunken coma and she somehow manages to get to her feet while I'm preoccupied.

It's at that point, the exact moment when for the first time in six years, I lay eyes on the guy who broke my heart, that Zoe hurls the content of her stomach all over my back.

Fuck. My. Life.

Two

eriously, what the actual, fuck? This night is beginning to feel like I'm stuck in a living, breathing nightmare. My arms hang loosely at my sides, as vomit drips from what feels like every part of my body (really, it's only the back of my pajama top, but still ...) I can feel tears burning my eyes in exasperation at the whole situation. They could also be from the rancid stench of vomit that keeps hitting my nose. I'm not sure which is worse.

My stomach begins to turn, and I'm at risk of sympathy vomiting. If we don't get out of the club soon, this has the potential to turn into a massive vom fest, and I promised Han that wouldn't happen.

Sophie has other ideas as she folds in half, creased with laughter while squeezing her legs together. The moment is causing her some major problems, as she tries not to pee her pants. That would be all we need to add to this shit show.

Standing for a couple of moments with my eyes squeezed tightly shut, I pray that when I open them again Jake won't be there, that this will all just be the horrible nightmare it feels like it is. But that would be cliché and far too lucky.

"Abby ... How are you?" His question comes plain as day and oblivious to the ridiculous scenario I'm currently stuck in.

After six years of no contact, he's acting like it's completely normal that we're here, standing together. His question gives me chance to quickly take in his full appearance. He looks older, manlier, more handsome than ever, with muscles that definitely didn't exist the last time we saw each other. A tattoo of fire covers his other arm and I briefly wonder what they all mean, and if he has more in unseen places.

It's infuriating how cool and complacent he's being, when I feel anything but. While I'm having my internal breakdown, Sophie returns to dancing and using some guys as her props. I'm assuming they're Jake's friends who have congregated around the spectacle. When she begins singing at the top of her voice, I decide it's time for us to make a move.

"Sophie. Will you *please* stop spinning in circles? We *need* to get out of here." Embarrassment pulses through my veins, but at least things can't get much worse.

Instead of helping, she collapses into the arms of a bemused looking guy, who, taken by surprise, loses his balance and they almost become the second pair to tumble into the puddle of beer on the floor. Luckily, he reacts quickly, finding his footing and somehow managing to keep them both upright.

"Before anyone else ends up on the floor, can we please stop her from moving, and get out of here?" I say.

The guy she collapsed into, looks at me with sympathy and shrugs. "Don't worry we'll get her outside in one piece. See you in a few, Jake?"

Jake breaks his gaze from me, turns to his friend and replies, "Yeah, man, I'll help with Zoe. Watch her though, she's a loose cannon." His friends leave with Sophie, and he turns his attention back to me. "Abby, will you please let me help?"

From his body language I can tell he's being sincere, and his expression is friendly and patient. Though I know he's finding the whole situation amusing, he's hiding it well. Just like old times.

"Do not think that if I accept your help it means you have suddenly become my knight in shining armor. I'd accept anyone's help right now, just to get us out of here." My words are harsh, and I know they sting, as he winces, but quickly recovers. The friendliness from his expression disappears.

"Fine, if it helps your ego, then I'm helping Zoe. Not you."

He turns his back and scoops Zoe gently into his arms. I can't stop myself watching his broad back, flexing, and straining under the material of his black shirt as he walks away, quickly towards the exit. I hate that the sight of him still makes my mouth water.

Every part of me screams not to follow, to stay away from him, but I need to make sure that Zoe and Sophie get home. Sighing, I follow them out of the club, receiving more funny looks than when I first came in, thanks to the stench of vomit accompanying me out.

New York summers are sweltering, but it's nothing compared to the sweaty heat of the club, and as I step outside, I feel like I can breathe properly in the 'fresh air'.

"I thought you said no vomit?"

I turn and find a stern looking Han, wrinkling his nose down at me.

"Well maybe if you'd let me inside quicker, I might've been able to intercept earlier. Does it count that I was the buffer and the vomit actually went on me not the floor?"

He stands for a minute, contemplating, and then responds, "I may let you off. You sure there's none on the floor?"

"None on the floor. As you can see, it's all over me." I gesture down at my vomit covered clothing.

"I suppose you stayed true to your word. If I don't have to clean any up, I'll let you off."

What a champion.

"Merely returning the favor, Han. I think this is the beginning of a beautiful friendship."

"And next time ..." he says.

"Yeah?"

I'm intrigued by what else he could possibly have to say.

"Try to wear some actual clothes, you'll get in quicker." He winks, ending our communication and turns back to the line of people still waiting to get into the club.

Looking around for Jake, Sophie and Zoe, I find them and Jake's friends, further up the block by my parents' car. Taking a deep breath, I try to mentally prepare myself for another few minutes of being close to Jake again. It's only a few minutes. I can do this and walk away in one piece.

A wave of nostalgia hits when I reach the group and look around, realizing that everyone apart from the guy Sophie collapsed into, is familiar. They're the old gang from back in high school, and it's understandable why they didn't register earlier.

Although the resemblance is there, most have changed their hair, they're taller, fuller and working the grunge look. They no longer fit the preppy boy mold they tried to rebel against in high school.

"Little Abby ..." a guy with dark blond hair, cut short at the sides and long on the top, styled away from his face steps forward. There are a couple of nose piercings that are new, but he has the same handsome face and friendly blue eyes.

"Sammy!"

I can barely contain my excitement at seeing him, and squeal, throwing myself against his chest. He engulfs me with his strong arms. Besides Sophie and Zoe, he's one of a few people I've missed since leaving home.

"I didn't recognize you all in there, thanks to being occupied with other things," I say.

I pull away and once again gesture down at my vomit covered pajamas, not that he'd need a reminder with the stench coming from me.

He laughs and his eyes crinkle at the corners as he smiles. "Some things never change. Not to worry, you can get your fill of me now."

He catches me off guard engulfing me in another friendly hug and it's hard not to bask in his warmth and familiarity. It makes me feel protected from the pain of seeing Jake again and right now I don't ever want to leave the comfort of his arms.

In less than ten minutes, this group of people I used to call my closest friends, are breaking through some of the walls I've put up over the years. I can already see my resolve beginning to crumble and I've not been home twenty-four hours.

A throat clears from behind us, and I turn to see Jake standing with his shoulders squared and arms folded across his chest. "We haven't got all night. What are you going to do with Zoe?" he says.

I try to keep the snappiness out of my voice when I reply, "Chill. You offered to help, remember? If you didn't want to, you shouldn't have gotten involved."

"I offered to help with Zoe, not stand around all night watching you and Sam grope each other."

"Jealous, I see." I place my hands on my hips and tilt my head to the side with a sweet smile. To everyone else it will come across as playful, but I know how to rub him up the wrong way.

His face flushes in surprise. The old Abby would have been too shy to challenge him, but times have changed.

He quickly recovers and says, "Hardly. Why would I be jealous, Abby? I was the one that ended things, don't you remember?"

This time it's my turn to be shocked. Shocked at how easily he's bringing up our past, such a sensitive subject, with little respect for my feelings. It feels like I've been punched in the gut, but I refuse to let him see how his words affect me after all this time.

"How could I forget? You're clearly still a douchebag," I say.

His face shows no emotion, but his eyes bore into mine.

Then he smiles and says, "You've gotten feisty."

He lets out a deep breath, which warms my cheek, and I can feel my whole body beginning to tingle, and my stomach flutter. When did we end up standing so close? How did I not notice myself gravitating towards him during our little sparring session?

Sam steps forward, recognizing that I'm in over my head and says, "Seriously, guys, you weren't even like this when you split up. Can we at least try and get along for a few minutes? You haven't seen each other in six years."

"Well, that would be because Jake doesn't like handling things like an adult, isn't that right, Jake?"

Jake doesn't say a word, just shakes his head and looks away.

Sam continues his intervention, more forcefully this time, and says, "That's enough, Abby. This isn't the time or the place to start rehashing things. It's not gonna be long until Zoe starts barfing again. Do you really want it to be all over your parents' car?"

I know he's right, which is reinforced by Sophie swaying from side to side, muttering, "Aaabbbuuu buuu buuu, I'm so tired and booooored. Can we please go home now?"

Resigned, I back away from my face off with Jake. "I guess that's my cue to leave. It's been emotional as always."

The guys help to get Zoe in the car, and in the process, Sam saves my cellphone number to his, declaring we need to make up for lost time. I laugh and agree to see him soon.

As I step back, Jake shuts the front passenger door, turns and crashes straight into me.

"Sorry, I didn't realize you were there," he apologizes and steadying me with his hands on my arms.

"It's fine. I should have said I was behind you."

I look up and everything feels like it stops. His stare holds an intensity that takes my breath away, but as with most of Jake's emotions, it vanishes as quickly as it appears, leaving me questioning whether I was imagining it.

"You look good, Abby. Drive safe."

With that he walks down the sidewalk, back to the club. I wait a moment, hoping he will look back over his shoulder. Any sign he was as affected by the moment as much as I was. He walks into the club without glancing back, proving he couldn't care less about seeing me again. If only I felt the same.

Three

I t takes a while to decide what's best to do with the girls. In the end I opt for taking them back to my parents, rather than trying to navigate each of them into their own home at this time of night.

The drive goes by quickly, as the roads aren't as hectic as they are in the day. Rolling down the windows, in an attempt to get rid of the awful smell coming from the three of us, I appreciate the feeling of the warm summer air blowing through my hair and across my skin.

There's a buzz about, as the smells of restaurants and late-night take-out's fill the car. Laughter and music fill the night as people bustle about on the sidewalks, creating an atmosphere that can only be described as New, Frickin, York. God, I love it. I love Brooklyn. Feelings of doubt already begin to creep in, as I wonder why I ever left.

I mull over the events of the night. Sophie and Zoe have always spent their time getting wasted and into trouble. They've taken the classic high school rebellion a step further and it's always been my job to make sure they're ok. My role hasn't changed regardless of where we've been. Whenever they've met with me at a new location for shoots, I've still had to step in and be their second mom.

I guess I wouldn't have it any other way, otherwise I would have put my foot down years ago. Despite their poor tolerance for alcohol and low inhibitions, they're my best friends and have been since we were in diapers. We live our lives differently. Zoe claims to be an *'influencer'* spending her time trialing new bars and restaurants, calling it work. Sophie refers to herself as the eternal student, each year changing her college major, stating that this time it's 'The One'. Luckily, they come from middle-class Brooklyn families that help to fund their antics.

Our parents started out working together in music and journalism. Although New York is a big and busy place, when you work in certain sectors the social circles are small and their paths crossed so often it was inevitable, they were going to become friends.

They all relocated from Manhattan to Brooklyn at the same time to start families. It was dead set their children would be friends from the get-go, and that's exactly what happened. We grew up together, vacationed together, went to school together. Even when I moved away at eighteen to pursue my freelance photography career, they followed me wherever they could, and when we spend time apart, it means nothing. All we do is fall back into old ways.

I smile to myself, as I look in the rearview mirror. Sophie is slumped against the window with her mouth open and Zoe has fallen forward with her head on her lap, a large spot of drool beginning to form. They may be a pain in the ass, but they're mine and I wouldn't change them.

I spend the rest of the journey home trying to clear up my plans for the summer in my mind. Keep my head down. Work while I stay in Brooklyn for a couple of months with my parents, rent free, to save some cash. At the end of the summer decide which of the two career making positions I will choose. As it stands, I'm confused about everything. It's going to take time to decide what path I want my future to take.

There is one thing that's clear as day. If I'm going to get through the coming months unscathed and with my sanity still intact, then I need to stay away from Jake. Having him back in my life just for ten minutes has resulted in him occupying my mind far more than I would like to admit.

Zoe grunts in the back, bringing me out of my train of thought. For now, it's best to put the confusion to the back of my mind. Tonight, has been an emotional rollercoaster, and even though they both drive me insane, the two friends in the back of the car are the ones that have stuck with me no matter what. They are what matters. They didn't leave or choose sides when Jake and I broke up like some of our friends did, and I need to remember that.

✷✷✷

After what feels like an eternity, I manage to drag Sophie and Zoe out of my parents' car and up the two flights of stairs to my room. Somehow, we haven't woken my parents in the process. Even if we had, it wouldn't have been anything out of the ordinary for them. Growing up this was a regular occurrence.

When we're finally settled, I find myself tossing and turning rather than giving in to sleep like my body craves. Exhaustion begins to take over, as the early morning rays of sunlight begin filtering through my blinds. As I finally feel my eyelids drooping and lulling me towards sleep, my cell buzzes ... again.

'Seriously? You've got to be kidding me,' I hiss at it.

I'm aware that I'm talking to an inanimate object, and all I need to do is turn it off if I want to get some sleep. But when I look at the screen, I see Michael's name flashing at me. Michael is my long-term boyfriend back in Florida, who I somehow neglected to inform I arrived safely in Brooklyn. He has every right to call because he will be worrying about me, and I know he isn't going to give up anytime soon.

Letting out a sigh, I reach for my cell and answer. "Hey you," I whisper.

Trying to be quiet and not wake the girls was a wasted effort.

Michael's voice wails down the line, "Abbbbbbyyyy beeee beeee beeee. Baby. I miss you, baby."

What is it with everyone getting wasted tonight? Getting wasted and preventing me from sleep, which is beginning to make me extremely grouchy.

"Have you been drinking?" I ask, trying not to sound too fed up.

"Only one, baby."

"Michael ... it's five am. Why would you still be up at this time if you only had one drink?"

"I miss you *so* much, baby."

I picture him in my mind, back in Florida, sitting in his home alone, running his hands through his hair in frustration. I can picture it clearly because it's what he does when he's drunk after a night out with the guys and we wind up having one of these conversations.

"We've barely been apart twenty-four hours! It's early and I've had no sleep. I'm tired and would like to get some rest," I say.

I hope he takes the hint and wraps up the call, but he chooses to focus on one of the minor details I let slip.

"Why've you had no sleep? Is there another guy? Already, Abby?"

Surprise, surprise, we're back going over one of Michael's favorite conversations when he's drunk. His insecurities regarding our relationship always rear their ugly head when alcohol is involved.

"I'm not having this conversation with you. It's too early and I'm tired of telling you there isn't anyone else. When are you going to trust me?"

"Baby, you're just so distant sometimes. I love you and it's like you're not all in like I am. Why do you think I'm wasted after you left?"

"You're going to blame your decision to get wasted on me?"

"Baby, I love you, I'm sorry."

"Please stop calling me baby. You know I hate it."

"I miss you. I don't understand why we need to spend the summer apart. Why wouldn't you want to stay down here with me in our home, where we've made a life?"

"It's *your* home and you know why. There's no work for me there right now. We've had this conversation so many times."

"Will I be coming with you at the end?"

I don't hide my sigh. Harsh, but he won't remember.

"I don't know if I'm taking either of the jobs yet. Even if I did, what would be the point in you coming? You're going to leave your career behind, everything you've worked for your whole life, while I follow my dreams?"

"Yeah, I would, Abby. That's what couples who are in love do. They support each other in their decisions, and they make sacrifices for each other. I should go. I just wanted to hear your voice. I won't bother you while you're away again," he mutters.

"I'm sorry. I'm just tired. I got a late call from Sophie and Zoe, hence the no sleep." I hope the small explanation as to my whereabouts this evening appeases him when he wakes up later. "I'll speak to you soon when things have settled down."

I know it's a poor excuse to avoid speaking with him, especially when he's obviously hurting. Luckily, he won't remember most of the conversation when he wakes up.

"I love you, Abby. Speak soon."

His voice sounds hurt as he hangs up. As his long-term girlfriend I should feel guilty for making him feel this way, but I feel nothing. I have yet to admit to myself why that is, even though deep down I know.

Four

6 years earlier

I *can't believe he's here, with me. I was sure he wouldn't come and that this was all a big joke to show up poor, shy Abby who daren't talk to anyone. It's the opposite. He's here and he's friendlier and more attentive than he was before.*

Over the past couple of months, we've only chatted on our cells. Sophie introduced us officially on a chat site, as he goes to a different high school in Manhattan, like some of the others in our group. She met him through Sam as they're in a band together.

It's incredible, but in the short space of time we've been talking, I feel like I know him better than anyone, even though I've never had the confidence to be open with him in person whenever we've crossed paths while out with the rest of the group.

Most nights we chat online and laugh over video camera. We talk for hours. Those moments are everything and I feel like he knows and understands me, even more than Sophie and Zoe.

I was sure when we first met, he liked Zoe. She outshines everyone around her, with her openly flirty and confident ways. Why would he prefer me, when I could barely open my mouth, barely look at him because I was so nervous?

But now ... he's looking at me. It feels like I've overcome a hurdle, one I was too scared to jump over. Now that I've finally found the confidence to be with him in person, we're moving forward. I'm not sure whether it's as friends or something more, but it feels amazing.

We run as quickly as we can to the nearest subway, but, typical of a fall downpour in New York, it only takes seconds for us to get soaked to the skin. Water droplets run down my face, clinging to my eyelashes, smudging my makeup. I don't care. Nothing could ruin this moment.

As the subway sways steadily from side to side I tilt my head upwards to try and look at his face without him noticing. I catch his eye and can't look away. I've wanted to know what it would be like to stare into those deep brown eyes for so long, but never thought I'd get the chance. Now, it's real. He's here, just a few inches away, with a genuine smile on his face.

He surprises me by leaning in slowly, our faces are millimeters apart and I swear my heart stops. I hold my breath waiting and hoping. Instead, he moves closer to my ear and whispers, "This is our stop, Abby."

Pulling away and moving quickly off the subway, he drags me with him.

As we're walking away, cutting through the crowds, he glances back over his shoulder with a knowing smirk on his face. A smirk that tells me he knew exactly how much I wanted him to kiss me.

Present Day

"Abby. Wake up, it's lunch time."

Somewhere in the distance, someone is talking and keeps shaking me. They keep doing it. Eventually it registers vaguely that it's Sophie's voice I can hear.

I feel groggy. Like I have the hangover from hell. Then it hits me where I am, and the hangover I'm feeling is in fact the exhaustion of dealing with Sophie, Zoe and Michael the night, (maybe I should say morning) before.

I remember the dream I had, and a wave of nausea creeps over me. It's been years since I've dreamt of Jake. This is not a good sign.

"Hey, Abs, you ok? Your face is doing this weird scrunched up look, like you're in pain, or taking a giant dump, or something," says Sophie.

I choose to ignore her comment. It's her roundabout way of showing concern.

"I had a dream about Jake ..." I admit.

"Oh? That would explain it. So, like a sexy one?"

"Can we not focus on sex for a minute? I had a dream about Jake, Soph. It's been six years since I had one, not that I was counting or anything. We see him last night and boom, off they go again. I've not even been back for twenty-four hours and already I'm on a downward, Jake-driven, spiral."

I throw myself back against my pillow with a thump and look up at the ceiling, trying to blink away the tears making my eyes burn.

"You ok?" Sophie asks, even though she knows I'm anything but.

"Not really. Why did you ask me to come and get you if there was a chance he would be there? I know you guys are all still friendly. Did you know he was going to be there?"

She holds her hands up in the air and shakes her heard. "I didn't, I swear. You know I wouldn't do that to you. I'm sorry I called. Zoe was wasted and I needed help. But then I got wasted too … I didn't mean for any of that to happen, I swear."

Zoe, who was dead to the world moments ago begins to stir thanks to our raised voices.

Without opening her eyes, she mutters, "What the hell? Where am I? Why do I smell so bad? Please tell me I didn't hook up with some randomer again. Please, God when I open my eyes let me be alone."

One eye opens into a slit and she peers around the room until her gaze settles on Sophie and me. She lets out a huge sigh of relief.

"Dramatic much?" I say.

"Thank you, God. Abby? You're back? When?"

I roll my eyes. "You don't remember anything from last night, do you? You were absolutely wasted … again. I had to come and get you."

"So, I didn't hook up with anyone?"

"The only people you slept with are in this room," I reply.

Sophie snickers, "It was an eventful night. You outdid yourself, babe."

Zoe groans and rolls over, so her face is pressed down into the pillow. "What did I do?"

I quickly summarize the events of the night, being extra careful not to leave out any of the drama and place emphasis on how embarrassing the whole thing was. Particularly for me.

"I'm so sorry, Abby. I swear, I don't mean to do these things to you." She's pale and puts her head in her hands. It's clear she's feeling guilty but I'm still annoyed. "Anyway ... Jake's back?"

Sophie nods. "Apparently so, and he chose last night to make his grand reappearance. Typical."

"Back?" I ask, looking between them both. "What do you mean back? Where has he been?"

They're reluctant to give me any more information, but I give them a pointed stare, making it clear I'm not amused they're keeping something from me.

"Are you sure you want to know this?" Sophie asks.

We've had an unspoken rule over the past six years, that anything related to Jake doesn't get mentioned. Ever. Rather than sticking with my guns, I nod my confirmation, unable to find the ability to say yes. Sophie shuffles back down the bed and gets herself comfy next to Zoe before beginning.

"He's been on tour ... He formed a new band with some of the guys a few years back. They started doing small gigs here and there and got a rep in the underground music scene. When they got some money behind them, they invested it in recording an album."

She pauses for a moment, trying to gauge my reaction, but I choose to give nothing away that would make her stop, so she continues.

"They made a music video that Jake's girlfriend helped put together, and it went viral on YouTube with like twenty million viewers or something ridiculous. With all the hype, they were approached by a bigger band and asked to support their tour along the West Coast, which is what they've been doing for the past three months."

Zoe chips in, "It finished this week, and they obviously hopped it straight back home. Word is a

38

record company is interested. Like *really* interested. Abby, are you listening?"

I must look like I've zoned out, but that's because all I can focus on is one thing. My heart is racing, and a distant ringing grows louder, as I feel the pressure of a migraine forming.

"Jake has a girlfriend?" I say.

It's irrational to feel this way. It's been six years since we were together, and we were teenagers in high school. It was never going to go anywhere even if we had lasted longer. Still, I feel physically sick at the thought of him with someone else. Jake was my first love, or maybe truer words would be that he was 'the' love.

He was the first one to capture my heart and when he broke it, I never quite got it back. Well … I did. Some broken, mangled version of it, that's been incapable of sharing those feelings with anyone else.

I've put up many walls over the years, after the train wreck that was our breakup. Mainly to block out the memories of being with him and how he made me feel. A therapist would say I've been sticking my head in the sand and delaying the inevitable feelings of hurt that will come when I finally face up to what happened. Basically, it's all going to come back and bite me in the ass.

"I'm going to sound like a bitch here," says Zoe, "but you can't act shocked. He has a life, and with that comes a girlfriend. We're all different to what we were in high school, even you. We've grown up." Sophie snorts at the irony of Zoe's last statement, which she chooses to ignore and continues. "People change. You have. And what about Michael? It's been four years since you met him, I thought you guys were doing great?"

The mention of Michael grounds me enough, that I'm able to reply. "They were ... I mean are. I don't know. I thought I was doing great and finally moving on, but then I bump into Jake and bam! All those memories come flooding back."

Sophie leans over and rubs my arm reassuringly. "We get it. I mean I bump into exes and it's always hard. There are some that get under your skin and you can't get rid of them. It feels like sometimes there's no closure ..." She trails off looking distant, as if she's being drawn into her own memories of heartbreak. She quickly snaps out of it and says to Zoe, "Stop rolling your eyes at me. Just because you're a cold-hearted bitch towards anything with a penis."

"I'm not cold-hearted. I just see them in a practical light, and I'm capable of having good sex without all the emotional attachment crap."

The truth is Sophie and Zoe are opposites when it comes to guys. Sophie has always been a big softie who wears her heart on her sleeve. Then there's Zoe. Sophie pretty much summed it up. She's hard as nails and uses guys for one thing, sex. Anything else she claims is a waste of time and energy. Sometimes I think she has a point.

"Which is also not healthy," says Sophie. "There's just something about your first ..."

"Not that I would know with Jake," I say. "We never even got that far and look at the state of me. Imagine if we had ..."

I face plant the duvet in frustration.

Sophie chuckles and says, "Stop imagining Jake naked. Things won't get any easier talking about him constantly. I vote we get more rest because I could sleep for years. Let's properly catch up in a few hours, when we don't feel like we've been part of a train wreck."

"I'm down for that," says Zoe, needing little persuasion as she snuggles back down to sleep.

"More sleep sounds good," I agree, noticing how tired I still am. As an afterthought I say to Sophie, "Although you are the one that woke me up in the first place."

"Things will seem better when we wake up later. Promise." She rolls over to her side of the bed and drops off instantly.

I doubt things will feel miraculously better just from sleep. That's not how my brain works when it comes to anything Jake related. There's a reason I've stayed away for so long, but I don't say this out loud.

Five

It's early evening when we finally resurface, something I rarely do, but by Sophie and Zoe's laziness standards this is nothing. For them working is a means to get by, and life is for socializing with friends, getting wasted and sleeping hung-over days away. We live our lives in hugely different lanes, but it's what works for us.

Congregating in my parents' kitchen and snacking on junk food, I give them a rundown on my plans while I'm back in Brooklyn for the summer.

"... so, Shaun dropped me a message on Facebook saying he'd seen that I was going to be back in Brooklyn. He said there was a job available, that the hours were flexible, and he would love to work with me."

I finish, grabbing a handful of chips and shoving them in my mouth.

"You mean he would love to work *in* you," Zoe snorts under her breath.

I reply. "He's Sam's older brother ..."

"Who has always had a crush on you, just like most guys have since we were teenagers. Just because you were too shy to notice them, doesn't mean it didn't happen."

"That's because she's gorgeous."

The grin that spreads over my face is instantaneous as my dad enters the kitchen, walking over to the stool I'm sitting on at the center island. He wraps me up in a warm hug and says, "Now, who has a crush on my little girl this time?"

"Come on, Dad!" I pull away, shove him jokingly to emphasize my point. "I'm not your 'little' girl anymore. And no one has a crush on me."

Not wanting to miss an opportunity to cause me some form of embarrassment, Zoe says, "It's Shaun. Sam's brother who owns the bar Riffs over in Williamsburg."

"I know the one," he nods. "Great place for getting spotted. Always full of new music talent."

"He offered me a job behind the bar over the summer. It's super flexible which means I can work it around my photography jobs. Plus, I get to control how much alcohol these two are allowed at the same time."

I wink and he smiles. I'm poking the bear with the stick, or whatever the saying is. Judging by how Zoe and Sophie are gaping at me open mouthed, it's working.

"If you shit on my parade, Abby, I swear to God, we are no longer BFF's. There are some things that friendship just can't survive and cutting off my beer tap is one of them." says Zoe wide-eyed.

I can't stifle my laugh. She's being ridiculous.

"Zo, chill," I say. "Do you really think I'd be able to get in the way of you and alcohol? You're a lost cause."

All I get in return is a "hmmmf." She begins shoveling food in her mouth and ignores me. She doesn't believe I was joking about supervising her nights out over the summer and is miffed.

"So, when do you start at the bar?" asks dad, steering the conversation away from what has quickly become a sore subject.

"I've a couple of photo shoots set up over the next few days. I said I'd go to the bar to discuss it once they're out of the way and I've settled back in."

"Sounds great, honey. Your mother will be back in a few days. Her work is hectic at the moment, but you can catch up with her then."

Dad leaves later for an event in Manhattan and I spend the rest of the night binging on Netflix and takeout with Sophie and Zoe.

I crawl into bed later, when the girls finally leave, and let out a content sigh. This is the most relaxed I've felt in months. In particular in the past twenty-four hours. Seeing Jake was a minor hiccup.

Brooklyn is part of New York, one of the biggest and busiest cities in the world. We don't have to be around each other if we don't want, and the city can help make an easy job of that.

✶✶✶

6 years earlier

Normally I hate the end of summer vacation. I love being on my own, taking photos, spending time with Sophie and Zoe and no one else. The thought of being thrust back into the cliques and daily drama of high school life, usually fills me with dread, but not this summer. Because of him I feel like a different person. I feel stronger, more confident, and excited for life in new ways.

44

I've lost count of the number of times I've ended up in a fight with my parents over my cellphone bill. But damn if I care, I can't get enough of him. We've spent the summer talking, getting closer, and now it feels like I know him better than I know myself.

Without realizing, he's gotten under the skin of the shy girl that barely spoke to anyone. He's become my rock, my everything. Sometimes, on days where I'm so happy I feel like I might explode, when we've caught rare moments alone together and he's really looked at me, I've dared to let myself believe that I'm his everything too.

It's been one of those long, hot, perfect days that I thought nothing could ruin. But as I look over at Jake, I see he's standing close to Zoe and insecurity creeps in. She leans in towards him, her long blonde hair falling over her shoulder as she giggles at something he says, and I feel a huge stab of jealousy.

I continue watching them and my mind races with a million different thoughts. Does she like him too? She knew how I was starting to feel about him. I love her like a sister, but she's so confident in her own skin, especially around guys. I wish they looked at me with the longing that they do her.

The memories of what had the making to be a perfect day feel tainted, leaving a bitter taste in my mouth.

Jake always feels close, but not quite in my grasp. Today, I don't have it in me to fight. So, I do what Abby does best, I turn and walk away.

Six

It takes longer than I anticipated to settle in at home, so I wind up pushing back my photo-shoots. It was optimistic booking them so soon after arriving, but luckily the clients are laid back and happy to delay them by a few days.

It's surprising how time can get away from you, and before I realize, I've been home for over half a week. Half a week of being consumed by all things Brooklyn. My time's been filled with unpacking, letting off steam running, catching up with old friends and spending time with my dad.

Finally, I feel like I've settled in, and I'm ready to face clients and get some good roots for work laid down. I book my first client of the day for mid-morning, as it's an outdoor shoot and the light tends to be better around this time of day. Making sure not to be late, I arrive an hour early. Killing time before the shoot, I meander around Carol Gardens with my camera, attempting to get in the zone and familiarize myself with the area I'll be working in shortly.

When I was younger, I'd spend hours wandering the streets of Brooklyn with the cheap digital camera my parents gave me for my fourteenth birthday. That was around the time I took a real interest in photography. It was the perfect hobby for someone as shy as I was at the time, someone who liked to stay off people's radar and observe from the sidelines. It allowed me an insight into people's lives and a view of the world that most don't get to see. It still does. Even though it literally takes me all over the world, and sometimes life on the road can be lonely, it's what I'm passionate about and what I've wanted to do since the moment I developed my first set of photos.

My first job in Brooklyn is with an up-and-coming blogger in the New York fashion scene. We spend hours moving from location to location and changing outfits and hairstyles with the rest of the team. Before I know it, it's late afternoon and I get a message on my cell from Sophie asking if she and Zoe can come over for food later when I've finished working. I quickly shoot back that I'll pick up some goodies from the local farmers' market.

✶✶✶

"Oh my God, Abby, it smells so good in here," says Sophie, as she wanders into my parents' kitchen-diner later that evening, after letting herself into the house with Zoe.

"I didn't know you could cook. I thought we agreed on takeout." Zoe seems anything but disappointed at the change in menu, as she begins picking at some of the food already laid out.

I swat her hand away. "It's Italian. But we'll end up having to get takeout if you keep eating it all. And most people learn to cook when they live on their own, how else would you eat?"

"Order takeout and eat cereal, obvs," she replies and slumps down in a chair at the table.

Sophie snickers. "Clearly we didn't get the growing up memo."

"Clearly," I repeat.

We're interrupted when both my parents arrive, dropping their work gear by the door as my dad chuckles.

"Look what the cat dragged in ... again," he says.

"John be nice. Girls, it's great to see you. It's been too long," says my mom, smiling warmly at them both.

She doesn't attempt to hide the emotion shining in her eyes when she looks over at me. It's the first time we've seen each other since I returned home, and it hasn't felt right being here without her around. "Baby, come here," she says.

I stumble and fall into her outstretched arms, as she envelopes me in the kind of hug only a mother knows how to give. Letting out a deep sigh, I feel the anxiety from returning home evaporate.

Zoe clears her throat. "It's really great to see you again, Mr. and Mrs. West, but can we please tuck into the food or I swear I'm going to die of starvation?"

She throws her arms in the air and collapses across the table, to emphasize her point.

"Still dramatic I see," mom chuckles, voicing the opinion of everyone in the room.

Once we're settled around the table, the food is devoured, and the atmosphere is light and friendly. My parents aren't exactly conventional. Dad works in the rock department for a major record label in Manhattan and Mom ... I guess you could say she's a bit off the wall, being that she's a sex columnist. Between them both, they're relatively chilled out.

48

"I swear, this is better than an orgasm," Zoe groans with a mouth full of food.

Mom being mom responds before I get chance to tell her to be quiet. "Well, you're clearly not getting the right kind of sex, Zoe."

I begin choking on my last fork full of pasta. "Gross, Mom."

"Tsk, always such a prude, Abby, you'd never know you're my daughter."

She smiles into her glass of red wine, knowing exactly how to push my buttons.

"No, really though," Zoe continues, "if your photography ever tanks, you could totally try your hand at cooking. This is great."

"Nice to know you have such faith in my career," I reply.

"What's got your panties in a twist? Or has nothing? Is that the problem?" she snaps.

"The food's great, honey. Anyway ..." Mom steers the conversation in another direction, "I saw Shaun the other week and he seemed excited that you're back and going to be working with him."

Zoe laughs into her glass of water. "I bet he was."

Seriously what is her problem? I narrow my eyes in her direction. When I glance at Sophie, I notice she's doing the same, unimpressed at the comments being made.

"Oh, he's interested?" Mom looks like a little kid at Christmas, fueled with gossip regarding my love life.

"No, Mom, it's work. Please remember I have a boyfriend. A boyfriend I've been with for *four years*." I'm hoping the emphasis on how long we've been together will distract them from the idea of Shaun and I together. Silly me, they're vultures.

"You mean on and off for four years," says Zoe under her breath.

"Ah yes, Michael ..." Mom has a funny look on her face, as if there's a bad smell in the room.

"What's that supposed to mean? And why are you pulling a weird face?" I say.

Really, I know why. It's no secret that my family and friends aren't Michael's biggest fans. They've supported our relationship over the years but haven't necessarily fallen in love with him.

"Nothing, sweetie." She reaches into the middle of the table, opening another bottle of wine and filling her glass, refusing to meet my eye.

"We bumped into Jake the other night," blurts out Sophie.

I put my head in my hands and groan, they know better than to mention Jake around my parents.

"Why am I even friends with you guys? I swear I need to sew your mouths shut or something."

Both my parents look at me, without attempting to hide the alarm on their faces.

"You saw Jake?" Mom asks, looking a little paler than a few seconds ago.

All the humor has gone from the conversation.

"Yes, and before you ask, it was fine." A small lie, but they don't need to know the details.

"Okay." Her response takes me by surprise, I expected her to pry more.

"That's all you've got to say?"

She places her wine glass down on the table, and says, "You said it was fine, so I believe you. Your father has had some contact with him over the years for work. He's a nice guy." She purses her lips. "I will never understand what happened with the two of you."

Hearing her speak positive about him seems wrong. When everything happened between me and Jake, her words were anything but. She went through the heartbreak with me.

"You're not the only one," I mutter.

I look at my plate and begin tearing chunks of bread apart, when the full extent of what she said registers. This time I turn towards my dad who has been unusually quiet. "What does she mean you've seen him for work purposes?"

He sighs. "We didn't think we'd need to tell you, but things always have a way of coming out, so it's best you hear it from me ..."

Closing my eyes, I struggle to swallow thanks to the huge lump that's formed in my throat, as I wait for what's going to come out of his mouth next.

"The record label has been following Jake's group for a while, and we're in talks of a record deal. It's not going to be an issue is it?" he asks.

Fuck. Of course, it's an issue, not that I say this aloud. I'm seriously beginning to question whether everyone in my life is on another planet.

Quickly getting it together, I force a smile on my face. "Of course, it's not going to be a problem. It's not like we're even guaranteed to see each other again. It's one summer, and Brooklyn is a big place. If we do see each other, we're adults now. We can be civilized."

"Yeah, because that was evident the other night," Sophie laughs, referring to our constant bickering after less than a half hour together.

"I was in shock and now I'm not," I say, hoping she gets the hint to leave it. "Jake and I will spend the summer not seeing each other and everything will be fine."

"I'm sure it will," Dad says quietly. "But for that to work, you have to not want to see each other."

Pretending like I haven't heard his comment, I stand and begin clearing the table to signal that dinner and the conversation have come to an end. Sophie and Zoe both remain seated with their heads down, not daring to look me in the eye, while Mom does the opposite, watching me like a hawk.

It's not until later, when I'm lying on my bed in my room, praying for sleep to come, that I find myself mulling over the conversation from dinner and wondering what the hell my dad meant. Jake and I clearly hate each other, so why would we want to be near each other?

Being back in Brooklyn was supposed to be about me gaining clarity, but if I thought running away from my relationship issues with Michael would give me a break, I was very wrong.

If I want this summer to go without a hitch, I need to stay away from all things Jake related.

Seven

I make my way over to Williamsburg to see Shaun the following afternoon. Zoe and Sophie are in tow, refusing to be left behind with such a good excuse to go to their favorite bar.

It's not at all what I expected, despite seeing pictures online. It's in a huge, old warehouse that's been converted into a mix of bars and eateries. Shaun's place takes up a good chunk of a side unit and even has an outdoor area, unheard of in New York.

It's seriously cool. I'm impressed with what he's set up. The high ceilings provide good acoustics and are perfect for live music, making it obvious why it's become the go to venue for bands. The large outdoor area has been landscaped with shrubs, tables and chairs, and an open-air stage for in the summer months. There's also a retractable ceiling which is genius, meaning no matter the weather, the space is still useable.

I'm so distracted taking everything in, I fail to notice Shaun walking over to us.

His gruff voice startles me from my daze. "Welcome to Riffs. How are you doing, Abby? Glad you could make it." He smiles down at me, then nods in the girls' direction "Soph, Zo ..."

Realizing it could be inappropriate that I've brought them if we're treating this as a formal interview, I gesture at the girls and say, "I hope you don't mind that they came? They refused to be left behind.'

He throws his head back and laughs. "No need to explain, they're part of the furniture."

I notice the way his smile reaches his eyes and softens his rugged image. He's aged well in the time I've been away, filling out considerably like the rest of the guys. The photos on social media don't do him justice.

Glancing between the three of us, his eyes linger a second longer on Zoe, but I don't have time to analyze it before he's directing us to a quiet table near the bar. Sophie and Zoe grab a separate one, and some drinks, while Shaun and I spend the next half hour going over the position he needs filling. I'm already sold on the job as I've done bar work in the past. He reassures me that the shifts are on a casual basis, meaning I can work them around my freelance photography work.

"... there might be a few other odd jobs I need you to do from time to time. If we get busy on food, etc. I might need you to jump in and lend a hand, but it's pretty basic bar stuff and you can cook, right? I mean you can heat things up because that's all it is really," he says.

I offer a reassuring smile. "I can find my way around a kitchen if needed."

"Great. The last guy made the microwave explode. I mean, who doesn't know how to use one of those?

Also ... there was something else I was wondering if you could help with?"

"Shoot ..."

He runs a hand through his hair and takes a deep breath. "Well ... we're getting quite a following in the music scene and we could do with some decent images. I know it'd help a lot of the bands out, and it'd be great for the bar, we need some proper marketing material. I need to start being all professional and shit."

I could let him carry on rambling, but I put him out of his misery, placing my hand on his arm. "Shaun, it's fine. Just let me know when you need things doing and we can figure something out."

"That was easy. Abs, you're a life saver." The relief on his face shows he appreciates the help.

"Remember though, I'm leaving at the end of the summer. No matter what."

"That's fine. We just need you while it's busy. Plus, it'll be good getting to spend time with you now that you're finally back. It's been forever."

His eyes crinkle in that friendly way again, and I feel slightly flustered under his gaze. Nobody could blame me, I'm human, and as Shaun has aged, he's also gotten unbelievably hot. Unlike his brother, Sam, his blond hair is long and shaggy, in that Kurt Cobain sort of way. A flame tattoo peeks out from underneath his shirt collar and a giant Enso sign inks his forearm. The eyebrow piercing finishes his whole grunge rocker look off to a T.

Throw in the rugged bar owner gig he's got working for him, and it's no wonder most of the women in the bar keep gazing over longingly. The undivided attention I'm receiving gets me a few hacky looks.

"You're happy then? Being back, I mean." It doesn't take a genius to figure out why he sounds concerned. It feels like all anyone wants to do is talk about Jake.

"Yes, I'm happy." I keep my answer simple, but he doesn't take the hint.

"It's been a long time since you've been back. Six years. A lot of things have changed."

"I know but it's fine. I'm fine." I shrug and look around the bar as my stomach churns. I don't want to talk about this.

"Have you seen Jake?"

His bluntness sucks the air right out of me.

I grind my teeth trying to hide my irritation as I choose my words carefully. "I've seen him. Not out of choice though."

Shaun leans forwards, eyes wide. "How was it?"

"Crap. How else would it be? We didn't exactly leave things on good terms."

He sighs, clearly not happy with my response. "He's changed a lot you know. He's grown up."

Great, another person that is team Jake.

"You could have fooled me. The guy I met was still an asshole. But I get what you're saying, we've all grown up. I'm not the pushover I was before I left. I'm back for the summer and that's it. I need to stay focused on my career and what's important, so I can leave without any regrets."

I'm fully aware it sounds like a speech I've rehearsed, but there's no other way I can convince other people, and myself, that my feelings for Jake are gone.

For a guy that plays the cool card incredibly well, he's always been intuitive with people. He raises an eyebrow and says, "Who are you trying to convince? Me or yourself? Don't forget where you came from,

Abby. Your friends and family helped you get to where you are. Remember that when you run off and leave us behind for another six years."

His last comment stings, but only because it's true.

"I have a life outside of New York now. I have a boyfriend and things are great. I'm finally happy and we've both moved on. I know he has a girlfriend ..."

I look down at the table and begin playing with a beer mat, attempting to hide my face because it will give away how I really feel about Jake having a girlfriend.

Shaun's too surprised to notice anything apart from what I've said.

"You know about Amanda?"

I shrug and reply, "Sophie and Zoe let it slip the other day. I don't get why it would need to be a secret?"

"Because he probably would have rather spoken to you about it himself-"

"And how would he do that, when it took less than ten minutes for us to be at each other's throats?" I say cutting him off. "It's not a big deal. Really. Plus, we're barely gonna see each other, if at all ..."

Shaun looks skeptical, "Come on, Abs. Who are you kidding? Brooklyn isn't that big, especially when you're trying to avoid someone as much as you are Jake."

I hate that he's right and I hate how it makes me feel torn up inside.

I should be feeling dread at the thought of bumping into Jake again, but all I feel is butterflies. It's too much to compute, especially when he looked like he did. My mind wanders, remembering how he towered over me in the club, piercing me with those dark brown eyes, and how his once boyish figure has filled out. Then there were those muscles, muscles covered in tattoos. God, I'm getting turned on in the middle of a job interview just thinking about him, and if I carry on blushing like I know I am, Shaun will know exactly what I'm thinking about. Cringe.

If he's noticed my suddenly flushed appearance, he doesn't say anything, choosing instead to move away from the topic of Jake. "Anyway, are you free to start tomorrow night? It'll be quiet, but better to get you started and familiar with the place as soon as we can."

"Sure, that sounds great. I don't have any plans, apart from those two tagging along with me wherever I go."

We both laugh, looking over at Sophie and Zoe, who judging by the empty glasses on the table have managed to make their way through at least three drinks and it's not even 4pm. Perfect.

Standing, Shaun beckons for me to join him. "I better make a move before it gets busy. Let's aim for you to start at six tomorrow. Get here a bit earlier so you're ready to start on time."

I lean in playfully with a smirk on my face and say, "Yes, boss." To the outside world it might look like I'm flirting, but Shaun will know otherwise, which is why I push it further, knowing I can get away with it. I stand on my tiptoes and whisper the last part in his ear. "Whatever you need ..."

"Eghem ..."

Turning around quickly, five pairs of eyes stare back at us with a mixture of expressions. Sophie and Zoe are both bright red in the face as they try to hold in their laughter at the irony of the situation. Sam and a guy I've not met before looking confused. And then, of course, there's Jake. To most people, his face would look unaffected by the scenario, but I'm not most people, I can see the storm brewing in his eyes

58

as he stares. He narrows them, glancing between us, trying to assess what exactly has been interrupted.

"So, what's going on here?" Sam asks the question everyone was most likely thinking.

Under normal circumstances I'd be open about what was going on, however the look of distaste Jake is giving me, has me acting out of character. He's making me feel like crap and I haven't done anything wrong.

I flutter my eyelashes and with an overly sweet tone reply to Sam, "I was just letting my boss know that I'm here at his beck and call for the summer."

I shrug my shoulders and look away innocently. The guys stand wide eyed, while Zoe and Sophie snort, unable to contain their laughter any longer. Zoe then complains that she's thirsty and heads to the bar with Sophie following closely behind.

My eyes fall on Jake, but he doesn't say a word and his expression is blank. He gives his head a small shake and follows the girls along with the other guy I have yet to be introduced to.

"Abby, really? You don't need to be such a bitch whenever he's around," Sam complains. The reason behind my little performance hasn't been lost on him.

"Tell that to Jake's judgey face." It's a struggle not to snap, but Sam doesn't deserve my wrath.

"It's not you I'm worried about," he mutters under his breath. I hear him loud and clear and narrow my eyes. Of course, I forgot that everyone was defending Jake these days, forgetting how he treated me back in high school.

Reading the frustration on both of our faces, Shaun steps in and says, "Guys, there's no need for this drama. Abby's only just got back in town, try and have a good time?"

Whatever Sam has left to say, he chooses to hold back. We join the rest of the group at the bar and I make sure I'm as far away from Jake as possible. choosing to introduce myself to the new guy in the group.

I focus my attention on the new guy to the group, extending my arm to shake his hand. "Hey, I'm Abby."

He takes my hand and smiles as he replies, "Zach ..." Then he gives me a look, as if he already really knows me, but I'm not sure how that's possible when we've never met. "It's nice to *finally* meet you, Abby."

Confused, I say, "Finally?"

Rather than answering Zach shrugs and turns to order a drink. As I hardly know him, I don't feel comfortable probing any further, so I make a mental note to chase it up later.

We settle at a table when we all have our drinks and some of the tension lingering from earlier disappears. Most likely because Jake chose to stay at the bar with Zach.

When the others appear to be preoccupied with other conversations, I hiss in Sophie's ear, "Who's the new guy? And why does he seem to know me?"

"It's Jake's best friend. They've been in the band together a few years," she replies quietly.

Not quietly enough, as Zoe jumps in to finish the explanation, "He's so sexy."

"You think anything with a penis is sexy," laughs Sophie.

Missing the humor in her voice, Zoe says, "Are you calling me a slut?"

Sophie shakes her head. "You call yourself a slut, all the time. You know I'm joking."

"Whatever ..." grumbles Zoe. Sophie's comments seem to be affecting her more than normal and they continue bickering between themselves.

I switch off and my eyes trail, involuntarily, to where Jake is standing at the bar. The tension he was carrying earlier has gone and he laughs at something Zach says.

I chew on the inside of my cheek. Just being in the same room together is stirring up feelings I'm not ready to acknowledge. After six years of nothing, everything is flooding back with an intensity that makes my pulse race. But it was always this way with us, and the emotions after we broke up were like nothing I'd ever experienced.

First there was a long period of pining, where I'd sit in my room crying for hours. Then there was the social stage, where I'd use any gathering as an opportunity to see him, in a last ditched attempt to change his mind. All of it was in vain because nothing changed.

When we broke up, the Jake I knew disappeared overnight, leaving me questioning whether our relationship had been a figment of my imagination. For at least a year I was a shell of myself, and I scared the hell out of my parents and friends. Finally, when it all got too much and the opportunity arose, I ran away from Brooklyn and didn't look back.

People keep saying that he's grown up and changed, but it feels like there's more to the story and I'm missing a piece of the puzzle. I can't help that everything still feels so raw. A part of me wants to fight, make up for what I didn't do back in high school, but doing so would create unnecessary drama for the group. They appear even closer than the old days, which Sophie and Zoe neglected to tell me.

It's obvious Shaun's bar is the group's main hangout, and if I'm going to work here, I need to get my shit together. Jake and I need to at least be amicable around each other and make life easier for everyone else. Tomorrow's a new day and all that.

"Right guys, I better get back to work." Shaun stands, bringing me out of my train of thought and back to reality. "I'll see you tomorrow, new employee."

He rubs my shoulder and winks before walking away. I look over to the bar where Jake is still standing. A wave of anger flashes through his eyes as he watches Shaun. It's subtle and I wonder if anyone else noticed.

"You're playing with fire ..." Sam murmurs, answering my question.

I roll my eyes. "He's a big boy, Sam."

"Let's not do another round tonight. We never let this get between us before, so why now?"

"Jake was non-existent before and refused to be in the same room as me. Things have changed and he keeps being very much existent."

"We'll get through it. What time does the slave driver have you starting tomorrow? We could catch up over coffee before?" The cheeky grin he flashes, wins me over, so I back down.

I shake my head. "No can do tomorrow, or the next few days. I have a lot on ..." His expression falls at my response. "... but I can do Friday?"

Visibly brightening, he says, "Great, you've got my cellphone number. Drop me a line later in the week and we'll sort something."

"Perfect. Anyway, I better get going I have an early morning shoot and need my sleep unlike you party animals."

Zoe and Sophie are unhappy I'm leaving, but I never get wasted before work. It's a rule I've stuck with all these years, and the reason I've done so well for myself. Some might call me boring. I call it professional.

When I manage to say goodbye to everyone, I stand up and offer a small wave, then leave the bar quickly, avoiding Jake and Zach. I keep my head down as I pass through the door, missing the look Jake gives me over his shoulder. A look that lasts a moment too long for someone who is meant to hate me.

Eight

6 years earlier

*H*e's standing so close behind me I can feel every part of his body, even the rise and fall of his chest. Our moments alone are made of this. Small intimate gestures and whispers to each other.

"Relax, Abby," he murmurs into my ear. "Just swing, don't over think it."

Turning slightly, I look up into his eyes. It feels like there's more to what he's saying.

"What do you mean?"

"Take the plunge and swing, what have you got to lose?"

Trusting what he's saying, I forget about making an idiot of myself. I draw back the hockey stick, and with Jake's arms still wrapped around me, guiding me, I swing. We both watch as the puck flies through the air, sailing into the makeshift goal he made earlier.

If only I had the courage to take the plunge with him.

Present Day

Thankfully, things continue drama free and I settle into a day-to-day routine, beginning to feel like my old self as I adjust back to life in Brooklyn. Days go quickly. It's what draws people in, making you never want to leave the hustle and bustle, the franticness of everyday life. I'm no exception.

Already I've found myself becoming distant with Michael. Between juggling photography jobs I've picked up and my nights working at Riffs, there's been no time to snatch even a few minutes for a quick call. It's the one thing he feared. That I'd come back to Brooklyn and forget about him. I guess his fears weren't without reason. I haven't forgotten that things were strained when we ended our conversation the night I first arrived. If I leave it any longer to clear the air, it will only create a bigger void between us.

If I'm honest with myself, space is what we need. I need time to breathe and get my head straight. Make sure we're on the same page before we move on to the next chapter of our lives. I'm determined to make this summer a good thing and gain some clarity.

It's already Friday, which marks the end of my first full week back home. Despite Fridays being busy, I've managed to bag a day shift at Riff's rather than what are becoming my regular evening ones. As I'm working the rest of the weekend, the sting feels a little less having the night off. It's also my first night without any plans, and the rest is needed, although I'm not sure how long my night will remain free.

I'm clocking out of my shift when Shaun walks over. "Hey, sexy lady, what're you up to tonight?"

"If you're coming on to me, be prepared for the mob to arrive soon."

"You know I don't mix work and pleasure."

I'm victim to another of his winks and I realize it's his signature move. Shaun is a winker. I chuckle to myself and he stares at me like I'm losing it.

"You mean you don't mix *the help* with pleasure. I'm pretty sure taking home customers is still classed as work."

It's not a secret that he regularly takes women from the bar to his apartment upstairs. Really, who would blame him when they throw themselves at him like they do?

He folds his arms across his chest and says, "Touché. Can't get much past you, can we now?"

"What can I say? I have a player radar that never fails." It's a shame my radar doesn't pick up when a guy is about to break your heart into a million pieces.

"Back to what we were saying before you decided to start calling me out on my promiscuous ways. What are you doing tonight?"

"I was hoping to get some chill time, but I doubt Zoe will let that happen," I reply.

"Good, she shouldn't. I know the last thing you want to do is be in work on your night off, but we have a big band playing tonight, they're great. I thought you could drop by as everyone will be here, and we can properly celebrate you being home."

He gives me puppy dog eyes and I can see how eager he is for me to say yes, but alarm bells ring. This isn't a good idea. If the whole group is going to be there, that also means Jake.

Despite the internal battle I'm having, I find myself reluctantly saying yes to Shaun's invite. As I leave work, there's a sinking feeling in my gut, knowing I've committed myself to a night full of potential drama.

✱✱✱

My cell starts vibrating and Sam's name flashes on the screen, along with a ridiculous picture he must have taken when he saved his number. Even though I'm running late getting ready, I quickly answer.

I'm greeted with his warm voice. "Hey, Abs, you coming tonight?"

"Of course."

I'm halfway through drawing on eyeliner with my cell balanced between my shoulder and ear. My response sounds a little off, but I'm too busy concentrating at the task in hand.

Sam picks up on my tone, misreading it. "We good?"

"Why wouldn't we be?" I place my eyeliner down so I can focus on the conversation, making sure I sound friendlier.

"I dunno. The other day was a bit weird, seeing you and Shaun so close."

Letting out a sigh, I reply, "We work together, Sam."

"I know, but it looked like more." He sounds unhappy at the idea.

"Believe me it wasn't. I have a boyfriend."

I don't know why I keep having to remind everyone of this.

"Yeah?" If he sounded unhappy before, he sounds almost pained now. I've no idea why. Sam and I have a small bit of history. The tiny, insignificant kind. Especially to him ... I think.

"Like four years yeah," I reply, "Soph and Zoe never mentioned it?"

"Shit, that's a long time." He sounds resigned, but I don't understand why. I would have expected my friend to be happy for me, not the opposite.

Choosing not to leave another question unanswered and another thing to dwell on, I ask, "Is that a bad thing?"

"For some yes ..."

"What do you mean for some? Who would it be bad for?" I try not to sound snappy but I'm becoming agitated by his cryptic answers.

I can imagine him shaking his head and rubbing a hand over his face as he says, "Never mind. It's me being weird. So, can we hang out tonight without any drama? I've missed you, Abs."

I choose to ignore the voices in my head telling me he's acting suspiciously. I reply, "Yes, to hanging out. Is it enough if I say I'll try my best with the no drama?"

"I guess it will do." I can hear his smile down the line, and I involuntarily smile back. Sam has that effect on people, his positive attitude and love of life can be infectious.

We agree to meet at Riffs in the next hour and hanging up, I realize I barely have time to finish getting ready. Luckily, I'm not one for high maintenance routines. As I've gotten older, I've begun to care less about what people think, so I often go for looking acceptable over making too much effort.

I avoid washing my hair and instead add some gentle waves with a quiff at the front to keep it out of my face. The copper highlights in my dark brown hair catch the light perfectly. I opt for some cut-off denim shorts, a black tank top and my converse. The past few days have been sweltering, and I refuse to be uncomfortable for the sake of fashion. Luckily, Riffs isn't that sort of place.

When I'm happy with what I see in the mirror, I make a move to leave, but when I catch my dad's reflection, I stop in my tracks.

"Hey, everything ok?" I ask.

"I just thought I'd catch you quickly. We've not seen much of you this week. Has work been good?"

"Yep, great. I've had positive feedback with the photos, and the bar is great. Besides that, I've, just been catching up with people, the usual. I'm actually off to Riffs now with the group to see a new band."

"Ok, just be careful."

I forgot that living under your parents' roof also came with their constant worry over what you're doing and where you are. Not that it ever goes away no matter where you are but it's usually less obvious.

"Come on, Dad. I've lived on my own for six years. I'll be perfectly safe at a small gig." I state the obvious but know what he's getting at. There's a hidden meaning behind his words which I choose not to acknowledge.

He frowns. "That's not what I'm talking about and you know it."

"Why don't you clear it up for me, because I'm not a mind reader." I hate the tone I've taken with him and that it's verging on rude, but I know we're about to have a conversation about Jake, and it's bringing out the worst in me.

"Watch your tone. You might be older but that doesn't mean you get to speak to your father like that." His eyes look hurt. It's not often we have disagreements but any we have had, are always Jake related.

"Sorry. I'm taking things out on you. Everyone keeps making these cryptic comments and I don't really know what's going on. It's frustrating." I look away and take a deep breath trying to calm myself down.

"I don't suppose they're trying to warn you off Jake?"

"Sometimes it feels like the opposite." I sigh. "I have a boyfriend, and it's been six years, all that stuff between us is in the past." I want the last part to sound convincing, but if I can't convince myself my feelings for Jake are in the past, how am I supposed to convince anyone else?

"Does Jake know that you have a boyfriend?" he asks.

"What does it matter? We've both moved on. Yes, I might bump into him, but we'll just get on with it and hopefully get through the summer in one piece."

My little speech isn't just to convince Dad, it's to remind myself what the game plan is.

"Just be careful. I don't want to see you getting hurt again." He looks sad and I know he's remembering the first time Jake hurt me.

"Honestly, Dad. I'll be fine. We hate each other, there's nothing to worry about."

"Abby ... Jake could never hate you." Oh yeah, I forgot they work together now. Apparently, he has knows more about our relationship than I do.

"Funny, it seemed like he did when we broke up. His face looks like he can't even stand to be in the same room as me, so I'd say otherwise."

He shrugs. "Maybe he has his reasons?"

Again, with the mixed messages.

I narrow my eyes. "Are you trying to make me stay away from him, or fight his corner? I'm confused."

70

"It doesn't matter. I know you're in a rush, but I did want to talk to you about Jake, before we even got onto that topic. I needed you to hear it from me before anyone else says anything. The label has decided to sign his band, imminently."

As hard as it is, I manage to contain my emotions and focus on putting his mind at ease. He obviously feels guilty for his connection to Jake, but it's important for the band and their success, that I don't let the past become a problem.

I paste on the most convincing smile I can muster. "Don't worry, it's fine. I'm glad you told me though. Like I keep saying, you don't have anything to worry about. When it comes to me and Jake, the past is in the past."

"I don't want to keep going on, but just remember, you're here for one summer. Trust your gut. You're both going places. Don't let things get in the way of that."

"I won't, Daddy, I promise. It's good to be home." I avoid saying anything else and stand on my tiptoes to place a kiss on his cheek.

He kisses me on the head in return. "It's good having you home, we've missed you. Have fun tonight. Let your hair down, you've been working too hard."

Alone in my room when he's left, there are far too many questions floating around in my head. I glance at the clock on my bedside table and curse. I'm going to have to run in this heat to make sure I get to the gig on time. Basically, I'm going to be a sweaty mess.

As I'm sprinting down the stairs, I fly past my mom, who, like Dad I've barely seen.

"You look nice, honey."

I feel guilty that I'm about to leave when she looks like she wants to talk.

71

"Thanks, Mom. Sorry, I'm already running late to meet everyone. Can I catch you later?"

If she's disappointed, she doesn't show it. "Sure," she says, "don't worry about it. Have a great night."

"Thanks, I'll try," I reply.

I let out a deep breath as I leave the house. I'd be lying if I said I wasn't nervous at the thought of bumping into Jake again. We need to get over the past and find a way to be around each other amicably. Hopefully, tonight can be the start of that.

Pulling on my big girl panties and making my way to Riffs like I don't have a care in the world, I decide that maybe in the process of convincing everyone else I'm fine, I can convince myself.

Nine

usk is setting in when I arrive at Riffs, adding a blue hue to the city. The light pouring from the bars seems to pop more than usual making them appear even more inviting. The heat of the day has yet to subside and there's a buzz in the air igniting my senses. The smells, the light, the atmosphere. Tonight, everything feels alive and different.

Stepping inside, I scan the room for the group. I don't have to look far despite it being busy, as I can clearly see Sophie and Zoe standing at the main bar with Sam.

"Abby, over here!" Sophie shouts excitedly, attracting attention from a few people surrounding her.

"I have eyes that work, you don't need to screech," I say when I eventually manage to maneuver my way through the tightly packed crowd.

"I can't help it! I'm so excited we're all back together again." Her voice gets gradually louder as she speaks. "This is the group's first night out in like forever!" She's only pint sized, but she can reach unexpected volumes. As she bounces up and down on her feet, it's like watching a pixie that's high. I refrain from rolling my eyes, accepting she's overly excited.

Instead, I turn to Sam and ask, "What are we drinking?"

"Shots!" shouts Zoe in my ear.

I wince and rub at it, flashing her an annoyed look. "Thanks for that. I'm not having shots I haven't started drinking yet."

"And that's why shots are a good idea," she grins, clapping her hands together.

"Seriously. I'm not playing babysitter tonight. How much have you had already?"

The fact she's stood upright is the evidence I need. She hasn't had anywhere near her usual intake, but after the puking incident last week, I'd rather stay vigilant.

"Not enough, you bore. You need to get drinking like now."

"Laaaaydeeees," interrupts Sam, hooking an arm around each of our shoulders. "No drama ... remember? Abby, you need to get a drink down you and chill out. Zoe, you need water. We're here to see a band, not go home before they start."

Zoe turns away, ignoring Sam's comment, choosing to chat with Sophie. They each throw me a look that says I'm shitting on their parade. Whatever, they'll forget about it after the next drink.

As we go to order Sam asks, "Beer? Please tell me you haven't become a wine bitch while you've been away?"

"I'll take the biggest beer they've got," I reply with a smile.

"That's my girl." With the arm that's still looped round my shoulders, he tugs me in close and murmurs into my hair, "Good to have you back, Abs."

74

"It's good to be back, Sammy." I gaze up at him with the familiarity only old friends have, and then Sam rings my order in.

It's getting busier but thanks to working the bar and being the owners' friend and brother, we don't have to wait long. When we have our drinks, we make our way outside for the gig, joining everyone else.

Outside has undergone a complete transformation. The tables which are usually scattered around, have been moved to the perimeter, providing room for standing in front of the stage. Overhead are thousands of fairy lights which create an ambient glow against the dusky sky, and lush greenery used to decorate the area. Despite being large and full of people, the space feels intimate, and chills run down my spine with excitement.

There are a few people I don't recognize when we join the group, and I assume they joined the ranks while I've been gone over the years. One person I do recognize is Zach, who I met during my first visit to the bar. I expect some animosity as he's Jake's best friend, but just like the first time I met him, he offers me a friendly smile. I smile back and mouth "Hi" at him, deciding he's a genuinely nice guy.

Taking a large swig of the beer Sam ordered, I choke as the taste fills my mouth.

"Shit, Sam, how strong is this?" I splutter. He's handed me the strongest one he could get, rather than the refreshing one I wanted.

"We told you to catch up," he laughs with no remorse. "Plus, it saves you having to go back for a while. You don't want to miss the band."

"With this, I don't think I'll need to go back for the rest of the night." I scrunch my face up as I take another small sip. It burns going all the way down my throat.

Zoe chips in, "Seriously, Abs? What've you been doing while you've been away? You're out of practice and no fun, you need to let your hair down for once."

"She's right you know," Sam agrees. He looks slightly apprehensive for my reaction, but there's already a buzz in my system from the small amount I've drank, and any fight in me has gone.

"I have been working a lot." A deflated feeling takes over. They may be on to something. It's been a long time since I really let myself go and enjoyed life without worrying about the consequences it would have on my future. A small part of me wants to let go and just be carefree.

"Let's change that while you're here," says Sophie, drawing me into a hug. "We need to make sure we have the best summer yet." Like my first night in Brooklyn, she's bouncing around, and raises her drink in the air causing some of it to slosh over the sides of the glass. "Come on, guys, let's do a toast to the best summer!"

Everyone raises their glasses and starts downing their drinks. Not wanting to be a party pooper, I join in the best I can, drinking as much as possible, despite how strong it is.

Sam points out my poor attempt. "You can do better than that, Abs."

I punch him in the arm. "If I didn't know any better, I'd think you were trying to get me drunk."

He leans in and says quietly, "That's because I am."

"Haha very funny, you can stop now." I turn away and catch Sophie and Zoe watching us with amused expressions. "What?"

"Are you two going to stop flirting so we can watch the gig?" Grabbing my arm, Zoe leads the way towards the stage, maneuvering us swiftly through the crowd.

We spend the rest of the time before the band comes on stage laughing and joking, buzzing with excitement. At one point the guys move away to grab more drinks, quickly returning before the gig begins. Thankfully my second drink isn't anywhere near as strong as the first.

The crowd roars in appreciation, as the opening notes from the band sound out through the night air. They're modern rock, the same genre we used to listen to when we were younger. Being here tonight is both refreshing and nostalgic. It feels good to be back to my old ways, letting go and enjoying life.

As the tracks go on, the night gets darker but warmer. The crowd presses in around us and I can feel my hair beginning to stick to the back of my neck, so I gather it up and sweep it over one shoulder. The band starts to play one of their most popular songs and the crowd sways from side to side to the opening riffs. I can't help getting caught up in the moment, swaying with them, closing my eyes and completely losing myself in the song.

The lyrics are a story about a girl captivating a guy, giving him everything she has, following him and trying to help him be the best version of himself. The story reaches to me, draws me in, and leaves me feeling breathless, as it hits a nerve. I'm still standing, eyes closed, listening, when a sudden feeling of awareness washes over me. Goosebumps cover my body.

Reacting to the signal my body is giving, I turn to speak to Sophie. Instead, I bump straight into a broad, firm chest. I look up, straight into Jake's eyes. It takes a second for me to gather my bearings, thanks to a mixture of the strong alcohol Sam has been ploughing me with, and Jake's sudden proximity. I blink a few times and realize I'm still staring straight into his eyes. Unfazed, he stares back down with an intensity that takes my breath away.

Disorientated, I stumble back, but Jake catches me quickly, steadying me with his hands firmly on my hips. His eyes never leave my face, and as hard as I try to fight the urge to look at him, mine betray me. Despite his serious expression, with the soft glow from the lights above and the slight sheen of sweat from the heat, all I can think is how beautiful he looks. He has the kind of masculine beauty that makes every woman give him a second, longing glance.

When I allow my eyes to meet with his, my body trembles. I'm sure he can feel it, thanks to his hands still planted on my hips, his fingers digging in. I will myself to move, or at the very least look away, but I can't. I'm desperate to take in more of the face staring back at me, in some ways so familiar, but in others, that of a stranger.

He's older and manlier. The scruff on his jaw is new and draws my attention to his mouth, where my gaze lingers. I lick my lips in anticipation. I've never wanted to kiss anyone as much as I do right now, but the thought of losing complete control with Jake terrifies me.

I'm not sure how long we stay staring at each other, but the moment is broken when Zach taps abruptly on Jake's shoulder. Looking between the two of us he seems wary, and it's the first time he's been anything but open and friendly towards me. He murmurs something in Jake's ear, which gauges a reaction, causing Jake to pull away quickly.

The sudden absence leaves me feeling embarrassed, but the rest of the group are too engrossed with the band. No one apart from Zach has noticed the moment that Jake and I shared. A riot of emotions course through me, mainly frustration. Frustration that despite telling everyone, as well as myself, that this summer would be fine and there was no need to worry, it's only taken us seeing each other twice, for my willpower to disappear.

A war is waging internally as I try to rationalize the situation. Maybe I misread the moment, and maybe thanks to the mix of alcohol and heat, my imagination is running away with itself. I tell myself that Jake was only helping to steady me, thanks to the crowd around us making me almost fall. And the look I mistook for lust, was obviously confusion. I was after all rooted to the spot, staring at him like a lunatic. A simple explanation. One that makes me look like a fool.

My cell buzzes in my pocket, snapping me out of my spiraling thoughts. I read Michael's name on the screen, and the realization I haven't given my boyfriend a second thought for the past week causes guilt to hit me. Yes, I've been avoiding contact with him, but all I want now is to hear his voice, to have something familiar ground and comfort me, after Jake has caused things to feel so unsettled.

With perfect timing the band wrap up for a quick break, as my cell continues vibrating in my hand. It provides the perfect excuse to put some distance between myself and Jake. A small part of me wonders if that's what I really want, but I quieten the voice, reminding myself that Michael is safe, secure, and with him there's no risk. He won't leave me like Jake did, because he loves me too much.

My voice is far too loud and over the top as I answer the call. "Hey, baby, I miss you."

The pet name grabs Zoe's attention, and she makes a vom motion at me. When her eyes settle on Jake, at first, she looks surprised. Then she rolls her eyes when it dawns on her why I've been over the top and using pet names which I hate.

"I can't hear you properly. Are you ok? Where are you?" Michael's voice draws my attention back to my cell.

"Sorry, I'm at a gig. It was a last-minute thing. I should have text you, so you didn't bother calling."

"I'm jealous. I wish I were there with you."

The crowd settles into the break time buzz and the noise amplifies. Plugging a finger into my other ear, I try to block it out, so I can hear what he's saying, but it's no good.

"Hang on a second," I say, "I can't hear you. Let me move somewhere quieter." I mouth to Sophie that I'll be back soon, then move away from the group, without so much as a backward glance at Jake. "Better?" I ask, stepping outside the front of Riffs.

"Yeah, I can hear you now," he replies.

"I've been wanting to say … I'm sorry for this week. You know, for not being in contact much." It takes a lot for me to own up to my mistakes, I'm stubborn like that, but Michael hasn't done anything to deserve my silence.

"I know you're busy. I'm just counting down the days till I can see you again. This summer already feels like it's been too long."

I surprise us both with the words that come out next. "I know. I miss you."

"You do?"

"Yeah, I guess I do. Is that so hard to believe?"

It shouldn't be hard to believe and that's what's sad about mine and Michael's relationship, that it's gotten to this point. Right now, truthfully, I do miss him and the simplicity of the life I had back in Florida. A life without Jake.

"It's not like you to say things like that," he replies skeptically.

"I may have had a couple of drinks," I chuckle, hoping he sees the funny side. I should probably be alarmed that my boyfriend of four years is surprised at me being openly affectionate.

"That explains it. Anyway, don't apologize. We both knew the distance would be hard, but we'll get through it. Right?"

"Of course." I hope he misses the slight falter in my voice. I'm going to hell for the lies I'm telling.

"In that case, go enjoy your night and we'll speak soon."

"Ok. Speak to you later."

As I hang up, a weight I didn't know was there, lifts from my shoulders. Although I have reservations about our relationship, Michael and I have still been together a long time, and I hate there being any animosity between us. Speaking to him has made things feel better.

The band has started the second part of their set by the time I rejoin the group. It's clear they didn't miss me, as they enjoy the music, drinks in hand.

Sophie hands me a beer, but as I glance around, I realize something has changed. "What happened to Jake?"

"He took off. Had to get to something apparently, but he seemed pissed. You two didn't have another altercation, did you?" She asks.

"Not that I'm aware of." There's a niggle in my chest. Maybe he overheard some of my conversation with Michael as he was leaving. But why would he be bothered?

I refuse to worry over yet another thing which is out of my control and opt for the *'fuck it'* attitude, knocking back my drink. I blatantly ignore my reservations about how I'll be tomorrow. It's what I've become good at, ignoring my feelings.

Ten

A high-pitched screeching noise jars me awake.

"What the fuck?" I vaguely remember Zoe messing with my cellphone last night, with a mischievous look on her face.

Groaning, I fumble about trying to find the offending object. Eventually, when I do, I spend another minute trying to silence it. Damn the effects of alcohol, I'm a mess.

The dull ache in my head intensifies, all thanks to the strong drinks Sam was plying me with all night. It seemed a good idea at the time, but now I hate myself for losing control. I decide that Sam must share the blame for my hangover, and I intend to make him suffer later when he's covering at Riffs alongside me. He'll have to carry my sorry ass through a busy Saturday shift. Lucky him.

Looking at the time, I curse Zoe again. It's only 7.30am and my shift isn't until later in the afternoon, but there's no chance of getting back to sleep. Rather than wasting away the morning feeling hungover, I drag myself out of bed and do something I haven't had a chance to since getting back to Brooklyn.

I run.

Once I've thrown on my gear, I head out quietly, not wanting to wake up my parents on their day off. Even though it's early, the heat is already rising, but manageable enough for a steady pace. I slip in my headphones and begin pounding the sidewalks in the early morning sun. Taking my favorite route from when I was younger, I make my way to Brooklyn promenade, enjoying the views across the Hudson, to Manhattan.

When I return home over an hour later, I'm grinning, relishing the burn in my lungs and the ache in my muscles. It's a feeling I've missed, along with the rush of endorphins. The run has done its job, clearing the worst of my hangover, maybe today won't be too bad after all. The positive vibes are out in full force, and as I step through the front door, the smell of fresh pancakes hits my nose, making my stomach growl.

I find my mom at the kitchen stove, still in her pajamas and the same apron she's worn since I was a kid.

"Morning, honey. Good run?" She looks happy to see me, but it doesn't stop her raising her eyebrows and wrinkling her nose at the sweat literally dripping off me.

"Yeah. Sorry for making a mess," I reply, looking at the puddle I'm creating on the kitchen floor.

"Nothing that can't be cleaned. Pancakes?"

"Do I need to answer that?" My stomach reinforces my answer, loudly.

"So, you had fun last night? I didn't hear you get in."

"It's been a long time since I've let myself have fun like that. Too long."

"It's good to have fun, Abby. You used to be carefree, maybe not as much as Sophie and Zoe, but still. You work too hard now and you'll run yourself into the ground if you're not careful."

"I know, Mom, I've just been focused that's all. I promised the girls last night that I would let my hair down more often."

"Good. Did you see Jake?" Straight to the point. I shouldn't be surprised that she's asking about him.

"Blunt much, Mom?"

"Well?" She refuses to back down.

"I did, briefly and it was fine."

The doubtful look she throws me, makes it evident she knows I'm lying. Still, I choose to omit the details of the moment Jake and I had. I'm not even sure it could be classed as a *moment*. With a clear head, it feels like I could have been imagining it.

"He's working with your father ..."

"It's not a problem. They're in the same industry. It was kind of inevitable. Plus, Jake and I can't avoid each other forever." I'm fully aware of the irony of what I'm saying. All I've done so far is try and convince myself and others that we won't see each other, yet here I am saying the opposite.

"Ok. I just wanted to check you're ok with all of this."

"Honestly ... everything is all good. I've already told Dad this."

I watch as Mom dishes up breakfast, then I tuck in quietly. Between us we have a silent agreement that the subject of Jake is closed. We sit in an amicable silence while eating, and I groan, rubbing my stomach in appreciation when I feel like I can't eat any more.

"Seriously, Mom that was *so* good." I've missed a lot of things in the years I've been gone, but her cooking, I've missed the most.

She smiles, then asks, "What are your plans for the rest of the day?"

"It's still early, so I think I'll get cleaned up and take my camera for a shoot around on my way to the bar. I've got a double shift this afternoon."

"Sounds great. Well, I'll leave you to it."

"Thanks for breakfast." I stand, then lean down and place a kiss on her head like I have done since I was a kid. I then spend a couple of minutes clearing the table before heading upstairs to shower and change.

Heading out with my camera later, I wind up walking the distance from home to Riffs, even though it's a trek. I need time to clear my head, so I take my time snapping everything that catches my eye. It's what makes me happy and it feels good to be photographing for fun rather than work. It reminds me that I do what I do because I love it, and it's a good distraction. Still, it's not enough.

In the fleeting moments where I'm not focused on keeping myself present, my mind constantly wanders back to Jake.

✶✶✶

6 years earlier

I look at Jake uncertainly and whisper, "I guess I'll see you later?" We've spent an amazing and rare afternoon alone together without the rest of the group. We've hung out in different places, laughed, talked and enjoyed being together. It's been perfect

86

and I keep pinching myself, trying to remember that this is really happening to me, and I get him all to myself.

"You sure you don't want to come back to mine for a while? We could just watch a movie or something ..." he scuffs his feet against the sidewalk, looking down. His tone is uncertain, which is unusual for Jake as usually he's full of confidence. But I get to see a different, more vulnerable side to him. When he glances up, he has a hopeful look on his face, and it breaks my heart a little that I'm going to take away the happy expression that's been on his face all day.

"I'm sorry, you know I can't. Dad will literally kill me. He's already unhappy with this." It's the truth.

My parents have always been cool with me hanging around with a mixed group, but they've caught wind that Jake and I have been spending more time alone, and Dad has pulled the reins in tight. He's not ready to let go of his baby yet.

Rubbing a hand over his face, he lets out a sigh. "I know, sorry. I shouldn't have asked again." He seems resigned but continues, "It's just today's been good, really good. I'm not ready for it to end yet."

Catching my eye, he wills me to change my mind. His gaze intensifies, as it moves down towards my lips, like he wants to move in and do more than just talk. I swallow nervously. It's all I can do. The truth is I've never been kissed, and the thought that Jake might want to, fills me with dread, because I don't have a clue what to do.

"I like that we talk in person now," he smiles. Reaching over he tucks a loose strand of hair behind my ear and his touch gives me goosebumps.

I know he's being playful, referring to the times when we only ever used to talk on the phone or online, because I was too terrified to talk to him in person. It's taken a long time for us to get to this point, and I'm surprised he didn't give up and walk away. Maybe I'm reading too much into the whole thing and all he wants is to be friends. But when he looks at me like he's doing now, my heart feels like it's about to leap out of my chest. I've never felt like this before. Ever.

The intensity is getting too much. As he refuses to look away, I tilt my head forward, looking down to break the moment.

"Well, it just took me some time to work up the courage," I say finally, and a little defensively. "I'm not used to all this attention."

He clears his throat and steps forward, eliminating the space between us. Grasping my chin gently, he encourages me to raise my face and look him in the eyes. "Well get used to it, cause I'm not going anywhere." With a tenderness that makes my heart pound he continues, "Please don't hide from me, Abby. You don't need to."

Instead of kissing me, he pulls me in for a hug. My limbs are everywhere as I'm not used to the physical contact and he's caught me off guard. He merely chuckles seeming nervous and unsure himself.

When he manages to engulf me in his arms, his larger frame covering mine, I can't get enough of the moment. The nerves seep away, and my heartrate slows as I begin to enjoy every second. I don't ever want to let go. My eyes burn, as I'm completely overwhelmed with how I'm feeling. I tuck my face further into his chest, breathing in his scent, trying to commit it to memory in case this is the only time I'll ever get to be this close.

He responds to my eagerness by leaning his head down and nuzzling my neck, then gently, he trails the tip of his nose up to my ear. His warm breath comes out quickly, and I feel like I'm about to combust as I begin to lose the feeling in my legs.

Just when I think I'm about to collapse in the middle of the sidewalk from sensation overload, he drags me out of my bliss-induced haze, by murmuring into my ear, "Next time … I want you and me alone. I want you all to myself with no audience." The last bit is followed by his signature chuckle, as he pulls away and begins walking backwards. "See you later, pretty girl."

I stand, gawping in shock at the loss of contact. Blood rushes to my cheeks and Jake laughs again, knowing the effect he's having on me. Then, he offers a small wave before turning and walking away. I watch his retreating form and notice an old couple sitting on a bench near to where Jake and I have been standing, with bemused expressions on their faces. I realize they are the audience Jake was referring to. It snaps me out of my daze, and I glance at my cell realizing the time. I don't have much time to get back before Dad starts to go crazy.

As the subway sways steadily, I think back to what Jake said. He wants to be alone, with me. Am I ready for that? Am I ready to take things further, from small touches to something more? I don't know. I've never even kissed anyone, but I know Jake would never pressure me to do anything I wasn't ready for.

I might not be certain how far I'm willing to take things yet, but there is one thing I am certain of. If there is anyone that I want all my firsts to be with, it's Jake.

Eleven

I agreed I would hold back a bit on the work front, but I can't turn away the money I'm being offered, so my work life feels busier than ever over the following week. Luckily, Sophie and Zoe understand when I explain that things will quieten off soon. I neglect to mention that my dad's been dropping hints about a big project working with his company that will take up a huge chunk of my time. That can wait.

I've managed to grab a Sunday night off from Riffs, which I use as an opportunity to spend time with the girls on their own, making up for my absence. We can talk freely without fear of the guys listening in, especially when we're talking about more serious subjects.

"Are you going to come for a wax with us?" asks Zoe from across the table.

"No." We've been having the same conversation for the past few minutes.

"Oh, come on. We've seen your vagina so many times, Abby, it's nothing new." She rolls her eyes.

"I'm aware of that. I just don't want it doing." I squeeze my thighs together at the thought of the pain. No thank you.

Sophie snorts into her drink and some of the other diners begin listening in to our conversation. It's hard not to with the volume Zoe's speaking at.

Getting louder, Zoe says, "But, babe, what do you do with it?"

"What do you mean, what do I do with it?" I hiss, feeling flustered. I suggested a smaller, more intimate Italian, close to where we all live and away from the bar scene. I hoped keeping the night low key would help to keep the girls under control. I should have known better than to try and contain the beasts. All I've done is move the humiliation to a smaller environment, where everyone can hear clearly the details of some of the awful conversations that I am regularly subjected to.

"Isn't it like fluffy and out of control if you don't wax?" Zoe continues, totally oblivious to our audience.

"It's not the dark ages, Zo, there are other options to maintain that area besides waxing." An old lady throws us a seriously dirty look, and it's then that I give up all hope of a civilized evening. "Fuck it, this isn't working. Let's go next door to the cocktail bar. At least there I don't have to worry about small children hearing the ridiculous shit you're both coming out with."

We quickly make our way to the hostess at the front of the restaurant, giving her enough cash to cover our meal even though we haven't even eaten yet, and then exit swiftly.

Behind me I can hear Zoe grumbling to herself. "Why is she always so grumpy? Is it permanently shark week or something?"

Meanwhile Sophie chants, "Cocktails!" over and over as she follows me into the bar.

I begin to relax when we eventually get settled with a selection of cocktails that are almost as big as me, and an even bigger selection of shots. The music is loud enough that people can't hear what we're saying which is a blessing as the girls have no filter.

Raising a shot glass in the air, Sophie encourages Zoe and I to do the same, and says, "To girls' night."

We clink our shots together, and then knock them back in one go. As the putrid liquid makes its way down our throats, Sophie and I begin choking.

"Fuck, Zoe, what the hell did you buy?" I barely manage to wheeze out, as the burn in my throat is strong.

"Teeeeeqqqquuuuuuilllllaaa," she shouts grinning.

"We need girls' night more often," says Sophie. "That woman's face every time you said vagina."

She begins howling with laughter, as Zoe chants, "vagina, vagina, vagina," getting louder each time. If I thought we wouldn't draw attention here, I was wrong. I can feel the alcohol kicking in though, and rather than telling them to shut the hell up, I join in, giggling and forgetting how immature they're being.

"How did we even get onto the conversation of why I need to wax my vagina?" I ask. Amidst the slight alcohol fog, I remember there was something Zoe wanted to speak about.

"Oh, I forgot to tell you," says Zoe, then screeches, "group road trip!"

"Group road trip? When?" I ask. "I can't just drop everything. I have to work you know."

"No, you don't. It's only for three nights and we're two weeks away from the 4th of July. Shaun said the bar is ridiculously quiet as everyone saves their energy for the big day. He said you can have the time off and even he's coming. Plus, we checked with your parents and they said your diary is free, so just don't book anything else in."

"My parents knew about this, but I didn't?"

"We wanted to keep it a surprise and tell you closer to the time. We knew you would say no otherwise and find a way out of it," murmurs Sophie into her drink, refusing to look me in the eye.

"When do we go?" I've resigned myself to the fact there's no way I'm getting out of it. "Also, *where* are we going?"

"Day after tomorrow, bright and early, leaving at five. We're tag teaming the carpool as it's a long drive to Lake Placid." Sophie clears up the minor details as Zoe has lost interest now the surprise is over with.

I raise my eyebrows. "So, we're basically going to Canada?"

"No. We're still in New York the state, just not the city. Come on, Abby, it's so beautiful. The group's been doing it the past few years, and we knew we had to take you there now you're finally home."

It's a completely unreasonable reaction, as I'm the one that's been working away all these years and refusing to come back, but I feel rather dejected at the news. It's hard not to focus on the fact I've missed out on so many memories with the group. There's only one way to fix that, I'm going on the trip and making sure I don't miss out on this year's memories.

One thing bugs me. They haven't clarified who exactly is going on the trip, and really, it's an important detail. "Who's *we* by the way?"

"Well ..." Zoe, quickly reels off a list of names. "There's me, you and Soph obviously. Shaun, Sam, Zach, Jake and Amanda." The last two names come particularly fast.

Clearly, she's hoping to get them by, without me realizing. The effort is pointless though, as my Jake radar is in full force. I dislike that his name has been tagged on the end with Amanda. It's a name I don't recognize, and it makes me feel uneasy.

"Who's Amanda?" I follow the question with a large gulp of my drink. I'm not sure why I asked when deep down I know the answer.

"Erm..." Sophie takes a deep breath then continues to answer. "She's Jake's girlfriend. She's been coming for the past couple of years they've been together. We weren't sure if she would this year as she's been away with work, but she got back last night and said she's game. I think you'd really like her if you let yourself. She's nice, and you're both similar in ways and totally have stuff in common."

"Things like Jake," I say, unable to hide the bitterness in my voice. I'm not sure how they expect me to make friends with the person who has everything I ever wanted. The person who got what I couldn't have.

"Come on, Abs," urges Zoe. "You have Michael. You've been telling us all you've moved on, so what's the big deal?"

It's possible the alcohol is taking over, as I didn't plan on anyone knowing this, (anyone apart from Zach) but I find myself saying, "Jake and I had a weird moment."

"What sort of weird moment?" snaps Zoe. Okay, so she's not a fan of the news.

"The night we went to the gig. I bumped into him and it felt like something happened between us."

"How did we miss this? Did you kiss?" asks Sophie. Her frown gives away that she also isn't impressed.

94

Trying not to get agitated by their reactions, I pause before replying, "Of course, we didn't. I'm with Michael. I would never do that to him. You guys know I would never cheat."

"With anyone else ... this is Jake though." Sophie's face is full of concern, making me feel worse than I did before. "We remember how bad it was. We were there, remember? He's changed, Abby, and he's not the same guy. He's grown up and it'd be easy to get drawn back in."

My voice goes a pitch higher when I say, "I'm not getting drawn back into anything! I promise. It was just a look. A slightly heated, get your panties wet kind of look, but that's all." Even I don't believe what I'm saying.

Zoe sighs and it feels like our roles have been reversed. "We get it. We just don't want to see you get hurt. He was *your everything*, and when all that went down, you were broken. You've never been the same since and I can't watch you go through that twice. I agree with Sophie though. He's changed. I don't think he would do that to you again, but still ..."

"He wouldn't do anything because he has a girlfriend and I have a boyfriend. He's not interested. He broke up with *me* remember ...?"

Zoe's answer is confusing things. Between them, they seem to be forgetting what happened between Jake and me, even though they're saying otherwise.

"You're both attached. Yes," says Sophie, "but the history between you guys is massive. Stuff like that doesn't just go away. Plus, Zach's been asking things since you've been back. He's definitely digging."

"What do you think he's digging for?" I ask.

"I'm not sure. He's just been asking whether you've mentioned Jake, things like that. Maybe they've been speaking about you. Fuck. I don't know.

Seriously, this is stressing me out. I need another drink." She stands up abruptly and walks to the bar.

Seeing Sophie stressed is concerning as it's not like her. Her and Zoe don't get stressed about anything.

I watch Sophie walk off and Zoe rubs my shoulder reassuringly. "Don't feel bad. She always gets emotional about the, you and Jake stuff. She hates seeing you hurting."

"Who said I was hurting?"

"Maybe you're not hurting, but this is going to affect you somehow. If you guys had a moment, it means something is still there."

I get what she's saying, and there's truth in it, but I'm in no place to begin acknowledging what it might mean, so I opt for my favorite thing. Denial.

"Nothing's there. We hate each other like we have for years, so everything's fine. Let's forget I mentioned anything."

"If you're sure?"

I'm not, but I don't say it out loud. There's so much left unsaid about how I really feel seeing Jake again. Then there's the state of mine and Michael's relationship and even my career. Rather than facing up to my problems, returning to Brooklyn has become an excellent way to ignore them and the decisions I need to make.

"I'm sure," I lie, putting an end to the conversation. With perfect timing, Sophie returns carrying another round of drinks for us all.

"I'm better now." She's relaxed considerably since going to the bar, and I wonder whether she managed to sneak in an extra drink to chill her out, before coming back. "So, we leave early Tuesday morning. Have your game face on because we are going to have *so* much fun. And you will be nice to Amanda, even if it kills you."

The last part is a little aggressive, but I'm proud of her for standing her ground instead of it being Zoe.

"Great." I take my drink and knock the whole thing back in one. "Can't wait. Wooo, Lake Placid!" The cheering motion may have been a bit over enthusiastic, as they both roll their eyes. The rest of the night passes without any mention of Jake.

Twelve

N ot that I'd ever mention it to Sophie and Zoe, but I've always wanted to go to Lake Placid. Knowing they've been doing it these past few years without me brings out some jealousy, but I stomp it down quickly because it's completely irrational. I try to focus on being excited about a break away with the group.

After girls' night, and a full day of work, there's been no time to pack, but hopefully it won't take too long later. I've managed to bag a later shift at the bar, the positive being that time passes quickly, leaving me with less opportunities to dwell on the potential disaster this trip could be.

Plowing my way through my end of shift jobs, I place my cell on one of the shelves in the stockroom with a random playlist on. I get to work on the final job, restocking the bar, quickly zoning out with the music playing in the background. There's no one around to laugh, so I dance around, grabbing bottles off the shelves and placing them into the crates, ready to be carried out front.

A throat clears behind me.

Spinning around in shock, I trip over one of the crates and fall back into the shelves, causing multiple bottles to tumble down. One hits me in the head. Others rain down on various body parts and, believe me, it seriously fucking hurts. By some miracle none of them smash but I've taken the full brunt and am going to have a few bruises to show tomorrow. Great.

"Shit! Abby, are you ok?"

My humiliation is complete, the voice belongs to Jake.

Internally I groan. Scrap that, externally I groan, and bang my already banged up head back against a shelf. I close my eyes and pray that when I open them again Jake will have gone, his appearance merely a figment of my near-death experience.

Luck is not on my side. When I open them, he's still there looking at me and I'm nowhere near death.

He looks even more gorgeous than the other night. Damnit. He's wearing a pair of tight-fitting black jeans, a white t-shirt and leather jacket. Without his tattoos showing, he looks more like the Jake I remember, and my heart flutters. Because I've been ogling his body, I've completely ignored him speaking to me.

He waves a hand trying to catch my attention. "Did you hit your head that hard? Can you hear me? Should I call for help?"

Three questions in a row. Is he for real? I rub my head and wince. "Jake, please just shush for a second."

I try to gather my bearings. Maybe the bottles did more damage than I care to admit, or maybe it's being alone in a storeroom with him. I don't know where to look, but I can't keep sitting on the floor like an idiot, not saying anything, as it's making the whole situation worse.

"Shaun isn't here," I say. It's all I can come up with.

"I know, I've already seen him." Jake's eyes twinkle with amusement and I can tell he's fighting back a smirk.

"Right. So why are you back here?"

"I came to see you." He shoves his hands into his jean pockets as if he's suddenly uncertain about what he came to say.

"Why?" I don't mean to come across sounding like a bitch, but the last thing either of us needs is for me to start swooning over the things he says. Walls, I need walls to keep him out. The only way I know how is with limited speech.

"Sophie and Zoe mentioned that you'd agreed to come on the trip to Lake Placid. I figured things haven't exactly been friendly between us and thought maybe we could clear the air?"

"Okay." I wonder if he's noticed that one-word answers have become my forte.

"Erm. Yeah ... So, how've you been?"

Never, in the time I've known Jake have I seen him act awkward, but as he's talking, he rubs the back of his neck with one of his hands. Why, after all this time, would he be nervous? What does he even have to be nervous about? He's not the one constantly making a fool of himself.

"I've been fine, just the usual, working ..." I reply.

"Yeah, the girls mentioned you're working a lot. Your dad too."

"I've had some great projects since I've been back. A lot of work locally. It's been good."

When I stop speaking, I realize I haven't asked anything about how he's doing, but it's too late to backtrack and it would come across exactly how it is, an afterthought. I finally let myself look up at him properly and he's smiling.

Suddenly I realize I'm still sitting here, on the floor, Jake towering above me.

"I seem to have a habit of falling at your feet," I say, wryly.

"Neither time has been your fault. Anyway, it's great that you're doing well. Seriously, Abs, finding your feet here again straight away ... you're doing amazing."

He extends his hand to help me to my feet. He's staring at me intensely, like he did when we were at the gig, and my heart pounds at his use of '*Abs*', but this time I won't allow myself to get caught up in the moment. I don't have alcohol clouding my judgment. I ignore his hand and struggle to my feet.

"Thank you for the compliment, but you didn't need to bother coming all this way just to say that," I say lightly.

His expression changes from intense, to aggravated. There's sadness there too, which is maybe why he tries one last time to win me over. "Can't we just be friends, Abby?"

I frown. "*Now* you want to be friends. That would have been great six years ago. You know ... when you broke my heart and left me alone. You even isolated me from some of my friends, but it seems like you've forgotten all that."

"I'm sorry." His jaw becomes tense. "There were things going on at the time that we both had no control of. I didn't mean to hurt you like I did, but it's been a long time and we've both changed."

"Yeah, we have. I don't accept bullshit as easily as I used to, Jake."

"It's not bullshit. I'm trying to clear the air between us. You're here for a couple of months and we're all going away on this trip together. The group is tighter than when you left, so we're gonna be around each other a lot, and I thought it would be unfair to the others if there was all this tension between us."

"Are you kidding me? The last few times we've bumped into each other, I'm not the one who's had a chip on my shoulder." I clench my fists at my sides, trying not to get too riled up.

His shoulders sag. Maybe he understands I'm right, and the animosity between us isn't just one sided. He's had his own part to play in why things are so awkward.

"It's my bad," he says, "I knew you were coming back, and I tried to get my head around the fact that we'd see each other. I didn't realize how difficult it would be. It's not easy being around you again, Abs."

"Why? I'm hardly a gremlin. I've barely said a word to you," I say with wide eyes.

He sighs dejectedly. "That's not it ..."

"Then what is?"

"I'm not quite sure what the answer is."

The twinkle he had in his eyes when he first came in the storeroom is gone. I feel a tug of guilt that it might be my fault, but him being nice now doesn't change the torment he put me through.

I shake my head. "Then neither am I. I'm not a mind reader, Jake."

"Can we start again? Pretend the last few meetings haven't happened? Or press pause and skip forward to the bit where we finally get along. If it doesn't work, then we go back to ignoring each other."

He rubs the back of his neck again, causing his shirt to rise, revealing abs that weren't there six years ago. My eyes do a quick perusal, observing how much he's filled out since we were together. I'm

102

mesmerized watching his now broad chest rise and fall rapidly as he watches me watching him. I can't take my eyes off him and would happily stand staring at his body for the rest of the night, but he clears his throat breaking the moment.

He sounds breathless when he asks, "You ok?"

My cheeks feel like they're on fire and I snap my eyes away from his body.

"Yep! Zoned out for a moment there. I must be concussed from those bottles to the head." It's cringeworthy how loud and chipper I'm being.

"Okay." There's a hint of a smirk on his face and then his eyes trail over me.

This is getting out of hand. We're both in relationships. He has a girlfriend who I'm about to spend two days in proximity with, yet here we are taking our fill of each other. What the hell is wrong with me?

"I should probably get back out there. Shaun will be wondering where I've got to, and I need to finish up and get home to pack."

"Are we at least a little bit cool? Cool enough to try and get along for the benefit of the group?"

"I guess so."

I step to the side, trying to create some much-needed distance between us. I pick up a crate and make my way to leave the storeroom.

"Great," he says quietly to my retreating form.

"Oh, and Jake ..." I look back, over my shoulder when I reach the door.

"Yeah?"

"Don't call me, Abs. You don't get to call me that."

I walk out of the storeroom quickly and try to ignore his sigh. A lot of things are muddled in my mind right now, but one thing is clear as day. Jake and I cannot be alone together again.

Thirteen

"**R**oad trip, baby!" Zoe bangs her palms against the steering wheel in a drum roll. "Seriously guys, this is going to be the best Placid trip yet!"

"I know!" Squeals Sophie from the back, leaning over the passenger seat where I'm sitting and pulling me into a bear hug from behind. "I can't believe we're finally getting to do this with you. You're going to love it out there. Have you brought your camera?"

I laugh and say, "Do you even know me?"

"Of course. Silly me." She rolls her eyes and settles back into her seat.

"Let's get going. We've got a long ass trip ahead of us," says Zoe. She hits the gas and pulls onto my parents' street, which is deserted with it being 4.30am.

My body is protesting at being up at this hour after so little sleep. The conversation with Jake played on a constant loop in my mind and I spent the night going over every detail, trying to understand why he said it was hard to be around me.

The first couple of hours of the journey pass quickly, and we take it in turns driving. We pull over regularly so we each get decent breaks. With all the stops, and hitting traffic, the drive takes longer than intended.

We finally make a pit stop for breakfast, pulling into a diner at the side of the highway. When any of us get hangry, it's not pretty, and we're fast approaching that point. If this place has coffee, carbs and bacon, I couldn't care less where we eat.

We relax back into our booth after ringing in our orders, and I almost kiss the waitress when she sets a vat of coffee on the table. The girls look at me amused.

"What? I'm exhausted," I say, "some of us worked a long shift yesterday."

Rather than feeding into my remark, Sophie asks, "Have you spoken to Michael much? We overheard the conversation you had that first night after you rescued us, but we haven't brought it up in case it was a sore subject."

"Yeah, we've spoken." I pause to take my first gulp of coffee, sighing in content. "Things weren't great when I left. He wasn't handling the fact I chose to come back to Brooklyn, instead of spending the summer with him, very well. Especially as he doesn't know what I'm going to decide with work and the overseas projects. I think we'll get through it though."

"Do you want to get through it?" asks Zoe, practically reading my mind.

There's no point holding anything back when I answer, they know when I'm lying. They know all there is to know about me and they know what I'm thinking and what I'm going to do before I even do it.

I ponder for a moment, then answer honestly, "I don't know. He wants me to move in with him ...

permanently. He wants me to be like all the other ball bunnies and follow him round while he works. But you guys know that's not me. I'm my own person and I love my work. I can't just drop everything for a guy."

"Especially if he's not The One," nods Sophie.

"He's a ball playing God. You'd definitely know if he was The One, and if you're having doubts when he looks like *that*, with all that money ... Maybe he really isn't The One,' agrees Zoe.

That's the thing, Michael is an actual God to most women. He's an NFL player. A tall, blond, muscular parcel of Greek godlikeness. Pretty much the entire female population would think I was insane if they knew I was having doubts about our relationship. Even though Zoe and Sophie agree he's attractive, they don't necessarily like him. He has a bad rep for being an ass, but I know there's more to him.

"I love him. I guess I'm just not *in* love with him. Our hand is being forced and we can't keep coasting by. I've realized there's no spark there anymore." I run my finger round the rim of my coffee cup, avoiding any eye contact that will give away the full extent of my feelings.

Zoe's brows draw together and she says, "Keep explaining ..."

"I dunno. I don't think about him all hours of the day, how I feel isn't all consuming. I'm fond of him and like him being around, but I don't *need* him in my life, and that's not fair on him. Especially when he's talking about marriage and making babies."

"Shut the front door," says Sophie and her mouth hangs open. "He actually wants to make gurgling shit machines. We're like only twenty-four though? What about all the partying and stuff we still have to do?"

"Exactly my point. I suppose I'm not ready for all that commitment. We're not on the same page, and it's not fair that I keep him from finding the person who is The One. I'm just too scared to break up with him because it's going to be hard."

"Abs, you really need to sort your head out. Things are a bit of a mess in there, aren't they? Undecided on the boyfriend, undecided on the living situation, undecided on the job ..." Zoe picks up her coffee, takes a gulp and then continues, "Even me and Sophie have our shit together more than you, and that's saying something."

"Lake Placid will be the perfect time to gain some clarity," agrees Sophie. "We should definitely do yoga, it's great for your yang and yin."

Zoe spurts her coffee everywhere laughing. "Very deep of you, Soph, but I think you mean yin and yang?"

Hysterical laughter takes over me at the irony of the whole situation. I'm sitting in a dive in the middle of nowhere, getting advice from my friends, who are even bigger screw ups than me.

"Thanks, guys," I say, "I know I can act high and mighty sometimes, but I appreciate you listening. I swear, sometimes I feel like my head is about to explode because I'm constantly going around in circles with it all."

"That's what we're here for," says Zoe and offers a warm smile. "We always have been, and just because we're not perfect, doesn't mean the advice we give isn't good. We just don't follow it ourselves, obviously."

We sit in silence waiting for our food to arrive, mulling over what's been said. After what feels like forever, the smell of sweet sugary pancakes and bacon reaches my nose, as the waitress makes her way to our table, balancing three of the biggest plates of food I've ever seen.

My eyes bug out of my head when I take in the sheer volume of food. There's enough between the three of us to feed a football team. Not that this stops us annihilating the whole lot. When we want to eat, we can really eat. The guys have always laughed at us for it, saying we're like a group of six-foot guys with the amount we pack away. Really, we're pint sized, each just over five-foot, packing it in like energizer bunnies.

"Oh my God, I think I need to nap," groans Sophie, lying down and stretching out in the booth.

Zoe whacks her in the arm. "Not a chance. UP. We gotta get a move on. We're way behind the other guys after this pit stop."

After giving Zoe the finger in disapproval, Sophie stands up and we throw down some money to cover the meal.

I strap myself into the driver's seat and it becomes clear I've pulled the short straw having to drive when I feel so full. I agree with Sophie, a nap is needed.

To take my mind off the tiredness, I ask, "Are the others travelling up now as well?"

"Yeah. We thought it would be better to spread over three cars. More space with it being a longer journey. They should be there about the same time as us, that's if they're not there already," replies Zoe.

I look in my rearview mirror and see that Sophie has given into her food coma and fallen asleep. I don't mention it to Zoe, as she will wake her up thinking it's funny.

We spend the remainder of the journey in silence and without any distractions the worry slowly creeps in. Worry over what the next few days have in store, especially meeting Jake's girlfriend Amanda, and seeing them together. It might be juvenile, but part of me hopes she's fat, ugly and boring. Of course, that's not going to be the case, and really, I shouldn't care, as Jake and I are in the past.

I wonder how much she knows about our past. Does she know we used to be a couple? Then there's the issue of PDA. Yes, it was six years ago since things ended between me and Jake, and I shouldn't be bothered if I've moved on like I keep saying I have. I pray they keep it tame in front of me, but if Amanda doesn't know our history, she wouldn't know to be mindful. I need to get out of this car ASAP and stop over-thinking things.

Of course, because she can read my mind, Zoe asks, "You ok? You've gone pretty quiet."

"I'm just worrying about meeting Amanda," I reply honestly.

"Ah ..."

"Yeah."

"From what I know she's nice. I think you'll like her."

"That's just it though. I don't want to like her."

"Sorry to burst your bubble, Abs, but her and Jake are very much together and happy. Prepare yourself."

"Thanks," I sigh.

"I'm telling you all this because I don't want to see you get hurt."

"I know. Let's leave it. I think we're here anyway?"

Zoe squints through the front windscreen and says, "Yeah, we are."

She directs me to come off at the next exit, and we make our way into Lake Placid along the winding, tree lined roads. I turn up the music to lighten the mood after dwelling for the latter part of the journey, which causes Sophie to stir from her nap.

Driving through the town I try to take in as much of the surroundings as I can. The main street is quaint without being Hicksville. It's incredibly picturesque, and although it's only mid-morning, crowds are out and about, bustling and laughing. The lake glitters behind the old buildings that house quirky stores, bars, and restaurants, and in the distance, there is the mountain. It's grand, without demanding attention, and adds to the outstanding beauty of the place.

It's not long before we're pulling into the lodge and exiting the car, getting ready to check in with the rest of the group. The lodge itself is huge but fitting with the area made completely of wood. The gardens surrounding it lead to the water's edge and are luscious and full of colorful flowers. I can't contain the squeal of excitement when I see the outdoor pool with sun-loungers and a hot tub. With the heatwave we're experiencing, my body is literally aching to get in the cool water.

"Oh my God, guys. This place is amazing!"

I jump up and down then pull Sophie and Zoe into a group hug. We stand laughing and squealing like teenage girls. When we finally pull apart, I'm aware my hair has gone crazy and I look like a maniac, with my head thrown back as I laugh.

"Nice to see you finally letting your hair down and actually enjoying yourself."

I turn to find Sam standing a few feet away beaming at us. None of us noticed Sam, Zach and Jake approach, too preoccupied with our group hug.

"Hardy har." I punch him lightly in the arm, as he tugs me in for a quick hug.

When we pull apart, he moves on to greet Sophie and Zoe in the same way. I look over at Jake and Zach, determined to keep my promise to try and keep things amicable.

I offer a small wave and smile. "Hey guys," I say. It's not much, but it's better than nothing.

"Hey, Abby, it's great to see you again. I'm glad you made it," says Zach with a broad grin.

The more I'm around the guy the more I like him and can see why he's become part of the group. All Jake offers back is a small smile, but it's enough. We didn't say we would be best friends, only that we would try to keep things pleasant.

It dawns on me that the whole group isn't here yet, so I ask Sam, "Where are the others?" I opt for the word others as I don't have it in me yet to say Amanda's name out loud.

Sam replies, "Shaun had a job to do for the bar, He started early and is bringing Amanda with him when he's finished. They should be here by this afternoon. Anyway, less about that, let's call dibs on rooms!"

Secretly I'm relieved, as I get a few more hours to brace myself before Amanda arrives. I try not to let the relief show on my face, but Sophie and Zoe will notice, probably Jake too.

We move on to check in, and the room situation is decided quickly. Zoe, Sophie and I are in one of the two larger rooms, and Sam, Shaun and Zach are sharing the other. Which means Jake and Amanda are sharing the final room. I try to keep my expression neutral, even though every irrational part of me wants to scream and protest. Out of the corner of my eye, I see Jake glance over. I look elsewhere, I don't want him to think I care.

We plan to drop our bags in our rooms, change and then meet at the outdoor pool, as it's already baking hot, despite only being 11am. After squealing and running around the room, bouncing on the beds like kids, I take my time unpacking. I pull out my bathing suit and Zoe looks over in horror.

"No way, you're not wearing that. Not a chance," she says.

I look down at the full swimsuit I've brought. It's practical and won't win in the fashion department, but it will do. I don't mind being covered up in front of the guys.

"I have nothing else."

"Well, it's a good job I always over pack." She begins rummaging through her suitcase, which is far too big for the short trip we have planned.

"Did you seriously need to pack that much stuff?" I grumble, wishing she didn't have spare things, as it inevitably means I'm going to wind up hitting the pool with virtually no clothing on.

"I had to pack double, as you always under pack. And you wear crap like that," she gestures at the swimsuit in my hand, "which doesn't show anything off. It's a sin not to when you have a banging body like yours." She scans me up and down, rummages in her suitcase some more, then throws some scrappy pieces of material at me. "Here, try on this."

I hold up the tiniest bikini I've ever seen. It's deep red with a few ruffles around the edge and will cover up about as much as Zoe's own turquoise bikini. Absolutely nothing.

Sophie comes out of the bathroom wearing an equally tiny yellow suit and chuckles when she sees what I have in my hands. "Good try, Zo. No way you're getting her in that."

"What's that supposed to mean?" I ask.

'There's only been a few times I've seen you in a swimsuit, and they've had about four times the material. There's no way you would dare wear that in front of the guys." She pulls her long blonde hair over one shoulder and smiles at me sweetly, but there's a challenge in her eyes.

I never back down from a challenge, so I say, "Fine, I'll wear the suit."

I quickly walk into the bathroom to change, leaving them laughing behind me. Laying the suit out on the side, I curse, realizing it's even tinier than I thought.

"Fuck," I hiss under my breath. Everyone is going to see everything, one of whom is Jake.

Once I've changed into the tiny bits of material, I look at myself in the full-length mirror, holding my breath. I'm surprised at what I see. It's cut in just the right places, and despite the lack of material, it flatters my figure, emphasizing how toned I am from all the running. The color is great, and thanks to the year-round Florida sun, I have a slight bronze tone to my skin, which the swimsuit compliments. My dark hair is in my signature waves, hanging around my shoulders, and it doesn't matter that I have on minimal makeup.

I take one last look, psyching myself up, and with a deep breath, walk out the bathroom to wolf whistles from the girls. We throw on our cover-ups and head down to the pool to meet the guys. The whole time I plaster a fake smile on my face, meanwhile, nausea sets in, as memories of the last time Jake saw me in a swimsuit flood my mind.

Fourteen

6 years earlier

"**A**bby, we're at a party in the middle of the wilderness. It's crazy and there's a hot tub! A hot tub, Abby," repeats Zoe. "You have to put a bathing suit on."

I cross my arms across my chest and shake my head. "No."

"I dare you," says Sophie, pulling out the trump card. She knows it's the one thing I won't back down from.

"You guys are unbelievable," I say.

"And you are going to look unbelievable in that bathing suit. Now get your ass moving, kegs are waiting for us." Sophie dismisses me towards the bathroom with a flick of her hand, making it clear the argument is over and I've lost.

Ten minutes later, I finally psyche myself up to go back into the room, in just the bathing suit. It's a two piece, which I've never worn in my life. Until recently, I hadn't grown into my body, and unlike

114

other girls my age, I've so far been too shy to show it off.

"Holy cow!" says Zoe. "Jake is going to blow his load when he sees you. Seriously, you look smoking hot, Abs. Now let's sort your hair out. We don't want it getting wet in the hot tub and going all crazy and shit."

I throw a short green dress on over my bikini to cover my modesty and then let Zoe get to work. After five minutes of Zoe weaving my hair into some sort of braid she saw on Instagram, we leave our designated room in the log cabin where we're all staying.

It's senior year, and my mom managed to convince Dad to let me come on the annual senior trip, which is a mix of students from different schools. I may, however, have neglected to tell them that Jake would be on the trip. That and a few other minor details, like the fact there wouldn't be chaperones, and there undoubtedly would-be underage drinking. Shoot me, it's the biggest trip/party of the year and there was no way I was missing out on this chance to spend time with my friends and Jake.

It's the end of November, and as we're up in the mountains, it's freezing and snowing outside. There's a warm glow to everything, making me feel fuzzy and excited. When we make our way down into the open plan kitchen area, the party is already in full swing. The music is loud, people are laughing and tumbling everywhere. Girls are dancing for the guys in their bikinis, even though we're inside and there isn't a pool in sight. The guys are chugging their beers, mostly shirtless and in board shorts. It's my first big party as I've never been overly keen to go to one until now. It's ridiculous, crazy and completely random, but at the same time the buzz is infectious.

Sam's familiar voice reaches my ears. "Laaaaaydeeeesss!"

We all look and find him standing in the middle of the kitchen with the alcohol. There's enough to rival some of the biggest clubs in Brooklyn. He hugs us all when we wander over and hands out drinks. The girls declare we have catching up to do, and before I realize what I'm doing, I've drunk two beers and a shot. If things didn't feel fuzzy enough before, they do now. I giggle to myself as I wobble.

A hand grasps my waist. I can feel how large and warm it is through the thin material of my dress. Then a familiar frame presses up against me from behind. I close my eyes, instinctively knowing who it is. I always do. My body is drawn to his like a magnet.

He squeezes my hip gently, then leans down and murmurs into my ear, "Hey you."

"Hi," I say breathlessly, struggling to find any other words. I'm completely overwhelmed by the feeling of Jake pressed up against me.

He chuckles, knowing the reaction he's causing. I've never felt comfortable being like this with him before now, but things are changing. Each time I'm with him, it becomes harder to contain my feelings. I know he feels the same. The glances between us last longer, they're more intense, and the small 'accidental' touches are more frequent. It's inevitable where this is leading, and I don't know if I will be able to stop myself when it does.

Jake begins slowly tracing circles on my hip with the tip of his finger and I shudder involuntarily.

"Meet me in the hot tub in five minutes," he whispers, placing a soft kiss on my neck just below

my ear. He walks away in the direction of the hot tub outside. It's the most intimate physical contact we've had and I'm about to turn into a useless puddle on the floor.

"Oh. My. God. I'm horny just watching you two," Zoe slurs. She slings an arm around me and breathes heavily in my face, the stench of beer brings me out of my Jake induced daze.

"Seriously Zo, keep your voice down," I laugh. Normally I'd be pissed at her for saying things like that so everyone can hear, but I'm too excited at the potential of kissing Jake to care.

"What are you waiting for? Go and finally get your guy." With a knowing look, Sophie pushes me in the direction of the hot tub.

I make my way over, stopping when I see Jake sat, facing out to the mountains with his chin resting on his arms. He looks so content and peaceful. I'm almost tempted not to disturb him. It's like he needs this time alone, as if something is troubling him.

But if he didn't want me to join him, he wouldn't have asked me to. I approach quietly. Before he can hear me and before I have a chance to get too scared and over think it, I pull my dress over my head and step up to the hot tub, hoping I can dart in before he sees me. I must make some noise because he turns around and his eyes widen as they take me in. His gaze trails slowly down my barely covered body, settling on my chest for a second. He swallows and looks up, meeting my eyes.

Trying to break the silence I say, "Hey, y-you." My voice falters, adding to the awkwardness. Even worse ... he doesn't respond, just sits staring at me. I lower myself into the water. "Is everything ok?"

The ongoing silence is driving me crazy. I need him to talk before I start to get cold feet about all of *this. My question startles him, and he blinks and swallows.*

Finally, he clears his throat and says, "Shit, sorry. Yeah, of cour- sor- I ..."

We're sitting at opposite sides of the hot tub staring at each other and I don't know if I've completely misread everything. I feel unsure and incredibly vulnerable. A wave of nausea hits me as my stomach churns.

I go to tuck my hair behind my ear, but I can't because Zoe put it in a stupid braid and now, I look like I'm doing some weird kind of wave at him.

"Maybe I should go?" I say. My eyes water and tears threaten to spill over. This is so humiliating. How did I ever think that I could waltz in, in a bathing suit? Did I think he would find me sexy? Of course, he wouldn't. Guys like girls like Zoe, not me.

"Shit. Why do I keep saying shit? Fuck." Getting frustrated, he stops and takes a breath. "Can we start again? I'm sorry. I'm being an idiot it's just ..."

Before I realize what he's doing, he leans over, grabs my hand and tugs me towards him. When I'm closer he places both hands on my waist and lifts me effortlessly through the water. My legs move involuntarily, and I wind up straddling his lap. My pulse skyrockets and I swallow, trying to relax.

"Is it me?" I ask. "Do I look bad?" I can't bare to look him in the eye when he replies, so I look down into the water between us.

"Hey," he moves one hand under my chin, lifting it gently so I look him in the eye. His expression is unreadable, and I have no idea what he's thinking. "You look amazing. Incredible. That's what's wrong - I'm speechless, Abs. You've turned me into a fucking mess."

Oh. No guy has ever said anything like that to me. I've never had such an effect on them that they would need to.

"Really?" I say taken aback by what he's said.

He nods and stares at me with an intensity that makes me squirm in his lap. Wrong move. In doing so I make accidental contact with his ... well you know ... which is hard, as, a, rock. I gasp. Partly from shock, and partly from the pleasure it sends soaring through every part of my body.

He glances down at my chest and then tips his head back groaning, "Abby you're killing me." When his eyes meet mine again, they're filled with need.

I might not have a clue what to do, but what I do know is that he's doing funny things to me and everywhere tingles. If there was ever a time to take a leap and do something daring and completely out of character, it would be now. So, I bring my hands up slowly and place them on his damp chest. He flinches as if my touch causes him pain, but I know that's not the case, as I feel his you know what twitch against my inner thigh.

"Sorry." He looks embarrassed, which is unlike Jake. "I have no control over how my body is reacting to you."

"What if I do this?" I start trailing my fingers up and down his chest, each time reaching lower. Towards his stomach ... then lower, towards the waistband of his swim shorts. "Or this?" I lean forwards and press my now wet chest against his, which rises and falls dramatically with each breath he takes.

Then I lean even closer and place a gentle kiss on the top of his shoulder, at the crook of his neck. I've never been this bold, because I've never done anything like this with a guy before, but with Jake I want to do everything.

I continue and say, "And what if I do this?" I move from the crook of his neck and trace the tip of my nose upwards, then gently suck on his ear lobe, something I've read guys like in books.

"Abby ..." He says almost as a warning, before he grasps my hair and pulls me back gently. He presses his forehead to mine and we both sit, panting. This is it. The moment we've been waiting for. We stay with our bodies pressed together until he nudges the tip of his nose against mine with a small smile on his lips. "I've wanted this for so long."

He licks his lips and then tilts his head, leaning in slowly to kiss me. I close my eyes and move to meet him.

There are only millimeters separating us, when Sophie barrels her way outside, screeching my name. "AAAABBBBYYYY!"

I fly backwards away from Jake, afraid of being caught in such a compromising position, although she's the last person who would care.

I turn, concerned at what has brought her out like this. "What's wrong?"

"Zoe has just spewed everywhere. It's so gross. There's no way I'm handling that shit alone. Sorry guys, I know you were all ready for bumping uglies."

I put my head in my hands and let out a groan. "Did you actually just say that? I've only been gone like five minutes. How could she be so sick?"

"We may have had some shots while you were getting ready." There's no hiding the sheepish look on her face. They know I hate it when they get wasted and I end up having to clean up the mess.

"You owe me, big time." I glare at her and climb out of the hot tub.

Grabbing a towel and my dress, I turn back and look at Jake. Everything inside me screams in frustration, telling me to leave Zoe and climb back into his arms, so we can finish what we were about to start. But that wouldn't be me and Jake knows that.

"It's ok. Go sort her out, there'll be another time," he says with a reassuring smile. His eyes tell another story, and I know they reflect the same longing in my own.

I wave Sophie back inside with a stern glare, then I walk around the tub, lean over, and place a kiss on his cheek.

"I can't wait much longer," I whisper. And then I walk away ... Again.

✳✳✳

Present Day

It might only be the end of June, but the weather is amazing. We haven't hit the peak of summer, yet the guys couldn't have picked a better time for the trip. We walk around the hotel grounds and I can feel the sun beating against my skin, it feels good.

It's early in the day, so it's quiet and doesn't take us long to find the guys at the main pool area. They've grabbed enough sun loungers for us all, and once we're settled, the drinks start. When I frown because of the time, Zoe looks at me pointedly, stating that it's vacation and anything goes. I refrain from saying that they don't need the excuse of a vacation, they would be drinking regardless.

We spend the first hour lounging, drinking cocktails and beers, and catching up. The early start was brutal, and mixed with the early drinking, exhaustion takes over. I lay back listening to the group chatting and soon find myself lulled into a deep slumber.

I feel like I've been out forever when Zoe wakes me. "Hey, Abs, time to get up," she says, giving me a gentle shake.

"What time is it?" I reply groggily.

"Just after one."

"I've been out over an hour? Why did no one wake me?"

"Believe me, I would have been the first one to wake you. But you looked so peaceful and you were working late last night, so I thought I'd leave you a while to catch up. I thought it might help you be a little less bitchy." Reinforcing her last comment, I throw her my best bitch face on purpose. "Or maybe not," she laughs. "Here, I grabbed you another drink as your last one went all warm and gross."

"Thanks," I say, taking the ice-cold, girly looking cocktail. I relish at how refreshing it is in the heat when I take a sip through the funky pink straw.

Sophie and the guys are in the pool throwing a football between them. Sam glances over and when he sees I'm awake shouts, "Yo, Abs, get your ass in here."

"Pass," I say in an overly sweet voice. The thought of the guys seeing me in Zoe's tiny bathing suit is not appealing, even though the heat is becoming unbearable and I know the water will cool me off.

He splashes water in my direction, with a mischievous look. "Come on, don't be such a bore."

"Nah, I'm ok." I take another sip of my drink, then turn to Zoe for back up.

"No way, lady. I'm not getting you out of this one." She starts laughing and stands up. Her cover up was removed hours ago and she already looks like a bronzed goddess. I can't help feeling envious at how effortlessly confident she always is. She leans over and with a wink says, "Come on, *Abby bear*, I dare you ..."

"Bitch."

Totally unphased, she leaves me behind and dives into the pool with the rest of the guys.

I sit and contemplate what I'm going to do. I never back out of a dare, but I really don't want to take the cover-up off. Maybe I could get in the pool with it on? But then I would look like an idiot.

Sam and the others have lost interest and have gone back to throwing the football around. I decide to suck it up, stop being a loser and join them. I work on the premise that if I'm in the pool, they won't even be able to see the bathing suit.

I choose a moment when they're engrossed in their game and stand, pulling my cover-up over my head. What I don't bargain for is my hair getting caught in the clasp at the back. Rather than the discreet entrance I was going for, I spend the next few minutes making a spectacle of myself, as I tug and try to get my hair out quickly.

A pair of wet hands rest on my shoulders, stopping me from dancing around like an idiot, but I can't see anything in the mass of hair and material covering my face.

"Here, let me help. You need to stay still for a second." I don't need to guess who it is. Jake. Of course. I feel his hands at the nape of my neck, pulling gently at my hair, attempting to loosen it from the clasp of the cover-up. Cursing under his breath, it's clear he's struggling. "Sorry. I need to get closer so I can see better. That ok?"

I panic, but can't exactly say, "no I'm fine," because clearly, I'm not and I need his help.

I murmur, "Yeah, sure." Luckily, my face is covered, as it's likely to be the color of a tomato. I can't decide if it's Jakes proximity, his touch on my almost naked body, or the cool water droplets that are dripping off him and running down my skin. I shiver despite the relentless midday heat.

"You good?" He asks under his breath, so only I can hear.

"Mortified, but what's new?" Embarrassing myself around Jake is becoming the norm so I might as well go with it.

"I've almost got it, and don't be embarrassed."

I smile to myself at the kindness he's showing, when really, I deserve anything but after how I left things with him yesterday.

Then he says, "I'm the only one that noticed." I wonder if he's realized that he's given the game away by informing me he was watching. "Done. Hold your hair out of the way and I'll pull it off, so it doesn't get stuck again."

"Great," I squeak. My conversational skills have reached their peak.

I still can't see a thing when he turns me, and I assume I'm now facing him. His hands gently skim my chest when he grasps the cover-up and pulls it over my head. My breath catches in my throat and I cringe trying to stop my body from reacting. Once the cover-up is over my head, it takes a second for me to gather my bearings. When my eyes adjust, I look up and see Jake staring back down at me with a frown.

"Thanks," I say sheepishly.

"Is that all you're going to wear?"

"E-excuse me?" I stutter, confused.

Before he has a chance to answer we're interrupted by the rest of the group.

"Holy fuck, Abby," says Sam. He follows with a loud wolf whistle, drawing even more attention to me, in case the situation wasn't embarrassing enough.

"What?" I'm seriously hating Zoe right now. I knew this was a bad idea.

"When did you get that body? Loving the bathing suit by the way."

He's only being playful, but this is my worst nightmare. I don't do being the center of attention. I especially don't do being the center of attention when I have little to no clothing on.

"Really, Sam?" I raise an eyebrow. Deciding if you can't beat them join them, I laugh and make my way into the water. Knowing he can take it, I say, "You've finally stopped loving yourself so much you've noticed that other people around you have grown up then?"

"Ha de ha. Believe me, baby, I noticed that you grew up a *long* time ago."

"You're such an ass." To emphasize my point, I splash water at his face.

A voice says loudly from behind us, "You're really going to speak to her like that, man?"

Sam and I both turn to see Jake still standing at the side of the pool with his arms crossed tightly across his chest. I don't want to look like an idiot again, but the way his arms are flexed draws my attention to the tattoos covering them.

Sam raises his hands in the air, and shrugs with a mischievous glint in his eyes. "Hey, man, she's fair game." He's baiting him for fun.

Jake shakes his head angrily. I have no idea why he's getting so worked up, but then it registers what Sam has said. If there's one thing I hate the most, it's being spoken about like a piece of meat.

"That fair game, you're talking about is one of your oldest friends," I say. "If you'd like to keep it that way, I suggest you stop talking about me like that."

Realizing his mistake by using me to annoy Jake, Sam says, "Sorry, Abs, I didn't mean it that way." He moves through the water and pulls me into a hug, which is awkward considering how few clothes we have on.

"Just don't do it again." I have no fight in me when it comes to Sam, he always finds a way to win me over no matter what he's said or done.

Sophie wades over and throws her arms around mine and Sam's shoulders. "Now that everyone is friends again, I think a round of drinks is in order."

"Hell yeah," hoots Sam.

"And shots!" Shouts Zoe from somewhere in the background.

The tense moment has passed, and we all make our way out of the water and head towards the bar. Jake and Zach don't follow. I look back over my shoulder and can see Jake still rooted to the spot where he helped me out of my coverup.

The two of them appear to be sharing heated words. There are a lot of hand gestures, as Zach whispers at him with a serious expression on his face. Every now and again they look over in my direction, and I try not to make it obvious I'm watching them. Zach says something and Jake throws his hands up in frustration.

They look over in my direction one last time and Zach shakes his head before walking away from Jake to where we're standing at the bar. I offer him a sheepish smile as he passes, which he doesn't return, and I feel a tug of guilt that I might be the reason for the animosity between the two best friends.

But that would be ridiculous, right?

Fifteen

The rest of our first day at Lake Placid is a blur of cocktails and lazing by the pool. It's the perfect first day of vacation and the down time I needed. I'd never admit it to the others, but the past couple of weeks have been crazy, running from one job to another, I'm exhausted.

Not long after the little cover-up drama, Shaun called saying there had been an issue at the bar and he had to stay until it was resolved in the afternoon, meaning him and Amanda would be arriving later that evening. The lodge has its own restaurant, and we agreed to meet there and hold off on food until they arrive.

Once we're ready, we meet the guys in the restaurant, where they've already grabbed a table, and ordered drinks. Luckily, with there being so many of us, the table is long, and I choose to sit at the opposite end to Jake. The less drama, the better.

When I sit down, I glance around, taking in the cozy surroundings. My eyes find Jake, who is frowning at me, again. I look elsewhere, choosing to ignore him. I don't have to justify my reasons for not wanting to sit near him and his current girlfriend.

"Are they going to be here soon?" Zoe moans. She's made it more than clear she's unhappy we're having to wait for the others to order food. "I could literally eat my own arm."

"Feel free if that's what it takes to keep you quiet," says Sam with an evil smile.

A napkin hits him square in the face, coming from Sophie's direction. "Don't be an ass. You know what she's like when she's hungry," she says.

Zoe's incessant moaning might be annoying, but none of us can disguise the loud noises coming from our own stomachs. The afternoon has been filled with plenty of drinking and not much eating, so we order a few appetizers from the menu, not knowing exactly when Shaun and Amanda are going to arrive.

The food arrives and I tuck straight in. The second I shovel a huge scoop of nachos into my mouth, a hand squeezes my shoulder from behind. "Couldn't wait for us I see," says Shaun's husky voice.

Sam holds up his hands, acting as if he had no part to play in ordering any of the food in front of us. "Sorry, bro. Zoe was getting hangry, you know how it is."

Shaun shakes his head. Losing interest in his brother he turns his attention back to me. "No hello, Abs?"

He stares down at me, so I look up and point at my overly full mouth, exaggerating chewing. Then my eyes focus on the person standing next to him. She's gorgeous, very blonde, very leggy, with huge breasts and golden skin. A bit like a real-life Barbie. My stomach plummets and I'm suddenly not interested in the food in front of me. We've not been introduced, but I know this is Amanda.

So here we are, like chalk and cheese. Her looking every bit the blonde bombshell, and me with cheese and salsa falling from my mouth. There's no question why Jake made the choice he did. Keeping my promise, I offer up a food filled smile, to which she wrinkles her nose, obviously repulsed at the churned-up food that keeps dropping down my front. It's an afterthought when she offers a smile back. Feeling humiliated yet again, I look down and focus on my nachos.

When I recover from my embarrassment, I look across the table, and Sophie catches my eye, offering a look of sympathy. True to form, I watch as both her and Zoe shovel huge mounds of nachos into their mouths, and then begin cackling and spraying food all over the table.

"Gross, guys," I say.

Really, I'm laughing on the inside and thankful these are my best friends. It's not often you find people willing to embarrass themselves to help you and it reinforces why we're such a strong unit despite our differences. We well and truly have each other's backs.

Out of the corner of my eye I see Shaun and Amanda move around the table. Shaun sits next to Zach and of course Amanda settles down next to Jake. I smile at Shaun, having finally cleared my mouth of food. I don't know where it comes from, but I gather the courage and turn to directly speak to Amanda.

"You must be Amanda," I say with an extra sweet smile, then continue, "sorry I couldn't say hi before, I had a bit of a food predicament. It's great to meet you, I've heard a lot about you."

The whole group stares silently, and you could cut the tension with a knife. I get that it's surprising I would be the one to instigate a conversation with her, but they could at least attempt to make it feel less weird.

"Not from Jake you haven't," mutters Sam under his breath. I kick him under the table, hard. "What the fuck, Abs?"

"Oops, sorry, my foot slipped." I shoot daggers his way, as a warning not to make any more remarks.

Amanda looks between us with an amused expression. Finally, she says, "That's so sweet. Jake's told me that you used to be close friends. I hope we can be friends too. Any friend of Jake's is a friend of mine."

Her smile seems genuine but I'm not too sure. It's obvious though that she believes whatever Jake has told her. Whether he has blatantly lied about our past relationship or merely chosen to omit a large chunk of the truth, that's their issue. Right now, my issue is that this girl I want to hate, seems nice and I feel torn, not knowing how I should react.

The waitress picks the right moment to walk back over to the table which distracts Amanda from our conversation and gives me time to think. Jake told her we were just *'good friends'*, which means he neglected to tell her our real history and that we had a relationship. What the hell? I knew he didn't think much of our time together, which was evident in how he ended things, but completely dismissing that we were together at all ... I don't know what to make of it.

I look around the table. Everyone's attention is on ordering food and more drinks. Jake stares at his menu intently, refusing to look at anyone. Then my eyes land on Zach. He must sense me watching him because he looks over with a sad smile, then shakes his head ever so slightly and mouths, "he's an idiot," which turns my frown into a smile.

When she's placed her food order with the waitress, Zoe whispers to me, "You ok?"

"Ma'am what can I get you?" I hadn't even realized it was my turn to order food, I'd been too focused on answering Zoe.

"You know what, I'm ok thanks." Zoe looks confused so I explain. "I think I'm gonna head back to the room. I'm suddenly not feeling that great."

It's not a lie. The last five minutes have turned my stomach, so I push my chair back, and stand. I offer the table, apart from Jake a wave and make my way back to the room. Collapsing on the bed, I will sleep to come quickly, which thankfully it does.

My last thought is that maybe after a good night's sleep, this won't all feel quite as bad as it does right now.

✳✳✳

"Rise and shine, sexy lady!" I wake up the following morning to Zoe diving on the bed and engulfing me in a giant bear hug. "Feeling better?"

I groan into my pillow. "Since when are you so chipper in the morning?" I don't feel like I've had anywhere near enough sleep, but then again, I would happily stay in bed forever if it meant I didn't have to face Jake and Amanda again.

"Since we have to be up and at 'em."

"Why?"

"Had you stayed at the meal … you would have been privy to our plans for the day. Whiteface Mountain," she states bluntly.

"Did I just hear you say mountain?" Suddenly I feel more awake. There's nothing I love more than getting outside.

She nods. "Yep. Please tell me you brought your sneakers?"

"Of course." My grouchy face is swapped for a smile. The days plans lift my spirits from the night before. I had intended on spending the morning in bed resting, but after the crap from last night, a bit of physical exertion is exactly what the doctor ordered. We didn't come all the way to Lake Placid to stay inside. Remembering some of the beautiful scenery we saw on our drive in yesterday has me literally buzzing to get out with my camera.

"Well, that got you out of last night's funk. Soph and I figured that the more distracted we all were, the better."

"Plus, it might be a chance to break the ice between you and Amanda?" says Sophie, walking in from the bathroom, towel drying her hair. I didn't even know she was listening.

"It's not Amanda that's the problem," I huff, as the conversation from last night comes flooding back.

Sophie smiles weakly, knowing my feelings have been hurt. "We know, but there's no point in dwelling on it. Whatever Jake chose to tell her or not tell her about the two of you is his choice. If you want to take it up with him, I suggest you do it when his girlfriend isn't around?"

I consider what she's saying. She's right. It's Jake's business, and nothing to do with Amanda.

"Soph, you're far too wise sometimes," I say.

"It's hard being this brilliant." She shimmies her Lycra covered ass to emphasize her point, and I roll my eyes. "Now, get up and get ready. We have a half

133

hour before breakfast, then we need to get out before the heat gets too much."

"Yes, sir!" I salute her, then jump out of bed and run straight into the bathroom.

Over an hour later, fresh, and full of breakfast, we make our way to the car so we can meet the rest of the group. They've gotten a head start on us, and we meet them at a small visitor car park at the edge of a forest. Even though it's only 8am, the heat is rising at a rapid rate.

"Nice to see you girls are punctual as ever," says Shaun, smirking at Zoe.

She narrows her eyes and struts past him. It's impossible not to notice his eyes following and taking in the view of her when he thinks no one's looking. Interesting. I never would have guessed there could be something between them, but it's been a long time since we've all been together like this.

"Almost ready to go?" Sam comes up behind me and pulls me into a hug.

"Yep, we just need to load up a couple of packs with water. Did everyone bring snacks?" Sophie asks to the group. They nod their confirmation and it's clear this is a regular part of their annual Lake Placid trips.

We take the primary trail, along a long open forest route and it's incredibly beautiful as the sun peeps through the trees. The guys tell me it's a long, steady slog, and although the route isn't too far, distance wise, the climb is the killer, especially in the summer heat. I don't mind though, because I get to take photos of the stunning scenery along the way.

We amble along, joking and chatting. I don't see much of Jake and Amanda thankfully, as they stay ahead of the group. I don't think it's a coincidence, as I saw Jake powering off at full speed with Amanda struggling to keep up behind. As far as I'm concerned, the more space between us the better.

Even though it takes time, when we get to the top, it proves to be worth every bit of sweat and pain, as the views are breathtaking. They're panoramic and we can see everything for miles.

While the rest of the group unloads their packs and sits down for a long overdue water break and snack, I pull out my camera and set about taking photos. I'm off work duty but I can't help myself. It doesn't feel like work when we're out here, above the world. These are the photos I rarely get to take, and it's refreshing. I wind up in my own little world, snapping away. Everything around me disappears, so I'm surprised when a sweet voice sounds next to me.

"Can I see?" I turn and find Amanda looking at me expectantly.

I tell myself no animosity, take a deep breath and say, "Sure."

I open the preview screen, so she can look at some of the images I've captured.

"Wow. These are good. Like really, really good, Abby."

"Thanks," I reply, trying to sound friendly. "They're not perfect but they're fine for just messing around."

"They're some of the best I've seen. If this is you just messing around then you must be really talented." I can tell from warmth in her eyes as she speaks, that she means it. Even though every part of me is screaming to hate her, I can't help but like her myself. Damnit.

"We should probably start heading back down. It's starting to get really hot out," I say changing the subject. There is only so much bonding with my ex's girlfriend I can take.

"You're right," she agrees.

Once the group finishes rehydrating, we steadily make our way back down the mountain. I take my time, wanting to put distance between myself and Amanda. Although we shared a friendly moment, I'm not keen for it to become a regular thing, and don't want it to go beyond this trip.

I trail at the back and Zach comes to join me, for a while we walk in amicable silence. We hear cheering down ahead and Amanda throws her arms up in the air in celebration. Shaun yells something I can't make out and Jake throws his arm around her shoulders, pulling her in and placing a kiss on her temple.

Walking in the middle, Zoe and Sophie look back over their shoulders concerned at what my reaction might be. This is the first time I've seen Jake and Amanda show any kind of affection to each other, and it sucks.

I'm trying not to act irrationally. We broke up years ago and he's in a relationship, I know this ... so why won't my heart listen? Why does seeing them together like this hurt so much? After the conversation we had at the bar about trying to be friends, I thought he might be a little more tactful in front of me. I was wrong.

"He's a good guy you know," says Zach, looking ahead as we continue walking.

"You could have fooled me."

"It caught him off guard, you, coming back."

This piques my interest. "What do you mean?"

"He didn't think you'd ever come back. Everyone said you were done with Brooklyn, and he thought he'd never have to face up to the mess he made of things."

"Mess ... That's one way of putting it," I'm being grumpy and none of this Zach's fault. I tag on the end a quiet, "sorry."

"I know this must be hard, but it's hard on him too. It always was. Maybe you should give him a bit of a break. The last thing he wanted to do was hurt you."

"Which is why he broke up with me after telling me how in love with me he was ..." I say. I'm trying to make this friends thing work with Jake and I'm trying to be the bigger person. But who he is now doesn't change the past, it doesn't change how he treated me.

"Maybe he didn't have a choice ..."

I pause. That tidbit of information doesn't fit with the memories I have. "Do you know something I don't?"

"Potentially. But as his best friend I swore I wouldn't tell anyone. So, I'm giving you a few hints and you can make up your own mind as to what really went down."

"Thanks?" I'm not sure why I'm thanking him, I feel more confused than ever.

He shrugs. "I just want to see my best friend happy, and there are some things he isn't happy about, even though he would never admit it. He's always done things for everyone else. You're a perfect example, and I'd like to see that change."

"Right," I say bewildered. He's speaking in riddles and I'm getting more confused with each thing he says.

"I'd also like us to be friends if that could work for you? I have nothing against you, Abby, and I can tell that you're great. Sorry if it seemed like I was frosty yesterday, I just don't want to see my friend hurt."

What he's saying is ironic because I'm the one that was hurt in all of this. Jake was the one who walked away.

"I'm not here to hurt anyone. All I want is to get through the summer and then get out of Brooklyn."

"Do you really though? It seems to me like you've got everything you could possibly need right here."

"Apart from one thing." I'm not sure if he knows about Michael.

He makes it clear he does when he replies, "What if the person you really need is right here, but he just doesn't know it yet?"

He places a hand on my shoulder and gives it a squeeze before walking ahead to join Sophie and Zoe.

I continue trailing at the back, away from the rest of the group, mulling over every cryptic thing Zach said. I come to one conclusion. I have no clue what's going on.

Sixteen

The hike up Whiteface Mountain kills us all off, and I spend the rest of the afternoon listening to the girls bitch and moan about how they hate exercise and will never do any again. They soon perk up when food and drink is mentioned.

The evening goes without a hitch. Although Zoe tries to convince us to go out partying, we're all exhausted and promise we will party as much as she wants tomorrow. The evil glint in her eye makes it clear she's going to make sure we keep it.

The last day is like the first, spent lounging by the pool and taking in the beautiful surroundings. We don't see much of Jake and Amanda. They venture off to do couples things. I'm not complaining. I'd rather they do couples things where I can't see them. It's later in the day when Zoe decides we have to follow through with our promise of partying, so we leave the pool to get ready.

We meet the rest of the group on the main street to hit up a couple of the local bars. They have nothing on Riffs, there's lots of wood and they have a small-town vibe, but they're quirky and fit with everything Lake Placid.

Once we settle in, I never want to leave. The atmosphere is fun and relaxing, and we spend hours outside, drinking under the evening sun. As the steady flow of alcohol begins to catch up with us, we grow increasingly louder.

"I wub you, Abeeee," says Sophie, throwing her arms around my neck and swaying.

I'm feeling buzzed, but no way near as drunk as she is.

I pat her head and reply, "I know you do."

"Pweez don't weeb again," she says verging on sobbing. She's always one to get emotional when she's had too much to drink.

"You mean leave? Well, I can't promise that, but you're too drunk to be talking about this."

She nods in agreement then folds herself in half over the table, placing her head in her arms to go to sleep.

"Too much to drink again?" Asks Jake, sliding in next to me with a drink in his hand. I'm surprised he's here. The last time I checked he hadn't turned up with Amanda, and as the night has gone on, I assumed they weren't going to come.

"Of course. At least there's more of us to handle the two of them."

He chuckles and says, "I think Shaun's more than got Zoe covered."

I turn to see what he's talking about. It isn't surprising that Zoe is leaning against him for support, she always needs someone to prop her up. What is surprising, is the way Shaun is stroking her face affectionately. Clearly, he's tanked.

"When did that happen?" I ask, unsure whether Shaun is as drunk as I think, or if there is something more going on that I haven't figured out yet.

Jake leans back in his chair and takes a long drag of his beer, watching them before he replies, "It hasn't. Yet. I don't think anyway."

"Well, he better not take advantage of her being wasted."

He raises an eyebrow at my comment. "Come on, Abby. You know Shaun would never do anything like that."

"You think you know people, but sometimes they surprise you," I say offhandedly, but it's obvious what I'm referring to.

"Listen, I'm sorry about Amanda. I know you're mad I didn't tell her about us, but I don't want her to start reading too much into things."

"Like what?" I'm not sure what he's getting at. We can barely be around each other five minutes without there being some form of bickering, she wouldn't care about our past.

He sighs and replies, "I dunno. There's stuff going on and I need to keep things as simple as possible."

"Always the man of mystery, never giving anything away ..."

It's an opening for him to explain and I sit for a few seconds waiting to see if he will take it. He doesn't, of course he doesn't. Instead of engaging with him any longer I turn my attention to Sophie.

"Hey," he takes ahold of my arm and tugs gently, so I spin back around to face him.

My eyes meet his brown ones and I freeze. My skin feels like it's on fire where his hand is touching, and I suck in a sharp breath as my heart pounds. This needs to stop.

My eyes betray me when they flicker down to his hand. Before I speak, I exhale slowly. "Jake, there's nothing to say. Do us both a favor and rather than trying to please me, focus on the girl back at the lodge. You know, your girlfriend."

His hand snaps away and he grabs his beer, downs what's left then says, "Right. Forget I bothered. Clearly me and you trying to be friends isn't going to work. I'm done, Abby."

I watch as he walks away, back to Amanda at the hotel, and even though it's the right thing for him to do, I'd be lying if I said it didn't hurt like hell.

✶✶✶

"You just left it at that?" Sophie asks from the back of the car.

We're on our way home from the lake, and the journey feels longer than ever without all the excitement and anticipation. The trip felt bittersweet. It was great being back with the group and feeling close to them again, but it was also painful being in such proximity to Jake for so long. At least after last night we've drawn a line under things and can each get on with our summer.

"Yeah. Unfortunately, it's not going to work us being friends. It was a tall order to begin with."

"Maybe it's for the best," says Zoe, nodding in agreement beside me. "What good would come from you guys getting close anyway?"

"There's no need to worry about that now."

I want the conversation to end. I'm feeling flat as it is, and don't want to keep rehashing what happened with Jake.

I spend the rest of the journey home quietly staring out the window. The break was needed, but

I'm craving being back in the full throes of work to take my mind off the Jake drama. The busier the better.

My cell bleeps a few times, alerting me to messages from Michael. I read what they say and begin banging my head against the dashboard.

Zoe frowns. "Want me to pull over so you can finish the job properly, or are you going to tell us what's wrong?"

"Michael booked tickets to come to Brooklyn for 4$^{th\ of}$ July," I answer.

"Not a nice surprise?"

I sigh, "Not really."

He's picked the worst possible time to tell me. With the funk I'm in, my reaction was never going to be positive.

"Maybe it's what you guys need? Time away from your usual surroundings might help to rekindle the romance."

"Zo ... the group are spending it together. That means me, Michael, Jake and Amanda together for a whole day. What can go wrong?'

Realizing the potential train wreck, it could be, makes Zoe pause before saying, "Hmmm. Well at least there will be shots, and fireworks. That will make things a bit better."

"I don't think it will." I don't want to be the queen of negativity, but I can't see how anything good can come from this scenario.

"You could just get so wasted that you don't have to deal with any of them ..." What she's suggesting is wrong, yet it makes sense. It would be an easy *get out of jail free* card.

"I've seen some of the predicaments you've gotten yourself into ..."

"Yes, but watching you get wasted and trying to deal with them all will add comedy value to my day," she wiggles her eyebrows letting me know she's kidding.

I blame the hangover for the fact I bite back, "Nice to know you're being super supportive."

"There's no point in dwelling, Abs, he's coming. Look at it this way. It's either going to make or break the relationship. At least then you'll have clarity as far as your relationship is concerned, even if you haven't made a decision about work."

I focus my attention out the window and say quietly, "I guess you're right."

"I'm always right."

She pulls me over the gear box and gives the best side-on hug she can, considering we're still hurtling down the highway.

✶✶✶

It's later that evening when we arrive home. We were the last ones to leave thanks to the copious amounts of alcohol we consumed between us the night before. We opted to be safe and leave later which meant we hit traffic in a big way, when trying to get back into Brooklyn.

My parents are in the kitchen, where Mom is preparing a late dinner when I eventually walk through the door.

"Hey, honey. Good trip?" she asks with a smile that instantly lifts me out of the bad mood I've been in all day.

"It was great. The lake was beautiful, we climbed the mountain, drank a lot of cocktails." I purposely miss out the details of what went down with Jake.

144

"Would we expect anything else with Sophie and Zoe in tow?" Dad laughs from the where he's sitting at the kitchen table, typing on his laptop.

"Exactly. I'm not feeling too great today. I may have let them lead me astray."

"Tut tut. How dare you have fun and act your age?" Mom waggles her finger, being anything but serious.

"Yeah, yeah. Is dinner going to be long?" It's been hours since I ate, and my stomach is growling at the delicious smells filling the room.

"No. You got home just in time. It'll be ten minutes max."

I let them know I'll be back and head up to my room. I drop my bags on the floor, planning to deal with them later, like maybe a day or two later. I freshen up and ten minutes later, as planned, I'm settling at the table with my parents and a huge mound of pasta, salad and fresh bread. I will never get bored of the home cooked meals.

"It smells amazing, thanks, Mom."

"No problem. Let's tuck in before it gets cold," she replies.

I'm finishing my third huge portion when Dad clears his throat and looks at me. "Abby, I have a favor to ask."

It's not often he sounds so serious. I place my fork down on the table and say, "Okay ..."

"We've taken on a lot of new bands at the record label, and they're all in the early stages of rebranding and promotions-"

Before he can continue, I smile and say, "Let me guess. You need a photographer?"

"Well ... yeah. I know I mentioned there would be some work at the beginning of the summer, but quite a bit has come up recently and we're struggling to find anyone with enough time in their diary to do

145

everything we need." As he's speaking, I notice the stress lines etched on his face from too much frowning.

"You don't need to explain, I'd be happy to help. I might need to jiggle about some shifts at the bar, but I'm sure Shaun won't mind."

"Well, it works kind of perfect, actually," he continues. "We've heard that Shaun's bar is the up-and-coming place for live music, so we're in the process of setting up a lot of new gigs there as breakout performances."

"Which means I will already be at the bar..." I nod. Dad is incredibly good at his job, and always has a way of making things work for everyone involved, with the least amount of effort.

"Exactly. The rest of the work we need you to do will be behind the scenes. Interview shots, staged shoots for branding, et cetera. maybe even some cover shots."

I raise an eyebrow. "Sounds like a lot of work. Some would say it sounds like a permanent position ..."

He's up to something. He's had this card up his sleeve for a while, and I know it's no coincidence that suddenly, as I return to Brooklyn, there is an abundance of work available for me at the label.

"There may be an opening for a permanent self-employed position." He fakes an innocent look around the room, as if he hadn't already thought all this through, but it's wasted effort as I already know what he's up to. "You would still have the flexibility of being self-employed so you could do other things, but most of the time, work with the label would be a guarantee. I know you have other options that you're mulling over, which still have to hear about I might mention."

146

"I know, Dad. Truthfully, I haven't spoken with anyone about the work stuff yet. I'll tell you when I'm ready. I can do the work this summer for the label and add you to my pile of options. How does that sound?"

I'm praying he isn't offended that my answer isn't an instant yes. It would be so easy, and most people would jump at the chance and think I'm an idiot for not, but there's too much going on in my head to make any big decisions.

His face relaxes and he replies calmly, "That would be perfect. You will be helping us out of a sticky situation, even if it's just for the summer. Who knew there was so much new talent out there? They seem to have crawled out of the woodwork overnight."

There's one detail niggling at me. "You haven't mentioned who any of the bands are. Do I know any of them?" My stomach clenches as my parents share a knowing look, meaning that I'm about to hear something I really don't want to.

"About that ... I suppose I do need to tell you ... One of the bands you would be working with is S.C.A.R.A.B." The smile on his face is far too enthusiastic and he purposefully doesn't refer to them as Jake's band, as if it will soften the blow.

I purse my lips, trying to stamp down the anger that flares inside me. One minute everyone is telling me to stay away from Jake, the next they throw us into situations where we can't avoid each other.

"Seriously?" I ask, my eyes wide with disbelief. "You've both been warning me off him and now here you are pushing us together? It's ok for us to be around each other ... but only if it's on your terms, right?"

"Abby, I never said for you not to be around him. I vaguely remember telling you that I thought he'd grown into a great young man. *That's* the reason I'm telling you to be careful. It would be easy to get caught up in the two of you again and after last time ..."

"Well, you don't need to worry. This trip set in stone that we can't be friends, even for the benefit of the group." Tears burn my eyes. I'm trying to fight it, but the past few days have been an emotional rollercoaster. I'm exhausted and ready for giving in.

"Maybe that's not a bad thing," Mom says taking in my disappointed expression.

"At least it will make my decision at the end of the summer easier," I admit, then curse inwardly that I've revealed Jake might influence my choice.

"So ..." Dad says warily. "Do you think you'll be able to work together?"

"I suppose." I feel as uncertain as I sound. "I'm not saying it's going to be all sunshine and roses, but for the most part I don't need to engage with him. I just need to give the band direction and take photos."

"Well, that's it settled then." The relief on his face is clear, even though he wouldn't have put any pressure on me to say yes. "Would tomorrow be too last minute to start?"

I sit, blinking slowly, trying not to panic at the thought of having to work with Jake after the disaster that was the past few days.

The last thing I want to do is let Dad and the band down, which is why I reply, "It should be fine. Set it up and I'll be wherever you need me. I have a late shift at the bar, so most of the day is free."

The next few minutes are spent making plans for the following morning. The shoot is at Riffs, so we arrange to go together. It's the strangest, most informal job interview I've had, but it's with my dad so of course it would be. I feel sick with nerves, even though he's doing everything he can to keep things

148

positive and make me feel comfortable about working with Jake.

Once I've helped clear the table, I say goodnight to them both and wearily make my way up to my room. Collapsing on the bed, my body and brain ache in ways I didn't think were possible, thanks to the persistent hangover and emotional stress of the trip.

If I stand a chance of getting through the next day in one piece, I need a good night's rest. Instead, I wind up in a restless sleep, dreaming of Jake the whole time.

Seventeen

Waking up the following morning feeling refreshed was never going to happen. Especially when I spent the whole night tossing and turning, anticipating how today with Jake's band would go. To make matters worse, I sleep through my alarm, so getting ready is a frantic rush.

We're in the last few days of June, the run up to 4th of July, and along with the excitement of the celebrations to come, the temperature is rocketing. Perks of being self-employed – I get to pass on professional attire and opt for comfort in this heat.

I decide on a pair of black denim short shorts, a loose grey vest and tie my hair up in a messy bun. I slide a headband on to keep as much hair as possible away from my face. There's no point in makeup as I'm already sweating like a pig and it's unlikely to stay in place for longer than an hour. I merely slick on a bit of concealer to try and hide the rough night I had.

Glancing at the clock, I see I only have a minute until Dad wants to leave, so I slip on some sandals and grab my backpack with my camera and other gear in. Stupidly I take a quick look in the mirror as

I'm leaving my room. It confirms what I already know: I'm a hot mess, but right now I couldn't care less.

I rush down the stairs and find him already waiting at the door ready to leave. Rather than looking annoyed, he looks amused. "Running late?"

"Didn't sleep that great," I reply with a shrug. I can't hide anything from him, so there's no point in even trying.

"You don't need to be nervous, Abby bear. You've done bigger shoots than this."

"It's not the shoot I'm worried about, I can do that in my sleep. Let's just say Jake and I didn't exactly leave things on great terms when we left Lake Placid."

"Ah ... well I'm sure he will be professional. You have nothing to worry about."

He places an arm around my shoulder and gives me a quick squeeze for reassurance before we leave. Normally I'd opt for walking, but it's stifling so we agree the subway is our best bet. We're in Williamsburg within minutes, which gives us the chance to visit a small coffee shop I found a couple of weeks ago. We stock up on caffeine and bagels and sit at a small table on the sidewalk, while Dad catches up on emails, and I people watch in an effort to calm my nerves.

Riffs is virtually empty when we arrive, apart from Shaun and a couple of suits from the label. As the bar doesn't open for another six hours, I can spread out my gear and get set up.

Eventually, a young woman, who I'm guessing is the band's PR rep, walks in with an assistant running behind her, wheeling a rail full of male clothing, nodding frantically at what the woman is saying. It all feels very professional for little old Jake and his band, which is when it dawns on me what a big deal this is

151

for them. Today is about doing what's best for the band, putting whatever issues Jake and I have to the side.

"Aaaaabbbbyyyy," a voice hollers from the front door. I turn and find Sam striding towards me.

Confused, I ask, "Sam? What are you doing here?"

"Did I forget to mention that I was also in the band?" They were in a band back in high school, but I wasn't aware they'd continued their musical journey together.

"Yes ..." I reply shortly.

He holds his hands up and says, "My bad. Abby, I'm in a band with Jake, Zach and a guy called Ryan. Sorry I forgot to mention it, must've slipped my mind." He throws me a wink like he always does when he knows he's in trouble.

"Whatever ..." I go back to sorting through my gear.

"Come on, Abs," he says, urging me to look at him. "I didn't want you to get upset about me working with Jake. I thought I'd give us a chance to catch up before you found out, and then you wouldn't be able to bitch at me as much."

It's like looking at a lost little puppy, and I can see with those big blue eyes of his that he's genuinely worried at how mad I am with him. I remember that this is meant to be a big day for him and the band, so I'm forced to accept the news and move on.

I smile as a peace offering. "It's ok. I wish you'd told me earlier, but it's fine, really. I'm looking forward to hearing you guys play."

"Thank God. I thought for a moment there you were going to kick my ass." He pulls me into another one of his signature hugs and places an affectionate kiss on top of my head.

If I didn't know any better, the amount of physical contact he keeps throwing my way would freak me out, but we're just friends. Still, there's a niggle in my gut, warning me that maybe this isn't one hundred percent the case for Sam. There isn't time to worry about it, as a throat clears behind us. Surprise, surprise, it's Jake and his excellent timing. Always catching me in one 'embrace' or another.

"People just can't keep their hands off you these days, can they? I didn't know our photographer came with benefits. Where do I sign up?" he says smarmily.

I narrow my eyes and clench my fists tightly at my sides at what he's insinuating. It's all I can do to stop myself swinging at him.

"Not cool, man," says Zach as he walks over, having heard everything Jake said. "You said you would keep things professional."

"I'm not the one struggling to keep things professional," he replies, looking angrily between me and Sam. This is turning into a disaster.

Fed up with his bad attitude I snap, "Do you always have to be such an ass?" I had every intention of making sure today ran smoothly but his stubbornness is making it impossible. "I'm doing you a favor here. There's no one else to do the job. Or would you like me to leave?"

I'm calling his bluff. His expression softens and it's clear he understands we have no choice but to work together. If we're going to do so successfully, he needs to calm down.

"Whatever," he huffs. "Let's just get this over and done with." It's not exactly positive, but at least he's agreeing to carry on.

"The sooner the better," I say coldly and walk away from the group, back to where I left some of my equipment with Dad and Shaun.

My dad looks unsure how to approach me. "That seemed to go well?"

I want to tell him what Jake said, but doing so could ruin the bands reputation with the label, so I bite my tongue and nod. If he knows I'm lying, he doesn't say anything. I sort through my gear mindlessly and blink away tears I didn't even realize were there. All the walls I've built up against Jake are starting to crumble, but this isn't the time or the place to fall apart, no matter how much what he said hurts.

Raised voices come from the group on the other side of the room, all directed at Jake. I filter them out and focus on what I'm doing. When I look up, the room is emptying as everyone makes their way to the outdoor stage. For now, the drama seems to have passed.

Dad nods at me then heads outside too. It's a small enough gesture to stay professional but gives me the strength I need to carry on. I hold back for a few minutes, wanting to make sure I really have got myself together before I follow.

I feel someone next to me and turn to see who it is. Through the lingering tears in my eyes, I look up at Jake, taking in his torn expression.

"Fuck. Abby, I'm so sorry."

It happens so quick I can't stop it. Suddenly I'm bundled into his chest, with his arms wrapped tightly around me as I shake like a leaf. The emotion seeps out of me, and tears I tried so hard to hold back, pour down my face.

Jake stands, holding me, stroking my hair gently as he murmurs repeatedly into my ear, "I'm so sorry."

He pulls back, looks me directly in the eye and it feels like the world stops. As I look back up at him, I'm overcome with exhaustion from all the tension since I returned to Brooklyn.

Raising his hands, he cups my face and uses his thumbs to wipe away some of my tears, then quietly asks, "Are you ok?"

The way he's looking at me and holding my face, feels so raw and overwhelming, it's taking everything in me not to begin crying again.

When I do find my voice, it comes out shaky and unsure. "I'm not made of stone, Jake. You can't keep using me as your punching bag. I know you're unhappy I'm here and I'm not exactly thrilled myself, but what you said before was crossing a line. You know me and you know I'm not like that."

"I can't control my reactions when I see you with other guys. You bring out the worst in me," he admits.

We're still in the middle of the bar. At some point, I'm not sure when, we ended up on the floor, and now I'm sat in his lap. Being in this position and hearing him say these things is beginning to make me feel uncomfortable.

"We should probably move. People are going to wonder where we are." I go to stand quickly, but with the awkward position we're in, end up getting my legs tangled and take a hard fall, flattening Jake in the process.

"Crap," I grunt.

We're now sprawled out, flat on the floor with every inch of our bodies pressed against each other. Jake's hands are on my waist, and his breathing has increased rapidly. When I work up the courage to look him in the face, there's no denying the need in his eyes, backed up by the fact his dick is hard as a rock, as it presses into my stomach. All I can compute is how I want to jump his bones.

Reality comes crashing down when voices approach from outside and I jump away frantically. The fact we're both in relationships and keep finding ourselves in these situations, which are getting progressively worse the longer we're around each other, isn't good.

I tug at my clothes, suddenly feeling self-conscious about how little I'm wearing.

I try to make a quick escape before anything else can happen. Gesturing towards outside, I say, "I'll just go get set up ..."

"I'll see you out there. I just need a minute ..."

I nod and quickly grab my kit, walking outside without saying another word.

The rest of the day goes by without a hitch. I spend my time making sure to get a good mix of staged and natural photos, although the natural ones are easier said than done, considering Jake barely takes his eyes off me the whole time.

The final shoot is the bands stage performance, saved for last to avoid them getting too hot and sweaty, which would mean more outfit changes and makeup. I don't know what to expect, as I haven't heard them play, but the girls and my parents have been bigging them up, and the fact we're here with a record label means they must be a big deal.

At first, I'm distracted, as the light has changed, but then the opening riffs catch my attention. I try not to get distracted from my work. The purpose of today is professional and not for my own private performance. Still, they're tight as hell, even for a mess around jam, and the song they're performing is catchy.

Somehow, I manage not to lose focus and get some great photos. The work is different from anything I've done in the past couple of years and it has me buzzing with excitement. I feel like I'm back to my photography roots and it's exhilarating.

The band wraps up their performance and the room fills with an applause from the record label suits and Shaun. The guys' beam with pride and rightly so. When the congratulations are finished the pack up begins. I speak with Dad briefly, confirming that I got the material needed.

Exhausted, I collapse at a table by the bar, with most of my kit packed away, apart from my laptop. I decide to get a head start on editing before my shift behind the bar. I'm startled when my cell vibrates on the table, having been so engrossed in work. I glance at the time and am shocked to see over an hour has passed. The screen lights up again, persistently, informing me I have a message from Michael.

When I finally open it, it says, [Can't wait to see you soon, baby xxx]

Annoyed at his use of the word *'baby'* after I've told him before that I hate it, I simply reply, [xxx]

I place my cell back on the table and look up to find Jake hovering, looking uncertain. His cheeks are still flushed from our awkward moment earlier, and I can't help feeling satisfied that I'm still able to draw such a strong physical reaction from him.

"Can I help you with something?" I ask, looking up through my lashes.

The Jake in front of me isn't the Jake I know. He's out of sorts and not at all like the guy I fell for back in high school who was full of confidence.

"Can I chat with you really quick?"

"Sure." I close my laptop, giving him my full attention.

"So ..." He looks around the bar and shoves his hands into his jean pockets.

"So ...?" This is nice and awkward.

Rubbing the back of his neck, he lets out an embarrassed groan as he says, "I wanted to apologize for this weekend and everything that happened. I know I said a lot of this before we went away, but I mean it. I can't help the reactions I have around you. I say stuff before thinking it through."

I smile knowing exactly what he means. "I seem to be suffering with the same problem."

"I had a lot of time to think on the way back. Maybe we're going about this the wrong way?"

"How so?" I'm intrigued where he's going with this.

"Maybe we're putting too much pressure on ourselves. Everyone around us knows our past and it feels like they're watching us with expectations. Other people are always getting involved, and we never seem to get past the first step. I was thinking maybe we need to spend a bit of time alone. Get to know each other again. There was a time when we didn't hate each other ..." he tapers off.

Confused by what he's spewed at me, I say, "What exactly are you suggesting?"

"Give me one afternoon, we can do something fun. Maybe grab a coffee, have a walk. We could even get out of Brooklyn and head into Manhattan?"

Every part of me screams that this is a bad idea, we're meant to be spending as little time as we can together, not the other way around. The pleading look he gives me has me wavering.

"Come on, Abby. Please? I need you to see that I'm not the ass you think I am. What we're doing right now isn't working. Will you give me this chance?"

Before I know what I'm doing, words spill out of my mouth that I have no control over. "Ok, sure."

He sighs in relief and grins. It's the smile I fell in love with six years, and I don't know what to do with myself. All the fight I had to avoid Jake leaves me instantly. This is not good.

Eighteen

The next evening the girls and I decide on a night in, giving us a proper chance to catch up. The suggestion of drinks was on the cards but juggling shifts at the bar and the work load my dad has given me, has left me with barely any energy. I'm happy for the distractions, but I need a night in.

"You agreed to do what?" screeches Zoe.

"Shh, keep it down. I don't need the whole of Brooklyn knowing my business," I hiss.

She ignores me and shakes her head in confusion, continuing to speak far too loudly. "I don't understand. After everything he's said to you since you've been back, not including years ago, you're giving him another chance. Being friendly around the group is one thing, but being alone together ... are you really sure that's a good idea?"

I know she means well. She was my biggest supporter through everything that went down in high school. Together, her and Sophie were my rocks, which is why they're now so apprehensive. When Jake and I broke up, it wasn't just me who went

159

through the rollercoaster of emotions. It wasn't just me he broke. It was them too.

"He seemed desperate," I say, as if it explains away the huge mistake I'm about to make.

"Well, let him be!" she throws her hands up in the air.

"Really, what are you doing, Abby?" asks Sophie. She's the optimistic one out of the three of us, but not today, she's as concerned as Zoe.

"I have no idea," I rest my head against my arms on the kitchen table.

"Well, you need to get an idea."

I sit back upright, and we all look to the door where my mom is standing, I didn't even notice she was there. From the stern look on her face, it's clear she's overheard everything.

"Jesus, can I not get any privacy, Mom?"

"Not when you're about to ruin your life. No, you can't," she replies.

"Mom!"

"Abigail, I watched you go through months of hell when you and Jake broke up. For goodness sake, he drove you out of Brooklyn." My eyebrows shoot up in surprise, and she continues, "Do you think I didn't know the real reason why you left? I know you were both young, but you've never been the same since. After everything you've worked for and how far you've come, the potential you have with your career ... Do you want to put that all at risk for him ... again?"

I look down at the table. "It's just a coffee, Mom."

I'm not convincing myself, so I don't stand a chance of convincing her. As expected, she calls me out on it straight away, meanwhile Zoe and Sophie sit in the background, their heads bouncing back and forth between us.

"Bullshit, it's just a coffee. Go have one with your friends, not each other. You're both in relationships. How do you think your partners would feel if they knew that you were both running around with an ex?" That's the thing with my mom. Like my friends she doesn't hold anything back, especially when she thinks I'm making a huge mistake, like now.

"Don't beat around the bush or anything," I say quietly, refusing to meet her eye.

"You know she's right. This isn't going to end well," says Sophie agreeing with my mom.

"You're joining in too?"

"We all saw the heartbreak you went through, Abs, and it affected us all, the whole group."

"Seriously? You'd think someone died or something ..." I let out a shrill laugh. It's a poor attempt at lightening the mood.

"You left the state, Abby," says Mom, "that might not seem like such a big deal to you, but to us it was everything."

I sigh in frustration. The conversation is getting out of hand. I don't want to let Jake put a wedge between us like this, but at the same time I refuse to back down, they're blowing this whole thing out of proportion.

"I know, Mom and I'm sorry for leaving like I did, but I'm twenty-four years old. I can live wherever I want. My career has taken me all over the world. It wasn't just about a guy." Standing up, I say sadly, "I'm going to my room, I think we all need some space before we say things we'll regret."

Sophie and Zoe nod while my mom looks away with a sniff. I shuffle out and make my way up the stairs slowly, feeling like I have the weight of the world on my shoulders.

We've argued before. It's what comes with having best friends for life and a close relationship with your mom, but I've never walked out leaving things on such a sour note. It doesn't sit right, but we're all too worked up to come to any sort of reasonable conclusion.

I need time to reflect on the problem, which we all know is Jake. I was already feeling anxious for tomorrow, and now, my gut is clenched in dread.

✗ ✗ ✗

6 years earlier

Despite being December and freezing outside, we all decided to get away from the city. There's no better way to do it than on one of the tourist boats that go around the island. It's peaceful, watching the bustle of the city from a distance. Seeing it, but not being a part of it. Even though we rarely go into Manhattan, Brooklyn is still hectic, as the buzz of the city and its tourists filter their way over. As teenagers that need space sometimes, it can be hard to deal with.

There's no denying how cold it is. It's the sort of damp cold that makes you feel like you'll never warm up again, and it's making us all question whether this trip was really such a good idea.

Standing at one of the rails, I watch as Brooklyn disappears behind us. Exhaling slowly, I feel some of the tension from the past couple of weeks disappear. It doesn't last long though. When Jake approaches me from behind, I'm tense again, but for completely different reasons.

The weather howls around us and I feel him before I hear or see him. But I would feel his presence in a crowd of a thousand people, it's the effect he has on me. He cages me against the rail with his arms on each side of my body and I'm suddenly so nervous, my heart rate goes through the roof.

"God, it feels good to be away from all that crap," he murmurs into my ear. I'm not one hundred percent sure he meant for me to hear it.

"Is everything ok at home?" I ask nervously. I know he hates talking about it and don't want him to think I'm prying.

"The usual, but you don't need to worry about that."

I do though. Jake's from a wealthy family in Manhattan. The pressure they put on him is immense and far too much for someone our age, I'm surprised he hasn't broken from it already. They want him to go to an Ivy League school, just like his father did, and his grandfather. His grandfather has a huge influence over his life, especially since his dad passed away a few years ago. Being around them must be stifling. Music, which he is so passionate about, doesn't come into the equation as far as his family is concerned, and it's beginning to take its toll on him.

"You know you can talk to me about anything."

"Abby ... Sometimes, the last thing I want to do when I'm with you is talk." He begins to run his nose up and down my neck gently, inhaling slightly.

"Did you just sniff me?" I've never had a guy smell me before and I'm glad I'm facing away from him as my cheeks flush bright red.

"I can't help it. You smell good. Like vanilla."

He places a few gentle kisses up my neck, finishing at the soft spot right below my ear. It feels so good that I can't help the soft moan that slips out.

163

It's slightly embarrassing, but with the wind howling, I pray nobody heard.

We still haven't kissed yet and I'm not sure why anymore. There's been the odd moment when we could have, but something always seems to get in the way. The more time that passes, the more I build it up in my mind to be something much bigger, to the point where now, it terrifies me. I've never even kissed a guy before.

Maybe I have always been waiting for Jake. After so much time passing between us and so many promises, I don't want it to be anticlimactic and I certainly don't want it to be with an audience.

We're both there, hovering at the edge, too scared to make the leap. Our relationship already feels so intense and it's scary to think about what things could turn into if we moved into that territory. When Jake and I finally kiss, I want us to be alone and I want it to be life altering. I know I'm being too much of a romantic. A kiss is just a kiss, but I'm going to do whatever I can to make it the best kiss he's ever had.

Jake continues placing kisses up and down my neck and I let out another moan. It's embarrassing how worked up I'm getting when all he's doing is kissing my neck.

"Get a room!" shouts Sam from further down the boat, and the rest of the group start laughing.

I let out a frustrated sigh and my head hangs forward as I shake it. Jake leans in even closer, covering my body with his, then says into my ear, "I'm tired of waiting, Abs. I'm warning you now, I'm gonna kiss you soon and nothing is going to stop me."

Nineteen

I'm walking along one of the Manhattan sidewalks the following afternoon. The sun is high and beating down, so I keep my pace steady, not wanting to sweat any more than I already am. Saying I'm nervous would be an understatement, but it's not just nerves racing through my system, there's guilt too. Guilt that Michael is back in Florida excited for our future together, when I am anything but.

As if he has a radar alerting him to when I'm thinking about him, my cell rings with an incoming call. The universe is trying to tell me, as I'm on my way to meet Jake, that what we're doing is wrong. The guilt gnaws away, and although I'd normally divert the call to a time when I'm less busy, I find myself answering.

"Hey, you ok?"

"I'm fine, are you busy?" We've spoken so little since I left Florida, his voice now sounds unfamiliar.

"I'm about to meet a friend for coffee ..."

"Oh? Which friend?"

"One of the guys from our old group back in high school. We're having a quick catch up." It's the truth, but not the full truth. I feel a little sick keeping this from him, but him knowing everything would only cause him to worry unnecessarily.

He's going to be here soon for the 4th of July celebrations, then we can broach the subject of Jake. He knows our history and it's one of the reasons he was so unhappy with me returning to Brooklyn. It caused many an argument before I left. Maybe he wasn't too far off the mark with his insecurities. My stomach twists. More guilt.

"I guess I'll leave you to it then."

"Thanks, I'm almost where we're meeting anyway." At least this bit isn't a lie.

"Ok, well, have fun. I just rang to say that my flight's the day after tomorrow. I can't wait to see you."

"Great," I squeak. It doesn't register fully what he's said, and I don't have time to over think it, so I wind up the call. "Me neither, speak to you later."

"Love you, Abby. Bye." His voice sounds flat, he was expecting more from the call, he always expects more, but I have nothing left to give.

I don't have another lie in me. Saying the words, *I love you* to him doesn't feel right, especially when I'm unsure how I really feel. I hang up without another word.

Originally, I was twenty minutes early to meet Jake, but now as I stand near Central Park, staring at the coffee shop where we're supposed to meet, I'm ten minutes late. We're at the center of everything and not far from Times Square, but there's no hustle and bustle to be seen. Everything is typical Jake, understated and cool.

I'm standing just off the corner of the block so I'm not in direct sight. I can see him in the distance, standing with his hands in his pockets, looking around as he stubs his toe into the sidewalk.

I'm perfectly aware that what I'm doing is ridiculous, but I can't find it in me to start walking towards him. It doesn't help that even from this distance he looks gorgeous. He towers above anyone that passes him by, and his dark hair, which he keeps running his hands through, is brushed back in its usual style. The more time that goes by, the later I become.

My cell vibrates in my pocket, and when I pull it out, it shows a message from the number I saved as Jake's when we agreed to meet. I expect the message to say something along the lines of *'where are you?'* or *'are you still coming?'* but it reads: Are you going to stand there staring all day?

I look up and see him leaning against one of the cars parked in front of the coffee shop, his arms resting on the roof. He looks directly at me, an amused expression on his face.

My heart skips a beat.

Any hope of remaining unseen and running back to Brooklyn with my tail between my legs has disappeared, so, I take a deep breath and walk over to him.

"Glad you could finally make it ..." His mouth twitches with a smirk, he knows he's got me.

"I was just cooling off ..." Somewhat true, today it's sweltering.

"Nervous?" his lips twitch again.

"A little," I admit.

"Then I'm not the only one."

My eyes widen in shock at him being so open. I'm not sure what to say, so I move the conversation along. "Shall we go inside?"

"Yeah. That's what we're here for ... coffee."

We go inside and I take in all the quirky details of the shop. Small, mismatched tables are scattered around, with random ornaments and decorative features complimenting the dark walls and curtains. It shouldn't work, but it adds to the cute atmosphere.

We walk straight to the coffee bar so we can place our orders and end up standing next to a display full of cakes that has my mouth watering. This place could rival my favorite coffee shop in Brooklyn, which I've been a diehard fan of since my teens.

"Nice, isn't it. Is your mouth watering yet?" Jake's eyes follow mine to the display of cakes. "Want one?"

"I don't think I could choose just one," I chuckle.

He rubs at the back of his neck and says, "We could maybe, you know, share a couple. That way you don't have to pick just one."

What he's offering isn't really what casual friends grabbing a quick coffee do. It's giving off major date vibes and makes me feel rather uncomfortable.

I shake my head no. "Jake, I don't think that's a good idea."

"It's just cake, Abby."

Thinking about it for a second, I decide he's right. If we don't over think it, it's just cake. "Fine, you choose, and I'll tell you if you've passed the test."

He grins and says, "Deal."

We're next in line, and as I go to place my order with the barista, Jake jumps in first, ordering my favorite drink. "She'll have a caramel, cinnamon latte, with an extra shot."

He looks down at me with a twinkle in his eye, waiting for my confirmation that he's got it right.

I give a small nod to the barista, then say, "You remember what I like to drink?"

He doesn't answer, just shrugs, then orders his own drink before the cakes. I don't hear anything else he says because my heart is beating too loud. After all these years, he still remembers something as simple as my favorite drink.

I walk away and take a seat by the window. The squashy armchairs have been calling to me. Plus, I like the idea of being able to stare out the window and people watch, rather than being the sole focus of Jake's attention. A few minutes later, Jake walks over with our order, carefully arranging it on the table, before settling in the armchair opposite mine.

"So ..." he says.

"So ..." My palms sweat as I clench my hands in my lap, and I'm sure Jake can tell how tense I am. My mind comes up blank when I try to think of something to say. It's like we've gone back to the early days when I could barely find the courage to speak around him.

I'm relieved when Jake recognizes that I'm struggling and speaks first. "I'm glad you came. For a while there I thought you were going back around that corner." He chuckles trying to lighten the mood.

"So did I."

He looks down at the table and says so quietly I almost don't hear, "I'm glad you didn't." Then he looks back up and grins, "How about some cake?"

"What have we got then?" I feel like I can breathe a little easier now we're onto something more trivial.

"I went for: Death by Chocolate – my favorite. Pecan Crunch – our favorite. Birthday Cake – your favorite."

He leans back and smirks knowing he's done good. Once again, I'm surprised he remembers a small detail like what cake I like. I search his eyes trying to find some reason behind it but get nothing. Jake is back to being a blank canvas, refusing to give anything away.

He hands me a fork silently and we both tuck in. We spend the next ten minutes groaning at how good the cake is, which takes away the need for awkward conversation. When the sugar and caffeine hit my system, I relax back into the armchair and enjoy this small bit of time with him. This *just friends'* thing could work after all. It's been harmless so far and I let out a contented sigh.

"Better?" he asks.

"Yeah. I was starving," I say sheepishly.

He nods. "I remember what you're like when you haven't eaten."

"Ha de ha. So, how have things been? Really, I want to know."

His eyebrows shoot up in surprise. "You do? Well, the band has taken off. We've just got back from touring along the West Coast. It was amazing, Abby. I never thought I'd get the chance to do what I love. I was sure I was going to end up at some Ivy League and wind-up pushing numbers on Wall Street like grandpa wanted me to."

I smile as he rambles on, being so open, then ask, "How is he?"

"My grandpa? He passed away two years ago." His gaze flickers out the window, expressionless. I know they had a complicated history, but his reaction proves there's more to it.

"I'm sorry. I had no idea."

"You don't need to apologize. We've not spoken in years, so how would you know? This might sound awful, but things have been better since he's been gone. The band have finally been able to pursue things properly without him breathing down my neck. I mean we never would've split if it hadn't been for all his shit back then-" He stops abruptly and goes pale when he realizes what he's said.

"What are you talking about?" I ask, not missing a beat.

"Nothing, forget I said anything." He picks up a napkin and begins wiping at his hands, agitated.

"That wasn't *nothing*, Jake. Is there something I don't know about why we split up?"

"You know everything you need to, Abby. Can we just leave it? Please?" His eyes plead for me to listen and not push any further. The part of me that knows Jake better than I know myself recognizes when to back down.

"Fine. What else is new?" I narrow my eyes, letting him know that I'm not happy leaving the subject.

"You know the rest. There's Amanda. I live with the band now, which helps us grab practice time together between all our other jobs." He shrugs, still affected from almost outing whatever his little secret was.

I push some leftover crumbs around on my plate, trying not to let his change in mood ruin what has so far been a nice time.

"I bet you're all burnt out," I say.

"Nah, it's fine, we're just doing what we have to. Now, I want to hear about you."

He leans forward in his seat, resting his elbows on his knees. My eyes fall to his biceps, which bulge as he places his weight on his arms. He's wearing a fitted white band shirt that hugs his chest and stomach, and I feel flustered when my gaze trails over him. God, why does my body have this reaction? I have no control over it, and it's becoming embarrassing.

It registers that I've zoned out of the conversation and he was expecting me to respond. When I look at his face, blood rushes to mine, and I pray he hasn't noticed the reaction I've been having to him.

I know he has, but instead of pulling me up on it, he allows his own eyes to travel down my body. When he reaches my bare, tanned legs, he licks his lips and swallows hard. Letting out a barely audible groan, he leans back and rubs a hand over his face. This is what I feared would happen. We shouldn't be doing this.

We could argue that we're only looking, that there's no harm in it, but that would be a lie because with the two of us, it's always been so much more than that. If we were only looking, my heart wouldn't beat faster than it does for anyone else. My thoughts and dreams wouldn't be consumed by memories of the first guy I fell in love with.

The walls I put up around my heart, were to protect myself from getting hurt again, the way Jake hurt me. He gave up on me when he said he never would. Those walls were put there to stop anyone else from getting in and it's worked with everyone but him. There's no wall strong enough to keep him out.

Breathlessly I ask, "What are we doing, Jake?"

"I'm just catching up. It was you who started checking me out," he laughs.

But he's right, I'm the one that started this and I'm furious with myself. "I'm being serious. I'm sorry ... I don't think I can do this, it's too hard." My mom and the girls were right, this was a bad idea.

"Abby, I was kidding," he says, frustrated at my change in mood.

I ignore him and stand up, throwing down some money on the table to cover my food.

"Really ... You're not going to say anything? You're just going to leave?"

I should do just that. Leave without saying a word. But I feel I should at least make it clear why I'm going.

I lean over the table, hoping the rest of the coffee shop doesn't hear when I say, "I'm walking away,

Jake, because what we're doing isn't right. We're both in relationships. If you love Amanda as much as everyone says you do, maybe you should start acting like it."

He doesn't respond, just stares at me in shock. I might have been harsh, but one of us needs to face up to the reality of what we're doing. Judging by the look on his face, it isn't going to be him.

I swing my satchel over my shoulder and walk out of the coffee shop silently. The fresh air helps to clear some of the tightness in my chest, however, there are only two things that can help ease my anxiety: running or taking photos. I can't do either as I don't have the gear, so I head towards Central Park in a power walk, hoping the slight endorphins will help to lift my mood.

I'm there before I know it and pleasantly surprised to discover a music festival in full swing. It's one of those free outdoor events that are perfect for local bands, and of course the tourists love them too. It's just the sort of thing I need to take my mind off what's just happened.

When I find a spot in the crowd, I catch my breath, willing myself to stop thinking about Jake. Easier said than done when he grabs my arm from behind.

The music, the laughter and the chatter of people are all background noise compared to the ringing in my ears as Jake spins me around to face him. I tilt my head back to look up at his face. People are dancing together around us, so we don't look out of place when he pulls my body tightly against his, staring into my eyes and swaying slightly to the music coming from the stage.

My chest heaves. It's not from physical exertion, but from being so close to Jake. It would be embarrassing if his wasn't doing the same. His thumbs begin tracing small circles where his hands grip my arms. He's trying to help me relax, but all he's doing is firing me up, as his touch leaves goosebumps in its place. My eyes fall to his lips and I'm mesmerized by how full they look. The need to kiss them is all consuming.

I don't need to worry about my own self-control because his appears to have gone completely, especially when he leans down, closing the distance between us. My eyes involuntarily close and he almost reaches my lips when it dawns on me what we're about to do.

"Shit!" I jerk away and look at him in horror.

He groans and looks up at the sky, as if that will give him answers to the messed-up situation we've found ourselves in. His shoulders sag when he realizes that he was about to cheat on the girlfriend who he is *'in love with'*, or so he says.

"Fuck, Amanda. What was I thinking?"

"It's fine. Well, it's not, but we both have a part to play in this," I try to reassure him and myself at the same time. "Let's write it off as being caught up in old times. Easily done right?"

"Erm, yeah. This isn't what I had in mind for today. You have to know I'd never cheat on anyone." He looks distraught, and that's putting it mildly.

"I know, Jake, let's just leave it ok?" Nodding, he takes a step back, and turns to face the band, who thankfully have decided to play a more upbeat song. It feels like forever passes by as we watch them, neither of us sure how to move on from the awkward situation.

Of course, one of the worst things that could possibly happen next brings us crashing back down to reality with a thud.

We hear her voice at the same time, and glance at each other quickly. Jake's expression mirrors mine, full of fear, as Amanda's voice gets closer. Did she witness the almost kiss?

"Jake. Jake, here!"

We hear her before we see her, and Jake scans the crowd frantically. He's not just trying to find her. He's trying to figure out if she could have seen us from whatever her position was. Finally, he spots her and hurries off. Stupidly I follow behind.

"Baby, hi." He pulls her into a hug, while I hover in the background trying not to gag at his use of the word *baby*. Ironic, as it's the same pet name I used with Michael during our call a few weeks back to try and get the same reaction from him. The pain I felt seeing them together at Lake Placid, was nothing compared to what I feel now, after being in his arms. After our almost kiss.

I must be staring because Amanda breaks their embrace and looks over at me, confused and says, "Abby, hi?" A question, rather than a friendly welcome.

I can see the cogs visibly turning in her mind, trying to process why we're here, together. The only saving grace being if she's confused, it means she didn't witness the almost kiss.

"I told you I was meeting a friend for coffee, remember?" Jake chips in, before she has chance to ask any awkward questions. Questions to which the answers would have to be blatant lies.

"A friend, Jake. You didn't specify who, so I assumed it was just one of the guys," she says with a sickly-sweet smile.

She's pissed. I can read the insecurity on her face and in her voice, because I've been there before myself, with Jake. And the way she subtly narrows her eyes as she glances between us, tells me that there's more to the bubbly, sweet, blonde exterior she lets everyone see. She hasn't been fooled by Jake's simple explanation of our past. She knows there is more to it, and isn't happy we've been here together, alone. Rightly so. To say I feel like the world's biggest bitch would be an understatement.

"So, what are *you* doing here?" says Jake in a pathetic attempt to change the subject. We're standing in the middle of a music festival, it's obvious why she's here. I raise my eyebrows in disbelief that he could ask such a stupid question. He ignores me, keeps his cool and remains focused on Amanda.

"I told you I was going to a gig today," she says, matter of fact.

"Right, sorry. I forgot." He begins rubbing the back of his neck, which Amanda and I clock at the same time. I try to divert my eyes from watching him, but she catches me in the act, and she gives me a cold look.

She places her hands on her hips and with an ever so slight sneer to her voice, says, "So, what are you guys doing here?"

Jake's never been a good liar and begins to sweat as he tries to quickly come up with a reasonable answer.

Before he dumps us both in a pile of crap we can't get out of, I say, "It's my fault. I love being outside, and I was getting fed up with the coffee shop, so I suggested we went for a walk, and we found ourselves here. It's been over six years since I've been in Central Park. God, I forgot how great it is, especially in the summer."

I have no idea if my lie is convincing, her expression is unreadable. She looks at me and I make one final, attempt to win her over. "It's perfect that we bumped into you actually! Now Jake doesn't have to bother heading back to Brooklyn. I'm leaving in a moment anyway, so he can stay here with you. We couldn't have planned it better!"

I throw in an extra, over the top, grin, trying to emphasize that my intentions are good. Even though five minutes earlier they were anything but.

It seems to seal the deal and I ignore Jake's expression, as I've thrown him under the bus. He should be over the moon to spend the afternoon with the girlfriend he claims to love so much.

Accepting my explanation and visibly relaxing, Amanda replies, "That's *so* great! It was nice to see you again." Somehow, I don't think I'm the only one who is good at lying. "Will you be joining us all for the fourth of July celebrations? It's probably the last time I'll see you as I'm away working for the rest of the summer."

To most her invitation would seem nice and welcoming, however, I'm miffed at her insinuation I'm the outsider here, when these are my oldest and closest friends.

We had a close call though, so instead of biting I reply, "You bet. My boyfriend Michael is heading here the day after tomorrow. I'm so excited for him to meet you all!"

I'm cringing inside at how fake I sound and Jake frowns as if he wants to say something. "Anyway," I continue, "I don't want to keep Jake from you any longer, enjoy the rest of the gig." I wave awkwardly and back away before I can be drawn into another conversation.

"Bye, Abby. It was *so* great bumping into you," Amanda says. Her face says otherwise.

"See you later," says Jake. His face is blank when he looks away. I wouldn't expect anything else with his girlfriend right there. I leave without saying anything else.

Any hope of a peaceful 4th of July celebration has gone out the window. If only I knew how eventful it was actually going to be.

Twenty

It's the day before 4th of July and I'm pacing my room. Michael's due to arrive at any moment, after a two-hour delay to his flight. I hoped we would get to spend a couple of hours together before the family meal my parents have organized (family including Sophie and Zoe of course). I think it will do everyone good, including myself, to see my actual, real-life boyfriend and bring us out of this Jake bubble we all seem to be in.

The girls are downstairs, helping my mom to get dinner ready, my Dad's in his office and I'm just here, in my room, pacing and waiting to hear the cab pull up outside. There's not the usual excited anticipation, because we haven't seen each other in so long. No, I'm full of fear that he will somehow know everything that has happened with Jake.

Whatever hope there was of this trip helping us to salvage our relationship ended yesterday. I'm in over my head with all things Jake, but before I can decide what to do, I need to ride out the 4th of July with as little trouble as possible.

Each time I think about tomorrow there's a surge of dread. The idea of seeing Jake and Amanda together after the almost kiss Jake and I had yesterday, isn't something I'm looking forward to. Throw Michael into the mix and I have the feeling a disaster is about to unfold.

I hear the cab pull up outside. I freeze, staring out the window, waiting for Michael to get out. I smile to myself when he literally unfolds his six-foot four frame out the door. He's a blond, muscular, football playing giant. There's a warm, familiar flutter in my stomach, but unfortunately, it's not the lust filled kind, but the love-him-like-a-friend kind.

I genuinely love spending time with him ... just not in the rip his clothes off, want to marry him and make babies kind of way. I watch him lifting his bags out of the cab, the muscles rippling on his tanned arms and I wonder what is wrong with me. Any other girl would be living the dream right now, head over heels with an NFL player who's set for life. But I'm pining over the guy who dumped me six years ago. I'm an idiot.

I feel sorry for Michael because he never really stood a chance and that's what's heartbreaking. When Jake stole my heart all those years ago, every guy was done for. It didn't matter how much time passed, or how much soul searching I did, I was broken. It's as if I had to come back, to gain real clarity over everything that happened between us and everything I felt.

I wait until Michael knocks on the door, needing those last moments to get myself together. When he does, I make my way downstairs, just as Zoe shouts up that he's arrived. I pause with my hand on the door handle, take a deep breath and pray for a small miracle that we all get through this relatively unscathed. When I finally open it, he towers above me with a huge grin on his gorgeous face.

"Hey, you," he says and pulls me into his arms, nuzzling his face into the crook of my neck. "I missed you."

He pulls back and before I know what's happening, he's kissing me. It's weird at first because he's taken me by surprise. I snap out of it quickly and go through the motions, when inside I feel nothing.

He groans in satisfaction and his hands begin exploring, they move underneath my top, as he pushes me back against the door. I should be enjoying this, we haven't seen each other in weeks, but all I can think is that somebody is going to walk in at any moment.

"Michael, you need to stop," I say, just as a throat clears behind us. I peer round to see my dad. Great.

"Hello, Michael." He looks totally unimpressed at the display we're putting on in his doorway.

"Sorry, Mr. West, it's been a long few weeks without Abby. You know how it is." He winks, as if he genuinely believes my dad will want to share this sort of joke about his daughter. I can't stop my face from grimacing, this is humiliating.

Dad stands with his face reddening in anger. "I'm not sure I do ..." We're off to a great start, let the circus begin.

Mom shouts from the kitchen with expert timing, for us all to come through. Thankful for the save, I power off, dragging Michael away from my dad before he can say anything else.

"Michael, it's so good to see you again." Mom walks over from where she was standing and chopping, wiping her hands on the front of her apron. She doesn't give away any signs of insincerity, though I know he isn't her favorite person. She would never

181

put me in an awkward position, unlike my dad and best friends, who are all incredibly open in their dislike of him.

"Hi, Michael," says Sophie with a smile. She appears to be on her best behavior.

"Wine, anyone?" Zoe doesn't openly acknowledge him with a hello, but at least she's being civil by offering him a drink. It makes a change from their usual bickering.

"Please!" I shout, in need of something to numb my senses.

Zoe hands over a large glass with a smug look, to which I respond with my best death stare before taking a large gulp.

"Woah, slow down, Abby, babe. I don't want you to be useless later." Michael shoots me a totally inappropriate look. Both Sophie and my mom look at him with their mouths hanging open, while Zoe holds the wine bottle in front of her face, trying to hide her snigger. I squirm, wondering what is wrong with him. He's known for not having a filter on the things he says, but tonight it's like he's purposefully trying to piss everyone off.

"Seriously, Michael?" I take another large drink of my wine and walk out of the room. Michael follows me sheepishly into the living area where I'm pacing angrily. "What is your problem? That's my family in there. You can't say things like that!"

"Sorry," he replies, his shoulders slump in defeat. "I'm nervous and can't help it. I know they all hate me."

"They don't hate you," I say feeling sorry for him. Despite his size, he looks like a lost puppy that just wants to be loved. "They will do though if you keep this up."

"I'll try and rein it in. I promise. I really am sorry."

"Let's just get through dinner without any more inappropriate comments please?" I move towards him and even surprise myself when I wrap my arms around his waist. I've been cold with him since he set foot through the door and he needs the reassurance, especially with the vultures in the kitchen.

"Sure," he says, albeit a bit defeated.

Back in the kitchen everyone is sitting at the table with dinner laid out in the center.

"I'm sorry about before," says Michael as he takes a seat.

"Don't worry." Mom dismisses it quickly. "Wine?"

"Why not?" he smiles, and to my relief she smiles back.

Dinner goes by without a hitch, even with the offhand comments Zoe makes under her breath. Michael's so anxious he doesn't hear her thankfully. When everything's cleared away, Michael heads upstairs while I make plans with Sophie and Zoe for the next day.

When I get upstairs myself, he's waiting in my room. Amazing. I tell him I'm beat, and we should get an early night ready for tomorrow. He looks disappointed but rather than arguing, asks if he's staying with me. There's no way my dad would ever let a guy stay in my room, regardless of how long we've been dating. When I tell Michael this, I get another disappointed look. Giving up, he places a quick kiss on my lips before leaving for the room next door to mine.

I flop back on my bed and let out a sigh, relieved the night is over. I only have tomorrow to make it through and then I can relax. I lay awake for hours, like I do most nights, waiting for sleep to come. It's impossible when memories of Jake are constantly

running through my mind, no matter what I do to try
and stop them.

***

6 years earlier

*It's been a couple of days since the ferry ride, and
I've been a bag of nerves. Not the bad kind of nerves,
the anticipation kind of nerves. Time is running out
as it's only a few days till Christmas and my parents
have decided this year of all years, we're taking a
trip to LA for some winter sun.*

*My mind's been consumed by Jake and how much
I want him. The wait for our first kiss has been long
enough, and if we leave it to chance or 'the perfect
moment' then it's never going to happen. Throw in
the mix our three-week vacation, and I've decided to
take matters into my own hands.*

*He's a teenage guy, and as Zoe so kindly pointed
out, there's only so long a guy will wait to get what
he wants, otherwise he will move on and get it from
somewhere else. Apparently, that's how their minds
work. Deep down I feel like Jake isn't like that and
would wait if I need to. I'm done waiting though, I'm
ready.*

*Last night was spent with Sophie and Zoe, trying
to figure out the best way to encourage things along
without being full on and forcing myself on the poor
guy. Ironically, the least romantic of us, Zoe, came
up with the most romantic plan. We opted for a bit
of a festive theme. Mistletoe.*

*You'd think it would be easy to find, alas it's not.
I've spent most of the day racing around Brooklyn
trying to find some. Note to self, you shouldn't leave*

it till a couple of days before Christmas, most places sell out fast. Lesson learned. Luckily, I got what I needed after some hard work.

The snow started an hour ago, and already the sidewalks are covered. Even though it's early, darkness is closing in, and as the snow swirls around, the streetlights give off a soft orange glow. Everything feels peaceful, but as I walk along Jake's block, glancing around at the brownstones, I'm struggling to keep my nerves at bay. There's a strong possibility I'm about to puke everywhere.

I make it to the front of his home and mutter 'Shit,' under my breath, as it dawns on me what I'm about to do. I clutch at the mistletoe in my pocket, using it as a lifeline, to keep me grounded and stop myself from turning around and running away. Rather than running the risk of bumping into his mom, I drop Jake a message letting him know I'm at the front door and he needs to come down as soon as he can.

In hindsight maybe I should've kept the message more casual, as a second later the door is thrown open by a distressed looking Jake.

"Abby, what's wrong?" he asks, pulling me into his chest and wrapping his arms around me protectively, while looking frantically behind and checking I'm safe.

I feel rather sheepish for stressing him out so much, and reply, "Erm. Nothing."

"You made it sound like there was an emergency?" He looks annoyed, but I would be too if I were in his shoes. I didn't think this part of the plan through.

I look up and take him in. His face constantly amazes me. Even though we're still young, there's no boyishness to be seen. I'm turning into a puddle of mush, and I'm done for when my eyes meet his.

"Abby?" His voice softens, he knows something is bothering me. He moves away and scans me over to check that physically I really am ok.

"So, I have this …" with a shaky hand, I raise the mistletoe slowly in the air, so it's high above my head. He's so tall there isn't a chance it would go anywhere near his, but it doesn't matter as he gets the point.

"Is that-?" The concern on his face from a moment ago is replaced by an amused look.

"Mistletoe." I can't hide my smile, even though I wanted to come across all serious and sexy, I'm too excited.

He looks nervous himself, for a short moment. I could have been mistaken, but his expression then changes and to someone as inexperienced as myself, is unreadable. I soon understand that his expression is one of want, and the person he wants is me.

He raises his arms, slipping his hands around the back of my neck and begins rubbing his thumbs against my skin to soothe the nerves that must be written all over my face. And then he starts to pull me towards him. I don't close my eyes until the last second, wanting to remember every moment of what we've waited so long for. It feels like forever as he closes the gap between us, and then his lips press down on mine.

At first, he's gentle, almost hesitant. His lips feel warm and moist. I start to feel him pull away, but I'm in no way ready for the kiss to end. We've waited too long for it. A sudden confidence takes over, and I take control of the kiss, pulling him back to me and pressing my lips more forcefully against his. The kiss changes quickly, moving from being an

186

innocent first kiss, to a battle between two people desperate for each other. It feels like we're finally kissing for real, as his mouth forces mine open and he begins massaging my tongue with his. I've never felt anything like it before and my body feels like it's burning up.

Our tongues tangle frantically, and he gently tugs my hair so my head falls back, causing me to open up to him even more. I've never wanted anything as much as I want Jake. The chemistry between us is off the scale, and I can't understand why it's taken us forever to get here.

As far as first kisses go, I'd say it's pretty heated. We've gone from PG-13 to R in a matter of minutes, starting with me not really knowing what I'm doing, quickly followed by Jake losing complete control, groaning and pushing me back up against the door. It was still open and slams with a loud bang. Neither of us bother to take any notice because nothing else matters. We're consumed by how much we want each other after holding back for so long. He lifts one of my legs, hooking it round his waist, and cradles my ass as he pushes his crotch into my hips. This movement alone causes waves of pleasure to shoot through my body, heightening when he begins kissing down my neck, nipping softly.

"Jake ..." I groan, but he's relentless and I'm powerless to stop him.

"Jake, dinner's ready!" His mom shouts from down the hall, and we pull away from each other like lightening, scared of being caught in such a compromising position. We're both panting and my hair's a mess from where his hands have been tugging and pulling. Our cheeks are flushed, and our eyes are glazed.

After a second, he takes a step back towards me, with an expression I've never seen before on his face. It's the sort of expression that hints towards something big, but it doesn't feel like the right moment to push and ask what he's feeling. I let him lean back into me, and place a more reserved, gentle kiss against my lips. He lingers wanting more. We both do, but I get why he holds back, as neither of us wants to start something we can't finish.

When I think he's about to turn and leave, he murmurs against my lips, "While you're away, Abby, remember, we have unfinished business."

Twenty-One

The next morning, I wake up relatively early, feeling disorientated by my dreams. Dreams of Jake, that I shouldn't have been having when my boyfriend is in the next room. Michael's awake early too, so we head out and grab some breakfast and coffee for ourselves and my parents. We return with what feels like gallons of espresso and enough bagels to feed a small army. Mom croons with approval, the night before forgotten.

It's a beautiful day out, the skies are clear blue, and the sun is beating strong. We decided as a group to head to Coney Island. It's the perfect place for a group adventure where we can all let our hair down, enjoy the weather and rides and pretend to be kids again. When we're fed up, there will be lots of drinking on the beach while we wait for the fireworks later. I'm more than a little excited as it's another group tradition I've missed out on over the years. Since I left Brooklyn, 4th of July celebrations have never felt the same.

I opt for a short, white summer dress over my bikini and shove a change of clothes and some

189

essentials for later into my bag. The plan is to hit some bars once we've watched the fireworks. I'm struggling with applying my sunblock when Michael walks into the room without knocking.

"Need a hand?" His eyes run hungrily over my body, and I blush feeling insecure. I know he's going to try something on and I'm not sure how I feel about it.

"You should have knocked. I could've been getting changed."

I give him an annoyed look and hand the sunblock over so he can do my back and neck. He begins rubbing at my shoulders, and I can't help letting out a moan of satisfaction. Unfortunately, he sees this as encouragement, becoming more eager as he places kisses along my shoulder. The fact that I don't stop him gives him an invitation to take it further. He spins me round and starts kissing me eagerly. There's no build up, he's straight in there like a bulldozer, shoving his tongue in my mouth and backing me up towards the bed.

It happens so fast that it takes a second for my brain to catch up with my body. When it does, all I can think about is Jake and how wrong this feels.

"Stop," I say, pushing him away.

"Come on, baby, don't do this. I know you want me too." He reaches out to pull me back into him again.

"I really don't." The words are out of my mouth before I have chance to properly think, and I hate how harsh they sound and how hurt Michael looks.

"What's going on, Abby?"

"I don't know," I stutter. "I didn't mean I don't want you. I just meant not right now. We're going to be late meeting everyone." I'm clutching at straws, hoping he accepts the pathetic lie.

"No need to explain, I heard you loud and clear. I'll see you downstairs when you're ready." He leaves the room abruptly and I hear him thud down the stairs. My heart's still racing from the panic of the moment. I can't even pretend to want him anymore, meaning I have a big decision to make, and soon.

After our little argument, we leave later than I originally planned, and wind up missing the bus to Coney Island. I text Sophie and Zoe, letting them know we're running late and will be on the next bus. Sophie replies, telling me to meet them at the Lunar Park entrance as the rest of the group is already there. She asks whether everything is ok, but I don't have the energy to go into it, and don't want to ruin the day. I reply that everything is fine.

There's stone cold silence from Michael on the journey, he's still angry about being dismissed earlier. We can't get to our stop soon enough and I race off the bus, heading in the direction of the rest of the group with him trailing behind.

We reach them and everyone is in good spirits, saying *hi* to Michael. I don't need to worry about him letting our argument from earlier ruin the day. He's a showman: constantly being the center of media attention means he knows how to put on a façade that things are perfect even when they might not be, in order to keep his personal life out of the limelight.

We start walking towards the amusement park and the only tell that something is wrong, is that Michael doesn't offer me any direct eye contact. He chooses to walk ahead with Sam and Shaun, talking football eagerly. Of course, only Zoe and Sophie pick up on this.

"Is everything ok with you two?" asks Sophie.

"Not really," I reply honestly. "We just need to make it through today."

"Do you want to talk about it?"

"Nah, let's not ruin things. Anyway, where are Jake and Amanda?" I ask noticing the group is short of two members.

Zoe answers, "Amanda had to pack, as she's leaving for work tonight and has a late flight. They're meeting us when she's ready. Drink?"

I look at the water bottle she's holding which is full of clear liquid I know is not water.

I raise an eyebrow. "Vodka? Isn't it a bit early?"

"It's never too early on the 4th of July." She spreads her arms out, spinning in happy circles, loving life.

"I want what she's had," giggles Sophie, grabbing the bottle off her, and taking a large swig.

"If either of you barf on me, you're dead," I laugh. Their mood is infectious.

We spend the next couple of hours running around the amusement park like little kids at Christmas, laughing and taking it in turns riding together. The fight Michael and I had earlier has been forgotten, and for a while we have an unsaid truce, enjoying just being together again.

We make our way to the beach when we finally tire from the rides. Some serious fuel of the food and alcohol variety is needed. Despite it being insanely busy, we find a great spot near the water, and not long after we're settled, Jake and Amanda meet us.

I watch like a hawk as Michael shakes hands with Jake and then goes back to his conversation with Sam and Shaun. All my nerves of them meeting for the first time evaporate. Michael is none the wiser that there is anything wrong.

I'm a rollercoaster of emotions though. This is the first time I've seen Jake since the almost kiss incident in Central Park. The guilt of having both Michael and

Amanda around is a reminder of how wrong it was and makes me feel sick.

I try not to be judgmental when Jake simple says *"hello"* to me, but spends the rest of his time with Amanda hanging on his arm. He gives the impression of being this cool, independent guy in a band, and yet ironically, he now spends his time with someone clinging to his side, which is anything but cool.

"We're gonna grab some food, anyone want anything?" ask Sam to the group.

We ring in our orders, and my eyes remain focused on Jake and Amanda. She's constantly whispering things in his ear and giving him small kisses, but his attention isn't solely focused on her. Every now and again we catch each other's eye. If I thought it would go unnoticed, I was wrong. I turn to find Michael looking suspiciously with his eyes narrowed. He knows something is up and he's not an idiot. He walks off to help the guys carry back the food and drinks and doesn't bother asking what I want.

I huff to myself. A headache is forming and the need for an alcoholic drink is strong. I look over at Zoe, determined not to let the animosity with Michael spoil the great day we've had so far.

I stretch my arm in her direction. "Vodka. Now please."

"Seriously, what is going on with you guys? I'm getting major bad vibes," says Sophie.

Zoe snorts loudly as she hands over the bottle. "Isn't it obvious? Michael wants to bump uglies and Abby doesn't."

"Why do you always have to let everyone know my business?" I snap. I'm hot and bothered and annoyed at how loud she's speaking.

Out of the corner of my eye, I can see Jake watching us and he looks pissed. He has no right to be as he's the one currently sitting with a girlfriend on his arm, fawning all over him. I'm the one arguing with my boyfriend while he gets to sit back and enjoy the show.

Zoe doesn't get the hint to quieten down and continues, "He's acting like a puppy that's had its ball taken away. The ball FYI is your vagina." In case this couldn't get any more embarrassing, a woman next to us tuts, covering her child's ears with her hands while simultaneously shooting us a death glare.

I flash her an apologetic look, then say to Zoe, "How much have you had to drink?"

"Not enough my friend." She raises her glass in the air. "The day is still young, and the men are still fresh. Dear, Lord, please bring me some penis."

The woman gives us another disapproving glare as the child asks what a penis is.

"Maybe you need to keep it down a bit," agrees Sophie.

When the family stand up, gather their thing and move away, we burst out laughing at how ridiculous the conversation is.

"You shouldn't be allowed out," I say to Zoe when I manage to catch my breath.

She rolls her eyes. "I can't help it if I haven't been laid in a couple of weeks. I'm horny. Fuck knows what you're like, Abby. I bet you're ready to dry hump Jake's leg."

My blood runs cold.

At that exact moment, the guys return with the food and have heard every word Zoe just said. Michael drops down in the sand next to me, and practically throws the hot dog he's holding in my direction. I feel obliged to take it, although I've lost my appetite. The rest of the group has gone quiet and I feel a pair of eyes on me. Looking in Jake's

194

direction, I catch Amanda watching us with her eyebrows drawn together, the complete opposite to her usual cheery self.

"Zoe's drunk," I say to Michael. My anxiety over today was justified. I knew that us all being together was going to be a complete disaster.

"She doesn't seem that wasted to me." He shrugs and looks out into the distance, avoiding eye contact.

"Still, she doesn't know what she's saying."

He turns back to me and his eyes are full of emotion. I'm not sure whether what I see is anger, sadness or both. "Funny. She's one of your closest friends. I think she knows what she's talking about."

"All I wanted to do was enjoy today and it's a disaster. Can we please just enjoy the rest of the day?" I rub my hand over his back in the way I know he loves, and I can see he's beginning to lose his fight.

"Kiss me?" He asks with pleading eyes.

They don't have their usual sparkle, and I hate that I'm the cause of that. I resign myself to this one small, physical interaction between us. Anything to take away the guilt. I nod to let him know it's ok.

He leans in and presses his lips against mine. The kiss is slow and affectionate, as he pours everything, he feels towards me into it. Anyone else would be left like a puddle of goo on the floor, but I merely go through the motions, nipping at him in the way I know drives him crazy, while I feel nothing. I know Jake's eyes are on us the whole time. It's like a sixth sense. When the kiss ends, I refuse to look in his direction.

The next couple of hours are a blur and the animosity is forgotten as more alcohol is consumed. Finally, 4th of July is turning into what I wanted it to be.

After Zoe's moment of verbal diarrhea, Jake, and Amanda leave. I see them walking through the crowds up on the boardwalk, holding hands in their own world. When they return to the group, Shaun and Sam see them approaching and begin wolf whistling.

"Dude! Lasted longer than normal!" Shouts Sam, causing Jake to blush while Amanda giggles pathetically. Jealousy bubbles inside me, and I will it to stop.

"I have to go. My flight's in a few hours and traffic's going to be horrendous with people travelling in for the fireworks," says Amanda when she finishes giggling like a preschooler.

"That's a shame." My voice doesn't sound as genuine as I intended.

Zoe shakes her head, shoving her fist in her mouth in an attempt not to laugh out loud.

"Well, I'm sure you'll do your best to look after Jake for me." You'd have to be an idiot not to notice the bitterness in her tone and the group goes quiet, again.

The group looks between me and Amanda, as our interaction has become the main entertainment. She turns to Jake, who clearly wants to be anywhere but here, and snaps for him to walk her to her car, and stalks away from the group. Everyone shouts bye to her retreating form, even though there's little chance she'll hear it, or care.

The next ten minutes are spent in silence as nobody knows what to say. It isn't until Jake returns that Shaun announces it's time for a game of football. We managed to pick a decent spot and have enough room to play, even with how busy the beach is.

We split into teams. Michael, Jake, Sophie and Zach on one, while I've landed in a team with Zoe,

196

Shaun and Sam. The game starts out normal, with me and the girls proving to be useless. Soon the guys get carried away and are far too competitive for us to even try and keep up. When I catch the ball for the first time, a massive rush of adrenaline surges through my body and I run full pelt across the sand. That's until Sam screams at me angrily that I'm running in the wrong direction, to which I throw the ball down in frustration at his feet, walking away in a strop.

The second time I catch the ball, I'm determined not to make the same mistake twice and prove my worth on the team. Racing ahead in the right direction this time, I can hear screams all around me, but they're muffled due to the ringing of excitement in my ears. I feel invincible, until I'm suddenly taken down. A strong pair of arms loops around my waist and we tumble down into the sand. Disorientated, I try to gather my bearings. When I manage to pull my face out of the sand and roll onto my back, I unwittingly take down my tackler in the process. They were trying to stand and fall flat on top of me. I can't breathe.

They shift their weight and I feel temporary relief, that's until my eyes connect with a pair of deep brown ones and all the breath is sucked out of me. Time stops and I've forgotten where I am, or who I'm with, as I lay, staring. I can feel Jake's body pressed up against mine, but I daren't move and ruin the moment. I don't want it to ever stop. Everywhere his body touches mine, feels like it's on fire.

I don't know how much time passes. I'm struggling to come back down to reality. It would appear Jake is the same, otherwise he would have moved already. Somebody has other ideas, as a loud and pissed off '*eghem*' causes Jake to pull away and jump up. He walks away quickly, rubbing his hand over his face.

I remain sprawled in the sand, a sweaty panting mess, looking up into Michael's angry face, for what feels like the hundredth time today.

"We need to talk," he says, turning and stalking away from the group and across the beach, expecting me to follow. I swallow nervously and think how fun this isn't going to be.

Twenty-Two

"What the hell is going on here?" He's angry at what just happened, there's no way around it.

"I'm not sure what you're getting at?" I say, attempting to fake innocence, but who am I kidding? Jake and I were panting all over each other with everyone watching. The only saving grace was that we had clothes on.

"You know what I'm talking about. The fact my girlfriend of four years will barely touch me. I go to kiss you and it's like I have the plague, you shrink away from me that fast. But you have no problem rolling around in the sand with pretty boy over there."

Christ, he's more perceptive than I've given him credit for. I've been kidding myself, believing that he wouldn't notice how off I've been and the lack of affection I've shown him since he arrived.

"We were hardly rolling around in the sand, Michael. It's called football."

"You had no problem with his body being pressed up all over you, yet you won't come anywhere near

me? I'm not buying it. I'm not a fucking idiot, Abby."
I wanted to have this conversation in private, but clearly Michael wants to have it now. "I'll let this all slide, if you make a decision now."

I frown. "A decision?"

"Don't play dumb. About work. Where you're going to be at the end of the summer and what's going to happen with us and our future. I'm not waiting, Abby. I need to know and expecting me to be in limbo for over three months isn't fair."

He has a point. I know he does. What I've expected him to put up with over these past few weeks would be too much for anyone, and he's hit his limit. I'm not ready to decide what I want to do for work, and I'll be damned if he forces me to decide about my future, because he doesn't want to wait. However, I'll happily decide about the future of our relationship if that's what he really wants.

"Stop pushing me, Michael."

Heads turn as our voices gradually get louder.

"How am I pushing you? You've known about these jobs for six months and you've had weeks in Brooklyn on your own to think about it. We've been together for four years, Abby. This is a normal thing to expect from my girlfriend, that she would know where our relationship stands."

In the heat of the moment I say, "What if I'm not ready for everything you want?" There it is, out in the open, my biggest doubt.

He shakes his head sadly, knowing where this conversation is leading. "Then we're not on the same page. This is the normal path a relationship takes and progresses to. Living together, marriage, kids. I want it all and I want it with you. You know that. But for us to get there, you need to make a choice about work and where you're going to be. I won't keep waiting around."

Unexpectedly, I find myself saying, "I need more time."

I didn't think it'd be this hard to let go and I don't know why I'm asking for more time, knowing what the conclusion will be. I don't have romantic feelings towards Michael anymore, but it doesn't change that he's one of my best friends. A part of me isn't ready to let go of him and if I end our romantic relationship, that's what I'll have to do. It would be too hard for him to remain friends and unfair of me to expect him to do that.

"We don't have more time," he says, "we've been avoiding this for months, and I've been constantly wondering why you won't decide, but I get it now. Maybe you're not as into us as I thought you were, because this decision should be really fucking easy, Abby. It should be me you choose every time, because I would choose you in a heartbeat, no questions asked."

"Michael ..." There's an ache in my chest, and I know this is it for us. This is the pivotal point in our relationship where we realize that we're not meant to be. Even though it's been coming for a while, it really hurts. Tears burn at the backs of my eyes, and I don't try to fight them, I don't want to. I don't want him to think I don't care, because I do. Just not in the way he wants me to.

Resigned he says, "You know what, have your space. I'm out of here. I can't pretend things are ok anymore."

"Are we breaking up?" I mumble, looking down at the sand.

I'm ashamed of myself, that I've pushed him to this point, rather than having the courage myself to speak out and admit something was wrong. I've been a coward, forcing him into a corner, so he's the one who must do it, even though it's the last thing he wants.

"I'm not strong enough to do that: I love you too much. It's your decision to make, because a part of me still hopes that what we have isn't lost and you'll come to your senses. But I can't stand here and watch while you make love eyes at Jake. I won't. I'm better than that."

We both look over to where the group is sat. Jake's staring coldly at us and doesn't look away, as if he's trying to prove a point to Michael.

"Have your space, Abby. Do whatever you need to do. I'm not going anywhere. I have no choice over that because I can't not love you. But remember, I'm the one who has stood by you all this time and loved you despite all this shit. I'm not the one who walked away and broke your heart. He was."

✹✹✹

After our argument, Michael left, booking an early plane ticket to get out of New York asap. Shortest trip ever, but he always said he hates it here anyway. I should have saved him the effort of coming all this way and had the conversation on the phone, but after so long together it didn't feel right. Not that how things went down was any better. The better option would have been to act like a normal human, and end things a long time ago, when I knew my heart wasn't in it.

It takes an hour or so for the dust to settle after his departure. I think about leaving and going home to lick my wounds, but it is the 4th of July and with both him and Amanda gone, the group begins to relax, so

I decide against it. The group all feel the need to offer their own advice whether I want it or not.

Sam says I'm better off without and that he would 'do me' anytime, to which he receives a disapproving look. Shaun tells me the best way to get over a breakup is to work extra shifts to keep myself busy. I laugh, telling him I work enough. Zach simply says he's sorry it's ruined my day, but I let him know it's nothing a strong drink won't solve. And then there's Sophie and Zoe. They don't hide their excitement over the fact Michael, and I have broken up. I try to let Zoe know that we're not one hundred percent over as he said he would wait a while, but she dismisses them as small details, carrying on doing her happy dance.

"... I mean you have to be happy. He was such a douche last night," she says with more happy dancing on her towel. After all the drama, we decided the best plan was to relax for the rest of the day. We're currently soaking up the late afternoon rays before the heavy drinking and fireworks begin.

"Maybe he wouldn't have been, if he hadn't been so nervous. You guys did make the whole thing rather intimidating." He can be an ass at times, but he was my ass, which is why I'm defending him. Deep down he's a great guy and would have given me the world.

"But you weren't feeling it anyway, we just helped things along. Your mom and dad will be so relieved," says Sophie smiling. She isn't one to voice her opinion, but Michael brings out a different side to her.

Rather than causing any more drama, I shrug, place my headphones in my ears and ignore their post-mortem of my doomed relationship. I lie back on my towel and close my eyes. The day has felt like the longest ever, and we're only into the early evening. After a while, Sophie taps me on the shoulder, waking me from a shallow slumber.

The group is off on a food and beer run and I'm on bag duty, meaning I can't sleep anymore. I tell her to bring me back some goodies as a tradeoff for waking me up. It's nice having some space from the group for a while. I find myself daydreaming, watching a young family muck about in the water, while listening to an old playlist I created on my cell.

A hand taps lightly on my side and I freeze. I squint against the sun and look around to find Jake sitting next to me with his arms resting against his knees, looking out at the water also.

Clearing his throat, he asks, "Are you ok?"

"Fine. It's been a long time coming," I reply honestly. "He's put up with a lot, and my indecisiveness recently has pushed him over the edge."

"About your relationship?"

"Everything," I reply.

"Like what?"

I didn't expect to have to tell Jake anything to do with my career, or the choices I need to make. I never thought it would be an issue as he wasn't supposed to be part of the equation, but now I guess he is. There's nothing between us, yet I still feel like I owe him an explanation.

I look him directly in the eye. "You know I'm only here for one summer, right?"

He nods. "I knew, but thought maybe once you got back here, you'd change your mind."

"It's never been about what I want to do, it's what I need to do. I came back to save some money and get a bit of space to clear my head, so I could make the right choice."

"You're being a bit vague, Abby. I'm not really following."

I sigh and start to explain. "Six months ago, I went for two separate job interviews. I got both. They've each given me till September to make a choice. They're photography positions, obviously. One's in South Africa and one's in Australia and they're permanent."

I can't tell what's going on in his head because his face is blank, but if he could read my mind, he'd run in the opposite direction because I'm a mess. Even though nothing has happened, this is the moment it should become clear to the both of us that nothing ever can. I have two jobs waiting for me on the other side of the world. I'm about to completely uproot my life, move away from my family and friends, permanently.

It won't be like my freelance work, where I could hop on planes here and there, coming and going as I pleased, seeing people when I chose. I will be a long-haul flight away, that will have to be scheduled around vacation time. Mine and other peoples. It's my first big grown up decision to make, and I'm scared that whichever I choose, it's going to be wrong. I thought coming back here would help clear my mind and make the choice easier, but it's only made it harder.

Being back with my family and friends, who I love unconditionally, I can't imagine having to leave them again. The part of my heart that I closed off, so as not to get to close to anyone, to make moving around easy, has been opened by the bunch of idiots surrounding me, and I don't think I can close it again. Then of course there's Jake, who takes over every thought I have. I can't even sleep without him creeping into my dreams. If anything happened between us, it would be game over. My heart would be absolutely screwed.

I don't say any of this to him. The last thing we need is for me to open up and for us to get closer. We're treading a fine line as it is and if we crossed over into that unknown territory, there would be no coming back. It's easier to keep him at a distance.

He smiles weakly and rubs a hand over his face, the way he always does when he's overwhelmed or frustrated. "Shit. I mean shit in a good way, that's amazing. Have you decided which you're going to go for? If any ..."

"What do you mean if any?" I ask.

"I know your dad would love you to be back here working with him. The other day at the photo shoot, you could see how happy he was."

"Since when have you and my dad become best buddies?" This is the last thing I need. Them becoming close complicates things and blurs lines.

"It's not like that, Abby and you know it. We've been working together for the record deal. We got talking when he was trying to book a photographer and mentioned you. He said in the bigger picture he'd love for you to work with them. I assumed that wouldn't be what you wanted, to be back here."

"Right." I'm unconvinced. There's more to my dad and Jake's relationship than either of them is letting on. Ironic considering how anti Abby/Jake my dad was when we were younger. "Anyway, no." I continue, "I don't have a clue what I'll do. They're both amazing opportunities, but they're so far away. Michael wants me to stay with him in Florida, for us to officially move in together and start planning our future, have a family ..."

"But that's not what you want?" His eyes bore into mine, begging me to give him the answer I know he wants.

I look away when I reply, "No. That's why we broke up ... sort of."

"I didn't realize you'd broken up. I just thought you had a big argument and he needed time to cool off." As he speaks, the shine comes back to his eyes at the news and my first thought is that he's an ass. How dare he be happy that we've broken up when he has a girlfriend.

Even though I'm annoyed, I play the game. It's nice that we're not arguing for once. "Yeah, we've sort of broken up. I've been indecisive over all this for too long and it wasn't fair to keep it going. It eliminates one scenario from the equation at least, but there are still other factors."

"Factors?"

"Other people making the decision harder."

"People?" he says, swallowing hard. His eyes move down my body and I'm aware of how little I'm wearing. Every limb can feel his eyes move over them. My heart races, and my palms sweat. I can see in his eyes how much he wants me. Raising one hand he tucks a strand of hair behind my ear, murmuring, "Abby ..."

He leans in slowly, as if he's afraid I'll scare suddenly and run. Nothing could make me run, I need him to kiss me more than I need to breathe and I'm tired of waiting. He's about to remove the final bit of space between us, when we hear the group hooting from close behind as they return with the drinks and food. Just like that, Jake and I are back to how we always were. Chasing moments, only for something to always get in the way.

He pulls away quickly and shoves his hands into the pockets of his shorts, looking down at the ground. I can't look at him either. I won't be able to hide my disappointment. It dawns on me that it's so wrong because one of us is still in a relationship.

"Beer truck has arrived. Toot toot!" shouts Zoe, tumbling towards us with beers in her arms. She passes one each to me and Jake, plonking herself in the sand in front of us, shooting me an amused look. I raise an eyebrow at her, but she shakes her head and looks away. I know she knows they interrupted something between us.

We stay sat, as the sun begins to set, drinking and laughing and enjoying every moment. I can feel the drinks going to my head, but it feels great to let loose after the turmoil of the past few weeks. I feel like I can enjoy myself without the guilt of Michael looming over my head I can just be me and do what I want.

After a while Zoe clears her throat. "So ..." she says, with an innocent voice, glancing between me and Jake. "Michael isn't here, Amanda isn't here ..." as she trails off, she keeps looking between us.

"What are you getting at?" asks Jake, with a touch of annoyance.

She's unphased and smugly replies, "What I'm saying is, you're both here for the rest of the summer, alone. I'm declaring game on."

My heart skips a beat at the truth in her words.

✶✶✶

It's much later when the darkness has set in and the fireworks are due to start. We've been at Coney Island all day and consumed more than our fair share of alcohol. Sam and Shaun are in good spirits, being all brotherly lovey, trying to get Zach to engage in a

208

bromance, but he's having none of it. Sophie and Zoe are skipping around, loving life like always.

Jake comes over and stands closely behind me. Sophie looks over briefly, giving me a knowing look that I quickly dismiss with a small shake of my head. The fireworks start and music fills the air. It's one of those moments you wish you could never forget. Stick it in a bottle so you can remember it perfectly and preserve it. With my friends close by and Jake even closer, I allow myself to love this moment and how perfect it feels.

I look up at the sky, taking in the different colors flashing and merging, I feel Jake's hand brush over mine. It's only a small movement, but it's there. He moves in closer behind me, slowly so as not to draw attention to us, and his thumb begins drawing small circles on the back of my hand. I take a deep breath, scared that if I move even slightly, he'll stop.

Every circle he makes causes my heart to beat a little faster, my body to become a little warmer. By the time the fireworks are finished, I feel like I'm about to combust. I turn around to face him and he smiles back, with a cheesy, goofy, genuine smile I haven't seen in a long time.

"Enjoy the fireworks?" I ask.

He nods and replies, "I certainly did. Did you?"

"You know I did."

"Come on you guys, stop flirting. We have to get out of here before the rush so we can get to the bars," slurs Zoe, as the group begins walking away. I bend over and grab my bag, following them with Jake trailing closely behind. Every nerve is on edge and I can feel him everywhere. A rush of anticipation runs through me for the rest of the night to come.

Twenty-Three

It takes over an hour for us to find our way out of Coney Island and back to Brooklyn. We stop off at Riffs so we can freshen up in the living space Shaun has above. Sophie and Zoe both opt for short black dresses that don't leave much to the imagination. I go for black skinny jeans, with a black lace cami. It's revealing but the lace is designed tastefully so I'm completely covered.

Once we're ready, we leave Shaun's room to whistles of approval from the guys. My body erupts in goosebumps, despite the heat, as I feel Jake's eyes on me again. Shooting him an unsure smile, I follow everyone down into the bar, where we have a round of shots before making our way to a club.

It's not where we would normally go, as we tend to go lower key, less New York social scene, but we're all amped and in the mood for dancing. We wind up at a small club that has a mix of music, different to the rock and indie bars/clubs we like. We stick out a bit, of course we do. We're a group of rock heads, the guys all covered in tattoos, in a mainstream club. Thankfully, Brooklyn is known for its eclectic mix of trends, so we're not the only group that looks like they've rolled up to the wrong joint.

Thankfully, the drinks begin flowing again once we're settled at a table. My buzz from earlier had started to fade and a hangover was about to hit. I know I'm not the only one that was beginning to suffer from withdrawal, as between us all we knock back shots and bottles of beer like water. I'm laughing with Zach over some silly story he's telling me when Zoe bounds over.

"We're dancing. You can't say no," she says and pulls me up. I don't fight it, a true sign I've had more than enough to drink as everyone knows Abby never dances. Dragging me to the dance floor, Zoe weaves through the crowds just as an electric mix of one of our favorite songs rings out around us. Out of nowhere Sophie appears beside us and all three of us get lost in the music, dancing like we're the only ones in the room.

Wankelmut blares out from the speakers, and as the tempo slows right down, a couple of guys wander over. The beat is steady and the tune mellow, making the atmosphere go from buzzed, to slow and hot, and the dance floor pairs off on auto drive. The guys who wandered over, close in on Sophie and Zoe, but I stay on my own. It's amusing as I look around, some people look plain awful as they make out like their lives depend on it. I continue looking around while still dancing and a guy tries to catch my attention. He's attractive but not my type, far too preppy. I shake my head to signal I'm not interested, but he ignores it and moves towards me anyway.

A pair of hands firmly grab my hips from behind, pulling me back into their body. I feel disorientated from the forcefulness, but incredibly turned on, and there's only one body that can draw that reaction from me. I don't need to turn around to know it's Jake behind me, staking his claim and making sure no other guy can get their hands on me. My other potential dance partner stalks off, peeved that he missed out. I couldn't care less as I begin dancing back against Jake. We grind together, my back flush to his front, and I can feel how much he wants me.

The power I have over him makes me feel sexy and I push further. It's wrong after Michael and I left things as we did. Jake is still with Amanda, but I've stopped caring and evidently so has Jake. His hands grasp my hips, digging in gently with just the right pressure before they start exploring. One hand moves from my hip, up my stomach and skims under the hem of my top. He flattens his other hand over my stomach, pulling me in closer. The crowd is so dense around us and focused on their own exploits that nobody takes notice of what Jake and I are doing.

His hand moves upwards, towards my breast, stroking gently and then brushing against my nipple, which hardens at his touch. I'm incapable of anything, as he takes all my weight against him and I want him to keep touching me everywhere. I want more and I'm about three seconds away from dragging him off the dance floor into a dark corner, to show him exactly what I want.

Nestling his face into my hair, his voice is strained as he murmurs, "God, Abby, I need you." He flips me round effortlessly like a rag doll so I'm facing him, looking into his hooded eyes. Every inch of our control is gone, and I'm struggling to remember the time when we hated each other. Did it ever really exist?

"What are you doing, Jake?" I pull back, making one last effort to walk away before we do something we'll regret.

"I've no idea," he replies and tugs me back towards him by the belt loop on my jeans. Then his hands are squeezing my ass tightly, pulling our hips together. I can feel how turned on he is as he carries on dancing and rubbing against me. I could come just from moving against him like this, fully clothed in a room full of people. Everyone around us is reveling in their conquests and I want mine.

I reach my arms up, around his neck, and watch his breathing increase as though he's nervous. I feel the same, but maybe it's Dutch courage as I fight the nerves and pull his head down towards mine. All the time we never break our gaze and his lips part when he's just a breath away. I close my eyes ready for the kiss that will change everything for the both of us.

I don't get the chance to feel Jake's lips on mine, as Zoe comes barreling over with both hands covering her mouth, looking green in the face. She reaches out, tugging me towards her, but it's too late, and for the second time since I've been in Brooklyn, she pukes all over me. Fate has a nasty way of making sure we never get that kiss, just like years ago.

✗✗✗

"I threw up on you again, didn't I?" groans Zoe into her pillow, laying sprawled out on the floor.

We left the club rapido after the puking, because I reeked and demanded we go home. As punishment, Zoe was designated to the floor, not that she cared, as she was too drunk to know where she was and passed out straight away. I couldn't stand the stench even after stripping my clothes off and wound up dragging my sorry ass into the shower. At least I don't smell like Zoe does this morning.

"Yep," I say bluntly, making it clear I'm incredibly pissed off. "I hope this isn't going to be a regular thing. Twice is enough and I'm not a fan."

"I'm so sorry. I don't know why it keeps happening."

"I do. Because you drink too much and don't know when to stop."

"Abby, please forgive me."

I huff then say, "Make me coffee and you're partially forgiven. But only partially."

Zoe drags herself out of the room, moaning in pain as she does. A snicker comes from under the covers beside me, where Sophie is lying.

"From what I saw, she did you a favor," she says, "you and Jake were ready for ripping each other's clothes off.' She pushes out from under the covers and moves up the bed, resting against the headboard when she gives me a pointed look.

"How did you see that?" I ask. "You were occupied elsewhere."

"Eyes and ears everywhere, don't forget that."

Thumping her with my pillow, I confirm what my lady bits are still mourning over. "Nothing happened."

"But it would have if Zoe hadn't puked all over you."

I groan and place my head in my hands. "I don't know what I'm doing."

Not even twelve hours after parting ways with Michael, I'm ready for jumping into bed with my ex. My very taken ex. The pounding headache from all the drinks isn't helping things seem any brighter.

For a while Sophie doesn't respond, she knows I need time just to wallow. She rubs my back comfortingly, showing she's not trying to be a bitch by pointing out the obvious, just that she cares.

"I don't think he knows either. You're both screwed," she says.

"Thanks for those wise words."

"Have you heard from Michael?"

I glance at my cell to see if he's made any contact. He hasn't, so I reply, "Not yet. I guess he's giving me space. I made it pretty clear we were done, but I think he's going to hang on."

"He deserves better." The sadness in her voice makes it obvious she feels sorry for him. Not the same vibe her and Zoe have given off whenever they've voiced their dislike for him.

"You think I don't know that? That's why I tried to end things."

"Tried being the operative word, Abs. You should have left it with no room for questioning. Seems to me like you and Jake both want to have your cake and eat it too. You need to decide what you want."

"Can we not talk about this right now? It's making me nauseous and I have work at the bar in a couple of hours."

She laughs. "You agreed to work the day after 4th of July? Rookie."

I let out another groan. "I had no choice. Shaun pulled a few strings with shifts so I could go to Lake Placid and have yesterday off. I owe a lot of favors."

"Sucks to be you."

I sigh and reply, "I know, believe me I know."

The hangover is getting progressively worse the longer I'm awake and the thought of a shift at Riffs is overwhelming. The next few hours I have one plan, and that's to sleep for as long as possible, ignoring everything Sophie pulled me up on, for now. Trying to make sense of things when I feel like this is a lost cause.

When I agreed that it sucked to be me, little did she know that I meant it in every possible way.

Twenty-Four

The majority of the population may have over consumed during 4th of July celebrations and had the luxury of hiding away, moping over the drunken mistakes they made. I unfortunately wasn't one of them. After what feels like a million hours, I finally begin cleaning down the bar. Although it was a quiet shift, just the sight and smell of alcohol had me running back and forth to the restroom, dry heaving, after emptying my stomach hours ago.

I'm almost done, when Shaun walks over. "Nightcap? It'll make you feel better."

Although my face scrunches up in disgust, my brain isn't functioning properly, as the word "Sure" comes out of my mouth. Whatever, I can't feel any worse. If anything, it will help switch my mind off, which is going into overdrive replaying the events of yesterday.

"Whiskey ok?" he asks.

I shrug. "I'm easy, nothing can make me feel worse."

He laughs and gestures for me to grab a stool at the bar. I sit, watching as he pours two tumblers of whiskey. Sliding my drink across the bar, he gives me a mischievous smile. "So, yesterday was interesting."

I don't quite meet his eyes when I reply, "It was indeed."

He smirks. "Are you not wondering which part I'm talking about?"

"I'm guessing you may be referring to the part where I split up with my boyfriend?"

"Or the part where you and Jake were dry humping in the middle of a club ..."

"We were not!" My cheeks burn bright red, giving me away.

"Yes, you were," he says sternly.

"Maybe we got a bit close, but everybody was."

"Hmm. You know my brother still has feelings for you right?"

This catches me completely off guard. As I was mid drink, whiskey comes shooting out of my nose as I begin choking. Thanks to our drink of choice, everything burns, and my eyes begin streaming.

Finally, I manage to croak out, "Sam?"

Shaun raises an eyebrow and says, "He is my brother, yes."

"Why would Sam have feelings for me?"

"Because he always has. You know this, don't play dumb. I know about the time you two almost got together. He tells me everything."

"Almost but not quite. Plus, that was years ago." I take a sip of my whiskey, making sure to swallow it quickly this time.

"And so was Jake, but the two of you can't keep your hands off each other. The heart knows what it wants, Abby, and time doesn't affect that." He spins his own glass around on the bar, pondering.

"Are you being serious right now?" I ask. All I get is a nod of confirmation. "Damn." I let out the breath I didn't know I was holding.

How could I have missed this? Maybe there have been a couple of signs. Sam always seems very anti-Jake and I, and sometimes he can come across as overly friendly, but that's the way he's always been with me.

While I'm staring at the bar, mulling over what Shaun has said, he continues. "He knows how it is, he's not an idiot. He knows when it comes down to it, it's always going to be Jake over anyone. But that doesn't stop it hurting him sometimes. I mean Jake's one of his best friends and so are you. I guess what I'm trying to say is, be careful and remember that he's there sometimes. Last night sucked major ass for him, seeing the two of you together like that."

Swallowing a big ball of guilt that's built in my throat, I feel sheepish and incredibly selfish. All along, I've been thinking about my feelings, and how hard it's all been for me. Meanwhile I've been completely blindsided to what's right in front of me.

"Does he hate me?" I'm not sure I want to know the answer.

"Of course, he doesn't hate you. You know he worships the ground you stand on. We all do." Trailing off, he looks away and a horrible feeling begins to creep in.

"Shaun. You don't, you know ... too do you?" This could be very awkward.

He laughs uncontrollably, to the point he's red in the face. When he finally calms down, he says, "Don't worry, Abby. Not everyone around here is in love with you. I have my sights set on someone else."

This piques my interest. He's the last person I'd guess had his heart set on someone, especially with the amount of action his bed sees.

"Oh really? I thought you were enjoying all the attention from women at the bar?"

"It's fun, but they're just there to pass time. None have been The One for me."

"So, this person is The One?" My face gives away how shocked I am, but I can't help it. I hope he's not insulted.

"I guess she is. She's pretty special."

There's a shine to his eyes that I haven't seen before. I'm dying to know who it is, but a small part of me thinks maybe I already know. Now isn't the time to push and find out though, as he seems perfectly content keeping the secret to himself.

"She's a lucky girl, whoever she is, to grab your attention like this. How about a toast?" I hold my glass up in the air.

Leaning forward with his arms resting on the bar, he seems relaxed for the first time in our conversation and asks, "To what?"

"To new things."

"I like that. How about, to new things and new chances?"

I nod. "To new things and new chances."

We toast and knock back what's left of our drinks. The whiskey floods my veins, sending a warm buzz through my body, dulling the 4th of July hangover that's still lingering. But it's not new chances that are the problem, it's knowing which to choose.

Twenty-Five

We're midway through July when I get a message from Jake, the first after the 4^{th of} July. It's been twelve days, not that I'm counting, meaning it's been six weeks since I moved back to Brooklyn, and will be six weeks till I leave again. For what, I'm still no closer to deciding. I'm loving life being back home which isn't helping make anything clearer.

Life has settled into a routine of shifts at the bar with Shaun, along with freelance photography projects which have become a lot less since the bulk of work my dad sprang on me. I'm not complaining as I love working with the record label, but that's the problem. Every day I'm here is making the thought of leaving again harder, and the choice between Australia and South Africa, more difficult.

I'm sitting in the kitchen, eating a bowl of cereal and catching up on early morning emails before I start my day, when the message flashes up on my cell. I place it down on the kitchen counter, frowning, as I consider whether to open it or not. Part of me wants to open it straight away but the other part is majorly pissed I haven't heard from him in so long after how close we got.

It's possible I'm over thinking it all and romanticizing it into something it's not. He's not the one that split up with their partner, partly due to old feelings for an ex. We should put the 4th of July down to us both being wasted and not having any control over what we were doing, but that wouldn't explain the other times.

"Much on your mind?" I was so caught up in my own thoughts, I didn't hear my dad enter the kitchen. He's standing in front of me looking concerned.

"Nothing ... everything," I sigh.

"Sounds serious. Does it have something to do with a certain ex-boyfriend who also happens to be in a band?"

He pours a coffee from the pot I brewed a few minutes ago and then tops up mine. Taking a sip, he waits for my response.

"Everything and nothing."

He frowns, looking completely lost at my responses to his questions. "You're being very cryptic."

"I don't think anything is clear enough in my mind, for me to be able to talk about it."

"That bad, huh? Well contrary to popular belief, we parents have seen a lot and experienced a lot, so if you need advice at some point, I may be able to help more than you think."

"Thanks, Dad. I promise, if I need to, I'll come to you."

He gives my shoulder a pat. "That's all I ask. Remember a problem shared is a problem halved."

I smile to myself as he walks out of the room, leaving me to get back to my thoughts. Smooshing around the now soggy cereal in my bowl, my appetite gone completely, I finally open the message from Jake on my cell.

[Be at bar Baron @ 9. We need to talk x]

That's all I get, after two weeks of no contact. Everything in me tells me to stay away, but I know no matter how hard I try, I've no control over what I do when it comes to Jake. He's pulling all the strings and that scares the shit out of me. What I do know is that my heart doesn't have another break in it. If this all goes wrong, there'll be no coming back.

I reply, [I'll try]

***

6 years earlier

It's been over two weeks since I left for our family vacation in Florida over the holidays. Over two weeks since our first, very heated kiss, and I'm craving him more than I've craved anything before. That kiss seared into me and stomped all over my heart. I've woken up every morning a hot, tangled, grumpy mess. There's only one thing that will help. Jake.

We've kept in contact every day, messaging constantly. But my family have noticed how distant and distracted I've been over the festive period, resulting in some clashes. All I've been capable of doing is counting the days until I can see him again.

We spoke earlier on the phone and he sounded off, upset even. I didn't want to push it and risk him closing off, so I made the decision I would come to him as a surprise. He's been having issues with his grades and the pressure from his mom and grandpa has increased massively with it being our senior year. Perhaps all he needs is a distraction, something to take his mind off it.

I don't have the patience to trek to the subway, so I opt to use some of the few savings I have on a cab. The winter Florida sun has worked wonders on my pale skin, bringing out the light scattering of freckles on my cheeks and nose, and enhancing the copper highlights in my hair. I look good, I know it, and I hope Jake thinks so to. I also hope he likes the black lingerie that I'm wearing that Zoe bought me as a Christmas present. It came with a gift card that had a wink face on it, typical Zoe, but I'm thankful she got it. According to her this is what guys love. Even though I'm bundled up in snow gear, looking like an Eskimo, I can feel the material burning against my skin, heightening the anticipation of seeing him.

When the cab pulls up outside his house. I rush out, quickly making my way up the front steps to his door. I can hear shouting from inside. Loud, angry shouting, which is troubling. I knew things were rough at home for Jake but didn't think things were this bad. Ringing the doorbell, I don't care who knows I'm here. Besides the shouting the house seems quiet, almost deserted from where I'm looking in. But then a porch light flickers on, and his mom comes bustling towards the door with her bag in hand, shrugging her coat on quickly.

"Abby, hi?" she says, surprised to see me standing there, even though I rang the bell. Maybe she didn't hear it. "How were your holidays? Did you enjoy your trip?"

"They were great, Miss Ross, thank you. Were yours good?"

I try not to feel intimidated as I'm speaking with her, but she's a very powerful and glamorous woman. She's never given me a reason to feel uncomfortable when I've met her. But behind closed doors, she's made it clear to Jake that she's unhappy with his current lifestyle choices. One of which is me.

"I did, thank you. I'm heading out for a while. Jake is just upstairs in his room." With that she bustles past me and out the front door. Flying down the steps in a hurry, she still manages to look gracious.

I feel nervous. It's the first time I've been alone in Jake's home with him, and I'm not entirely sure what to do. Do I just go upstairs? Do I call his name out, so he's aware there's someone else in the house?

Not wanting to make too big a deal of the whole thing, I decide to go upstairs to his room quietly to surprise him. The door is slightly ajar, and I can see him sitting on the edge of his bed with his head in his hands. He looks lost and younger than I'm used to seeing him. It's as if he has the weight of the world on his shoulders. Rather than faking confidence like I'd planned, I gently push the door open, my need to check he's ok overriding everything.

"Hey, you," I say.

He rubs his hands over his face. My eyes are drawn to the tight white shirt that clings to his body, and how it flexes over his chest and arms as he moves. I can already feel myself getting worked up with how attracted I am to him, but it isn't the time to be feeling like this when he's clearly upset.

His voice is flat when he replies, "Hey."

"Is everything ok?" I try not to be disappointed at his lack of enthusiasm at seeing me.

"I'm assume you heard some of that?" He looks pained and there's a pang in my chest.

I don't know what else to do, so I try to just shrug it off.

I don't know what else to do, so I try to just shrug it off. "Nothing specific. I could hear some shouting and knew something was wrong, that's all."

After a minute, he says, "Things aren't great."

"I didn't know they were this bad. You should have told me."

"It wouldn't have made any difference, Abby. It is what it is. I can't wait till I'm eighteen and they have no say over my life. They're just so focused on money and society, all of them. It drives me crazy. They don't give a crap about what I want or what makes me happy. I can't stand being around them."

He thumps his hand down hard against the bed in frustration. I've never seen him so worked up. He's normally so calm and collected.

"Hey ..." I approach him slowly, place a hand under his chin and lift it so he will look at me properly for the first time since our kiss. "You can be whoever you want to be, Jake."

He looks torn and I hate seeing the pain in his eyes. "You sound so sure."

"It's your life. It might not feel like it right now, but it's your decision to do whatever you want to do. It might just be a bit harder to get there." I don't know where the confidence to speak like this is coming from, but he needs my honesty and my reassurance, so that's what I give him. "You're so talented and have so much going for you, don't lose sight of that. And remember, deep down they only want the best for you. Even though they might not be getting it quite right."

His eyes meet mine directly and he finally smiles, causing my heart to start beating erratically. It's crazy the effect this guy has over me. "I don't deserve you," he says, "you're the only one who gets this mess, who helps to make any sense of it. Anyway, I have something to show you."

He stands and moves over to his computer. The light is low in the room, the only glow coming from his bed side lamp and computer screen. After our little heart to heart, the atmosphere has relaxed considerably and feels cozy, so I take my coat and other outerwear off and settle in.

I approach him at his desk, feeling slightly self-conscious as I have on a few layers less. My skinny jeans and fitted black vest don't leave much to the imagination. Normally I go for baggier clothes that hide my figure, but tonight I don't want to hide from Jake, I want him to see all of me. My chest is rising and falling dramatically, I hope he doesn't notice how nervous I am.

When I get to him, he reaches an arm around my waist, pulls me into his side and trails his fingers over the small patch of skin on my stomach which has become exposed where my vest has risen slightly. With his other hand, he casually brings a video of his band up on the screen.

He's playing the guitar of course, and there are a couple of his other friends too. They're good, really good. They might not be up there with mainstream rock, but they're better than the average amateur band. Dad would appreciate the talent they have to offer.

I don't know what else to say apart from, "You guys are good."

"You really think that?" His voice lightens at the compliment.

"Jake, have I ever lied to you?"

He looks up and his eyes have darkened, causing me to bite my bottom lip. Being around him feels too much to bear. A throbbing starts between my legs *that I've never felt before. I squeeze them together trying to dull the feeling, as it takes everything in me not to jump on top of him. His eyes move from mine, down my body and he tenses his grip around my waist.*

"Jake ..." I say, breathlessly.

That's all it takes to obliterate every ounce of control either of us has, after months of dancing around each other and being careful. Swallowing hard, he looks back at me, with lust in his eyes like I've never seen. Before I realize what's happening, he stands forcefully and his desk chair flies backwards, then he's everywhere. His tongue is in my mouth, his hands in my hair are tugging back, encouraging me to kiss him deeper. He lifts me up, sitting me on the edge of his desk and I wrap my legs around him, pulling him in and thrusting my hips against his, needily.

"Fuck, Abby," he says harshly against my mouth.

He lifts me again, this time turning and carrying me towards his bed. Excitement floods me as his intentions become clear and I accept where the kiss is leading. Gently pressing me into the bed, his weight pushes down onto my body and it feels incredible. I feel safe and secure, like nothing else in the world matters. His hands explore as he continues to kiss me deeper. Wandering underneath my vest, they move up and move my bra so he can cup my breasts. As he tweaks one of my nipples, I cry out, overwhelmed by the sensations taking over my body. He groans his satisfaction, gently rotating his hips into mine, and I can feel how hard he is for me.

"Abby, I swear I'm about to come in my pants." *He breathes heavily, placing small kisses down my neck.*

228

I laugh, what must sound like a euphoric, crazy laugh. My voice is serious when I ask, "Do you have a condom?"

Keeping his body flush with mine, he stretches out, reaching over to one of his drawers, pulling out what appears to be the only one in there. I hope and pray it was there for the purpose of me and me alone. He comes back down to meet me, with the condom in his hand and our kissing becomes frantic. I pull his shirt over his head, my hands roaming greedily over his muscular chest and back, when suddenly he pulls away and I'm left feeling slightly hurt, wondering if I've misread the situation or done something wrong.

"Shit. Abby." Pressing his forehead to mine he tries to catch his breath.

"What's wrong? I thought ..." My eyes begin watering, as humiliation creeps in.

"No, shhh. Don't panic. I want you. I think that's obvious. Just, before we do this ..." He's struggling to find the words to say what he wants. He swallows and the emotion swirling in his eyes is unmistakable. "I-I love you."

Relief passes over his face as he says the words. It's as if it's caused him physical pain to not be able to before this. At first, I must look confused. Confused at how this beautiful, talented guy, could love me. Plain boring Abby. But I don't care why or how. All I know is I feel the same and want to let him know in every way possible.

"I love you, too. I can't stop myself."

He lets out a sigh of relief and then we're kissing again. This time it's more urgent than before. We're more confident, less hesitant, as we each know exactly how the other feels. We both want this so much, to be together, as close as we can. They say your first time is supposed to be awkward and painful, but I know that with Jake he'll do everything he can to make sure that's not the case.

I'm tugging at his pants, fumbling with the buttons as he kisses me. He grinds his hips into me, murmuring my name. Suddenly his bedroom door flies open revealing his mom in the doorway, a look of thunder on her face.

Jake moves quickly, positioning himself so he's shielding me from her sight. It gives me a chance to readjust my clothing, while he remains shirtless with his pants hanging open. Damnit this is mortifying.

"What's going on in here?" she demands. All traces of the graceful woman I saw earlier on the front steps are gone, now she more resembles a pit bull.

"I think that's pretty clear, Mom, do you really need to ask?" snaps Jake.

"I'd like to make it clear, you are both underage for this sort of activity, so I suggest less of the smart mouth. Abby, I think it best you leave now." There is no questioning her tone. I need to get out of here and fast, even if the last thing I want to do is leave Jake with the fallout.

"No problem." I scurry off the bed, grab my coat and glance over to Jake for reassurance. He's too occupied in a Mexican standoff, so I mutter "bye" under my breath, bustling out the room and past his mom, without looking back.

If only I'd known that would be the last chance that I'd get to see Jake like this. If I'd known, maybe I would have stayed longer and fought the battle with him.

Twenty-Six

I tried to convince myself this was a bad idea and to turn my back on this whole frustrating situation with Jake, but I couldn't stay away. I enter the bar much later than he told me to after spending forty-five minutes standing outside debating whether to come in or not.

The music is loud, haunting, and good, really good. It's a song I've never heard before. As I move around the dark room struggling to find Jake, my eyes fall on the small stage set up, where they find Sam as he starts singing again. To his side is Jake holding his guitar. He hasn't noticed my arrival, lost in performing with the band, so I hold back in the crowd, not wanting to distract any of them.

I make my way to the bar, settling on a free stool and order a beer as I chat with some of the people floating around. All the time my eyes keep flitting back to Jake, not wanting to stay away from him for too long. When they finish their final song, Jake glances around the crowd, and when his eyes settle on me, his face lights up. He moves over to Sam, whispering something in his ear that makes him also look up, beam and wave at me. They both appear happy I've made it.

Jake jumps off the stage moving towards me, cutting through the crowd, and ignoring the longing glances he receives from some of his fans. The same fans who are now throwing death stares in my direction as they notice I am the sole focus of his attention.

"You likey?" he asks, playfully wiggling his eyebrows. He stands next to me, casually placing a hand on my shoulder and massages away tension I didn't know was there.

"I love," I reply, trying to stay focused when all I can think about is how good the movements of his hand feel.

He looks taken aback at the boldness of my appreciation. The atmosphere becomes awkward, when he seems to read more into my statement than what was intended.

"Right, yeah," he says with a shrug. He then turns and disappears back into the crowd without looking back.

I focus on my drink, completely confused by his reaction, wondering why he invited me to come if he was just going leave me here alone. Everything with him feels so hot and cold at the moment and I never know where I stand. A couple of minutes later, Sam wanders over, just as I was contemplating leaving.

"Hey, you," he says.

Throwing his arms around me, he pulls me into a hug, which normally I would relish in, but after the conversation I had with Shaun I don't know how to react. I don't want to lead him on. I opt for playing it cool, as if nothing is bothering me and go for the safe topic of the gig.

"So, when did you guys get so good?" I wink to show I'm joking.

"We've always been this good, Abs. Don't act like you didn't know," he responds with a cocky smirk.

"I actually didn't know you guys were still in a band together until the day of the shoot. Something you kindly forgot to mention."

"Because you didn't want to know anything about Jake," he retorts.

"I guess. You still could have told me." He must think I'm crazy to still be grumbling over this.

He laughs and if he does think I'm crazy he doesn't let on. He opts for changing the subject. "So, where is Jake?"

"Beats me," I sigh. "He came over, then randomly his mood changed, and he abandoned me, despite being the one to invite me." I pick away at my beer mat, taking some of my frustration out on the pieces of paper I'm tearing into tiny pieces.

"Good old hormonal Jake. I suppose that means I can be your partner in crime for the night instead."

He looks far too pleased as he orders more drinks and the conversation with Shaun starts to feel more like reality. How did I never see this before?

As the night goes on, the drinks keep flowing, and I try my hardest to ignore the feeling of being watched. I know that it's Jake standing in the distance observing us, but I refuse to acknowledge him after he left me on my own.

I don't know when it happens, maybe after my third or fourth drink, but I feel myself becoming flirtier with Sam, which is completely wrong when I know how he feels about me. He's one of my closest friends and the last thing I should be doing is leading him on. Thanks to a mixture of strong cocktails and

233

being pissed at Jake, my morals appear to have left the building, and I carry on gracelessly.

There was a time, not long after Jake and I broke up, when Sam and I became close. He helped me through it all and it felt like overnight there was chemistry between us. I thought something more could have happened between us, then one day he just became cold and distant towards me. It was always the same with any guy, right up until I left Brooklyn.

I can tell I'm pretty gone, when I stare at him through hazy eyes. I'm mesmerized by how pretty he is with his bright blue eyes and crazy blond hair.

My inhibitions have gone out the window as I slur, "I missed you Sam. What happened to us?"

He chokes on his drink and struggles to clear his throat. He looks nervous and I'm not sure why. My suspicions rise when he brushes off the question as though I'm just wasted, "I don't know what you mean."

I've had a fair amount to drink, but I remember everything that happened back then.

"Yes, you do. For a while, there was something between us, wasn't there? Or was I misreading things like I did with Jake? Did I make it all up in my head? Did you not want me back either?"

I'm swaying embarrassingly on my stool, but at least I'll be able to pass this moment of insanity off in the morning for being wasted, and I know Sam will let it slide.

He looks at me with sad eyes, but there's definitely something more there. "Of course, I wanted you, Abby. You think I didn't feel anything back? Seriously? How many lingering looks did we have and how many times did we almost kiss?"

My cheeks begin heating up with embarrassment. This conversation feels far too intimate for the Sam I've spent time with this summer.

Looking away, I mumble, "I thought it was just me. After Jake and I broke up, I convinced myself it was all in my head and that I'd somehow pestered him into being with me. That he never really wanted me and was doing it just to please me. Why would he or anyone else want to be with me?" I can't look at him. The moment has brought up so many old feelings of rejection and hating myself. Feelings of not being good enough.

He looks enraged hearing me talk about myself the way I am. "Abby, you're gorgeous, talented and kind. Anyone would be lucky to be with you. Look at me."

I look up and catch his eye. More walls are being broken down, as we get to the real reasons why I've resented Brooklyn for so long. There's more to why I left with no explanation and didn't return. All the tainted, painful memories.

"We all knew you were the real deal. Yes, we were horny teenagers and went for the easy options. But we all knew you were the type you marry and keep forever. Look at you now. You're like a fine wine, you just get better with age."

I snort at his last statement, easing some of the tension that has built. "That was a very camp thing to say."

"You know what I mean. Sheesh kick a man when he's down."

"I couldn't help it. It's been a long time since I've taken a trip down memory lane and it was making me uncomfortable. If you're certain I was as amazing as what you're saying, then why was I so lonely before I left? Why whenever I got close to anyone, did they suddenly become cold and start ignoring me without any explanation?"

"Why do you think?" He stares at me, waiting for me to figure it out on my own, as if it's the most obvious thing in the world.

"I really don't know, Sam. That's why I'm asking you. Will you please give me an explanation?"

"Because we were all in the same circle. He knew when something was going on and he didn't like it." He looks resigned, knowing I'm not going to leave it at that and probe further.

"Who did? What are you trying to say?" I'm not sure if it's the volume of alcohol I've consumed, or that I'm finally getting answers after all these years, which is making me a bit slow on the uptake.

"He changed his mind, Abby. Jake did. But he thought it was too late. So, he did what he could to make sure you were unavailable to any other guys."

His words register, wiping the drinks we had earlier from my system. I now feel very much sober and incredibly pissed off.

"You're joking, right?"

The dots begin to connect in my brain. The memories of relationships that never quite were, never quite became what they could have been, all come flooding to the forefront of my mind. Suddenly it all makes sense.

"I'm not." Sam shakes his head defeated.

I can't believe he kept this from me all this time.

"So, you're telling me that asshole, after he ripped my heart out and stomped all over it, without a care in the world-"

"He got scared," Sam interrupts. "We were all young and had a lot going on. Maybe you don't know the real reasons why he did what he did."

"Don't make excuses for him!" I growl, my temper about to reach boiling point.

"Abby, you need to calm down." Sam looks helpless, the poor guy. But what did he expect opening this can of worms?

I throw my hands up in the air. "Calm down? You calm down. You're telling me that *he* is the reason I spent my last year in Brooklyn miserable and alone?"

"Potentially ..." He plays nervously with his glass and it's obvious he wants to be anywhere but here with me, having this conversation.

"Please expand on *potentially*, Sam and fast, because my patience is running thin, and I'm about to go nuclear. Tell me exactly what happened."

He exhales slowly. "Everyone liked you, all the guys. God you'd have to be blind not to," he gestures at me and continues, "look at you. But like I said, you're marriage material. But yeah, they thought you were sound. It was like five months later when you finally got the courage to talk to that guy Matt. Dou remember him?"

Remember him I do. The memory becomes clear as Sam is speaking. We had gotten close, but that hadn't been my original intention. My plan had been to get in his good books, so he'd speak to Jake about me, but then things changed, and our feelings began to change. I've always wondered where things could have gone, but one day he turned around and said he didn't care about hanging out anymore. Said he wasn't really feeling it with a girl like me.

The memory stings and there are more to go with it. All similar scenarios that wound up with me being pushed to the gutter when I thought things were going somewhere.

"There was a rumor that you guys had hooked up or were going to. I knew you wouldn't you were still too raw after Jake, but anyway ..."

"What happened?" I ask, swallowing the lump in my throat.

"Jake saw it all going down and it dawned on him what he was missing. To be fair, I think it did straight away, but he didn't have the balls to come back to you. I don't think he ever didn't want to be with you, Abby. There was something else that happened, I just don't know what. Then the guys were ripping him for spending so much time with you and it all got out of control." He looks down sadly, but I'm still confused.

"You're not being clear about what happened."

I'm trying not to get annoyed with him, as I know it's hard him being the one to tell me all these things, but still, I wish he would speed it up.

"Sorry. When he saw you guys in front of him, saw you getting close to someone else, he got jealous. He'd never admit it to us, so he called dibs and initiated the bro code."

My eyebrows shoot up. "Excuse me?"

"You know what I mean. He warned us all off you and said if we went near you, we were violating the guy code of trust, et cetera. Either we followed, or he'd smash anyone who went near you to pieces, that sort of thing. Why do you think I always pulled away? I wanted you, Abby, but I couldn't do that to my best friend who was, and still is very much in love with you."

Hearing Sam say Jake has always been in love with me and still is, hits a nerve. I've spent the summer stamping my feelings down, trying not to lose control and now I feel like I'm about to detonate. All the feelings of hurt and confusion are still so raw. How dare he feel that way and put me through all that

238

misery, leaving me wondering what was wrong with me ... pushing me away from my family.

Something in me snaps when I think of my family and friends, and everything I've missed out on over the years, all because of the shit that went down between us. It's time to finally get some closure, and there's only one person I can get that from.

Sam looks at me nervously. "You ok?"

I smile back, brushing some of the hair that's fallen into his eyes away from his face, then in the sweetest, most sinister tone I can muster, say, "I will be. Where is he?"

He gulps as he looks over towards the stage, where Jake has been standing watching us intently. "Abby, maybe you shouldn't do this here."

I climb down from my stool, spin back around and abruptly say, "I'm a big girl, Sam. I can do what I want when I want."

I stalk off in Jake's direction and all I see is red.

Crack

"Abby! What the fuck?" Jake looks back at me in complete and utter shock.

I could have gone for the stereotypical bitch slap, but that wouldn't do what I'm feeling any justice. I'm not like most girls, so I went straight in with a sucker punch to the face. Whatever. He deserved it and seeing him rub his jaw back and forth, trying to ease the pain, is incredibly satisfying.

"What did you do?" I hiss.

He looks at me in disbelief then grabs my hand and drags me to the side of the bar, out of the way of the audience we gathered.

"Have you lost your mind?" he says, "what are you talking about?"

My hands clench and unclench at my side, in an unsuccessful attempt to keep my temper under control.

"I'll ask you one more time, Jake. I want the truth and if you don't give me everything, I'll walk away, and we won't speak again. I promise."

"I don't know what you're asking me though."

I want to believe him, and hope Sam was lying, but I know Sam, I know he wouldn't. I also know Jake's tells better than most and over the years they haven't changed. When he rubs the back of his neck, I know that it's beginning to click what I'm talking about.

"Tell me what you did after we broke up. Why was I alone for so long? Why did guys always back away whenever we started to get close, even just as friends. What. Did. You. Do?"

He looks past me, looking to Sam for confirmation of what I'm referring to. I can't see him, but he must nod, because Jake closes his eyes and groans. We're having this conversation whether he likes it or not.

"I told them to stay away from you," he says solemnly.

"You're an asshole," I spit back. I'm handling this whole thing wrong, but I've gone down the rabbit hole, letting myself feel all the emotions I've suppressed for years and I don't think I can come back.

"I know." He looks pained. Good, he deserves it.

"Why did you do it?" I ask more calmly.

"Because I was an idiot. I'm sorry, it was a long time ago." If he thinks the excuse of us being younger is going to get him out of this, he's got another thing coming.

"That's not good enough, Jake. I want answers."

"What do you want me to say?" He throws his arms in the air in exasperation.

"The truth, please. I need it. After all these years and all the shit, you owe me this."

He looks away and when he looks back, it's straight into my eyes. His are filled with so many emotions, I don't know how the conversation is going to go. I can't read him at all.

"I missed you," he says. "I knew I'd screwed up and didn't want anyone else to have you if I couldn't, so I told them to stay away."

Even though I already knew the answer, hearing the words come from his mouth, is like having a bucket of iced water poured over my head. It takes my breath away.

"You had no right," I say in almost a whisper.

"I know. I was an ass, and I didn't know what I wanted."

"You gave up on us. You told me you loved me and then made me feel worthless, like nothing."

He looks up at the ceiling and replies with a sigh, "Abby, we were only seventeen, what do you want me to say, that I was ready for marriage and kids? Because I wasn't. But I shouldn't have given up on us. I should have grown a pair and fought for what I wanted, rather than doing what everyone else wanted me to do."

"You're a coward." I can feel how harsh the words sound after everything he's told me. He flinches and I wish I could take them back.

"You think I don't know that?" He surprises me by hitting the wall to his side with his fist. "We shouldn't be having this conversation. I have a girlfriend. You and Michael are up in the air. What we're doing is as bad as cheating."

I roll my eyes. "Grow up. It's not at all." It's a lie and I know it. It's all I've thought since Jake and I bumped into each other my first night in Brooklyn, that what we've been doing is wrong. Still, the words pour out of my mouth and I have no control over what I'm saying. "We're just two adults rehashing some old memories, so that we can move on with our lives."

He takes a step towards me and his hands wrap around my arms. He lowers himself to look me in the eye and his voice drops a level. "Us even being near each other is bad. We might not be together, but my feelings for you never changed. You were everything, Abby, you still are."

This is what I've wanted, for months. Hell, if I'm being honest, years. This is what I've longed to hear from him. I dreamed sometimes about him running through the crowds, admitting he'd made a mistake and telling me he still loved me. The reality though, after years of shit and built-up resentment is much harder to swallow. I don't know what to do with this new piece of information he's thrown at me.

I take a step back to shake him off. "I can't listen to this."

"Now who's being the coward?" He steps back in towards me, forcing me to press my back up against the wall. I'm terrified he's going to kiss me, because if he does, all rationality will go out the window.

I turn my head away, to break some of the intensity. "I thought we couldn't have this conversation. Amanda, remember?"

"Tell me one thing." He places his hand under my chin, lifting it so I look back at him directly in the eye. My stomach swirls with nerves at what else we're about to reveal to each other. How much more can there be?

"What?" I swallow hard, waiting.

"Why does all this old crap matter so much to you?"

"I'm not telling you that." Nausea kicks in at the thought of telling him how I've really been feeling being around him again.

"Come on, Abby, if we're being so fucking honest with each other. I had to open up and tell you my feelings and everything that happened. So, you need to tell me yours. What's so bad about hearing how I feel about you after all this time? It shouldn't matter if you're over me." He narrows those huge brown eyes, challenging me.

"Because it's all I've ever wanted to hear," I reply quietly. At first, I'm not quite sure he's heard, but his stance relaxes somewhat, so I continue talking. "Because my feelings for you have never, ever changed, Jake."

There, it's done. The floodgates have been opened. After weeks of built-up tension and frustration, snappy comments, hidden moments where we both wanted more, everything has been laid out on the table.

Jake was right. Everything about this is so wrong, because whenever we're around each other, all I can think is how much I want him and no one else. Knowing he's been feeling the same really is as bad as cheating. We might not have been together physically, but emotionally, the things we're both feeling for each other is so much worse.

He strokes my cheek, still staring me in the eye. Every part of me wants to just get it over with and kiss him. Why prolong the inevitable? In this dark corner of the bar, nobody would notice, and we could hide here without a care in the world. But there's still a small shred of dignity left inside me.

If Jake and I are going to be together, I want him to be mine and only mine.

With every ounce of strength, I have inside of me, I push his hand to the side, shaking my head. This time, I'm the one to walk away.

Twenty-Seven

The following days are quiet on the Jake front. I avoid seeing anyone where I can. I'm not ready to talk about what went down between us and I'm trying to get my own head around it. I've done what I always do when things aren't going my way, absorb myself in work. Between the piles my dad has for me at the record label and extra shifts at the bar, my time and mind are occupied. The extra money is nice too.

I'm finishing up an early shift at the bar. Shaun was adamant I take it, rather than a double late one, making it clear there was no arguing about it.

"You're working yourself into the ground. You need some time off. I know what you're doing and it's only going to make things worse." I didn't have it in me to fight with him, so I have an afternoon free of work.

Zoe and Sophie come bounding in, conveniently five minutes before my shift ends. I narrow my eyes at Shaun, and he shrugs in amusement then walks away.

"Why have you been ignoring us, bitch?" Zoe's face is serious, well, as serious as she gets. She's pissed I've been avoiding them, and she's let me know as much in the message she left on my cell.

"I haven't been ignoring you," I say.

"Yes. You have." Sophie looks equally as pissed as Zoe. "We've barely seen you since 4th of July and when we have, you've had some excuse to run off. What's up?"

"I've got five minutes till my shift ends, then we can talk." I walk away and go about finishing up. I'm dawdling in one of the back rooms when I hear Zoe calling my name, refusing to let me get away without facing up to the music.

"New turf is needed for this," she says. I laugh, shaking my head at how dramatic she's being. "I'm being serious. The guys have eyes and ears everywhere in here."

"There's a place a few blocks away that does great cocktails and fries," says Sophie, so we head out.

Before I know it, we're chilling at a table on the sidewalk in the sun, mammoth cocktails in hand while we wait for our order of fries.

"So. Spill." Too busy playing with my cocktail and replaying the other night in my head, I'm not sure who it comes from. Not that it really matters.

I take a deep breath and begin speaking rapidly, wanting to get it all out as fast as I can. "Jake told me he never stopped loving me, and that he still does. Oh, and admitted to singlehandedly destroying any potential relationships I had before I left Brooklyn."

"Damn." Zoe and Sophie both say in unison. The expression on their faces is comical. I've never seen them so shocked.

"Exactly." Taking a big swig of my margarita, I relish at how cool and refreshing it is, as it slides down my throat. "Needless to say, it's messed my head up, and I'm not really sure what to do."

"How did you leave things?" asks Sophie.

I shrug. "I walked away. What else was there to do? He has a girlfriend and I refuse to be a cheat. You know that isn't me." It makes me feel sick just thinking about how hurt Amanda would be if she knew what's been going on between us.

"There have been a few close calls ..." Zoe isn't really one to talk. She's not exactly the queen of being faithful.

I narrow my eyes at her, making it clear I don't appreciate her stating the obvious. "Unlike some, I've always come to my senses."

"I suppose." We sit looking at each other unblinking.

I finally let my guard down. This situation isn't their fault and they're only pointing out the obvious. "I know what we've been doing is wrong."

"Mmmm," they murmur, again in unison.

"Nothing has actually happened or will happen. Especially not while he's in a relationship and things are still up in the air with Michael."

"Speak of the devil," states Sophie. We all look down at the table where my cell has lit up and Michael's name flashes on the screen. "Maybe now is the time to clear things up with him? You at least owe him that. Hell, Abby, you've enough on your plate, you owe it to yourself."

It feels nice that she's empathizing with me, rather than telling me off for doing things I shouldn't. All I've been doing is trying to keep everyone happy and I may have let that affect my judgement rather than following what my heart really wants.

"We'll get another round of drinks while you take it." Zoe stands and Sophie follows her inside to the bar, urging me to answer as they go.

I down the rest of my margarita. I'm need it for this conversation. I quickly answer before it rings off and I have a reason to avoid the conversation again.

It feels awkward and like forever since we last spoke on the 4th of July. It's the longest we've been without speaking in four years.

"Hey you ..." I say.

"Abby. I'm so sorry, baby. I miss you like crazy." This wasn't what I was expecting.

"Michael-"

He cuts me off speaking rapidly. "I've been wanting to speak to you since the moment I left, but I'm stubborn, you know me. I'm sorry. I shouldn't have said what I did, and I was just being jealous. I made assumptions I shouldn't. I love you and just want us back together. I'm sorry, ba-"

I hate this. I hate hearing him so hurt and desperate. It's going to make it so much harder. I wish he were screaming and angry, at least then I would feel justified doing what I'm about to do.

"You were right," I interrupt.

"I know you don't care about him any- what do you mean I was right?" He stops abruptly and the tone of his voice changes.

"You were right about Jake. I'm still in love with him."

It's like ripping off a band-aid. I hold my breath anticipating what will come next.

All I get is silence that goes on so long I begin to wonder whether we've been disconnected. That's until I hear something in the background smash.

It's so loud and sudden I flinch, then ask, "Michael, are you ok?"

"How can you ask me that when you've just ripped out my heart? I thought we had something. I thought we were going to get married, kids, the works."

I take a deep breath, then say, "I don't love you, Michael. I love you as a friend, but that's all. I'm not *in* love with you. I don't know when it happened, or if I ever really was in love with you. Maybe you were just someone there to catch me when I was falling."

It's harsh being so blunt and some of the things I said aren't even true, but Michael is the hopeful, forgiving type. The only way to clearly end things, is to make sure he won't pine over us and try to give the relationship a second chance. To end things properly, I have to squash any positive memory he has of us into the ground.

His voice wobbles when he says, "You don't mean that."

I try not to picture in my mind what he looks like, how broken he will be. I never thought I would have to put someone through the same pain that Jake did with me. I never thought I would be capable of that.

"I do. Look ..." I need to wrap the conversation up quickly before we get into anything else, dragging it out longer than necessary. "I'm out with Sophie and Zoe and they should be back any second. I should get going."

All the fight in him is gone as he replies, "Ok. And Abby ..."

"Yeah?" A part of me hopes that he gets it. That he understands why I've said what I did, and we can leave things on relatively good terms.

What I get is an unfamiliar, bitter and cold voice. "You're not who I thought you were. You're just a cold hearted, using bitch."

The line goes dead. My heart knows that's the last time I'll hear from Michael.

Around four hours later, after multiple cocktails, we're dancing carelessly around the annual Brooklyn music festival. It was Sophie and Zoe's solution to cheering me up, after the disaster that was my final conversation with Michael. Their answer to everything is always alcohol and music. For once I don't disagree.

My spirits have lifted as the afternoons gone on. I have to admit, finally clearing things up between us has made it feel like a weight's been lifted off my shoulders. At least it's one part of my life where there isn't any uncertainty anymore.

We dance around, lost in the music and the sun starts to set in the sky. I feel euphoric, like I could do this forever. We're drawing attention from a lot of guys, a standard reaction when the three of us are out together like this, but as always, we stay in our own little bubble.

"Shaun and Sam are coming," shouts Sophie, over the music. "They should be here soon."

"Yaaaay!" I slur, throwing my hands above my head and spinning around. "My two favorite guys."

I'm heading towards being a little wasted.

Sophie giggles. "If you had to screw one which would it be?"

"Shaun!" shouts Zoe.

Under normal circumstances I'd pick up on how quick her reaction is, but I've drank too much to focus properly.

"Sam is pretty hot," I slur.

"You're not too bad yourself missy." A deep voice chuckles into my ear, pulling me in towards them. I should be embarrassed at being caught out in my honesty, but I'm too far gone.

Tomorrow might be a different story.

"Sammmmmyyyy!" I sing, swinging myself around and nuzzling at his neck. God, he smells good. Does he always smell this good?

"Down, girl," he laughs, gently pushing me away. "As much as I'm loving the attention, the person who really wants you is here, and he looks like he's about to come over and rip my balls off."

His words take a second to register, as everything in my mind is rapidly becoming a fuzzy mess. When they do, I turn my body away from Sam and narrow my eyes at who I assume is Jake.

"What are you doing here?" I sway, struggling to stay upright.

"Nice to see you too, snarky pants." It's definitely Jake, I'd know his voice anywhere.

"Please leave. No one wants you here," I say childishly.

"I'm not here to get in an argument. I wanted to tell you something but seeing as though you're wasted, I guess it's not a good time."

If I could see his face clearly, I'd bet money on him frowning at the state I'm in.

"Anything you want to say, you can say now, in front of our friends."

He steps forward, so he's closer to me. I sway, struggling to keep my balance and find myself placing my hands on his firm chest to steady myself.

He whispers close to my ear, "No, I can't actually. What I have to say is for your ears only."

Although it seems like I'm losing complete control over every part of my body, he still manages to make me feel like I'm on fire. His proximity is overwhelming, and I push away, stumbling back into Shaun.

He places his hands on my shoulders to steady me and says, "Woah, buddy. I think you've had way too much to drink. We need to get you home."

"I'm fine, really. I just need to lie down."

Not caring that we're in a crowd of thousands of people, I fall to the ground, curling into a ball and closing my eyes. It's like I'm having an out of body experience, I'm not just wasted anymore, something doesn't feel right. I don't fall asleep, but I'm incapable of moving my eyes or any part of my body. I will myself to get up, move around, hyperaware of how wrong this all is. My mind and body are two separate beings and it's terrifying.

"Fuck! How much did you guys drink?" I hear Jake shout at Sophie and Zoe. I can only imagine how angry he looks.

"We had a few cocktails and we're tipsy. You all know Abby can drink us under the table though, and that was hours ago." It's Zoe speaking now, and she sounds desperate, like I've never heard her before. I must look bad.

"Wait ..." Comes Sophie's voice and she sounds as concerned as the rest of the group. "There were some guys that bought us drinks about half an hour ago."

"God damnit!" Jake shouts again. "How many times do we have to tell you to stop taking drinks off guys? This is why. How long did it have to be until your blasé attitude caught up with you and you had a near miss? Now look at Abby. What would you do if we weren't here?"

Zoe whimpers. I can picture how scared she must look and how guilty she must feel. I want to shout at Jake that it's not her fault, that I willingly took the drinks, knowing what the risks were, but I'm incapable of doing anything.

"Look at the state of her," Jake continues. He's in no way ready to slow down his relentless telling off for our reckless behavior. "She's like a rag doll. Anybody could do whatever they want to her. Do you get it now?"

"Come on, man," intervenes Sam, keeping his voice calm. "This isn't helping things. We need to get Abby out of here and seen to, quick. Do you need help moving her?"

"No, I've got it," snaps Jake somewhere in the distance.

A giant set of arms lift me in the air, pulling me up against a firm, warm chest. It's as if I'm floating, and it feels like heaven.

Then everything goes black.

Twenty-Eight

I feel hot, really hot. It takes a while for me to figure out why and then I understand it's the sun glaring on my face. My head is pounding. No, that's an understatement. I feel like I've been hit by a freight train. I don't have a clue where I am or how I got here. It hurts too much to even try and open my eyes.

Wherever I am, the bed feels like a big fluffy cloud and I want to stay here forever. Alarm bells start to ring. This can't be my bed. My bed at my parents' house is firm. Where am I?

The last thing I remember was Zoe handing me a drink which a group of guys we don't know gave her, at the festival. Everything after that's a blur. Dread creeps in. I've totally screwed up. I really don't want to open my eyes and find out how badly.

When I dare to open them slowly, I look around the strange, unknown room that I'm in. It's quite modern and has a lofty feel, with its exposed brick walls. It's also clean and doesn't seem like the den of a serial killer. Then I notice a guitar in the corner. I pray it means what I think it does.

"Morning, sleepy head."

I startle and look over at Jake, who is sitting in a snuggle chair by the window, on the opposite side of the room.

My throat feels raw as I croak out, "What happened?"

Standing up, he walks over, settling down beside me on the bed. He brushes some hair out of my eyes and trails his hand down my clammy face, finally resting it at the crease of my neck. He rubs in a soothing motion.

"Shhh. Don't talk, just listen. You need to save your energy." I nod and wait for him to continue. "Your drink was spiked."

Terror washes over me and I'm afraid to hear what he has to say next. I don't want to find out the potentially awful things that may have happened. He must see my eyes widen in horror, as he begins stroking my hair to calm me down.

"Don't worry, nothing happened to you. Me and the guys arrived just in time. Whoever gave you the drinks must have left when they saw us. When we realized what had happened to you, we tried to find them, but we couldn't." He growls the last part and his jaw clenches.

I grab the hand that isn't stroking my hair, squeezing it with the little strength I have, to remind him that I'm here and fine. It seems to work as he calms and continues talking.

"When we knew something was really wrong, we took you to the hospital and they did tests to check you were ok and find out what was in your system. They discharged you when they were happy with your vitals, but we found out that your parents were in the Hamptons, and we couldn't get into your house. The girls wanted to take you, but I didn't really trust them

255

after what happened. Sam and Shaun were needed at the bar, so I brought you here. Plus, I didn't want to let you out of my sight ..."

He looks down and swallows. I can see tears in his eyes. "Abby, if anything had happened to you ... if I hadn't got there in time ..."

My eyes begin welling with tears too and then I find the courage to ask, "How long have I been here?"

"Four days." I gasp at how much time I've lost and how dangerous the situation I'd been in was. "The doctors said that whatever it was they gave you ... it was the strongest around. You were lucky we got to you when we did. I don't want to scare you, Abby, but I need to. What the fuck were you thinking taking drinks off people you don't know?"

It hurts how angry and frustrated he is, but what hurts more is how disappointed he looks in me. There isn't much I can do or say to change that, it will just take time.

"I-I don't know. I'm sorry," I say.

I finally let the tears that have been building fall and before I know it Jake's arms are wrapped around me tightly, as I sob and whimper into his chest.

If my head wasn't screwed before, it certainly is now.

Twenty-Nine

Since the incident at the festival, I haven't been capable of much. Mom and Dad have stuck to my side like glue, both taking time off work so they can keep an eye on me. I tried to tell them I'd be fine, but they were having none of it. I know they feel guilty that they weren't here for me when it happened. Stuck in the Hamptons and unable to cancel, they left everything to Jake until I was ready to come home. It irked them – relying so heavily on him. It still does.

Since then, I've been subject to hundreds of lectures about how they expect more of me, that I should be more responsible, that I was lucky Jake, and the guys were there to help me. Things I know already, but with the guilt consuming me, I sit back and take each and every one, which always finishes with them telling me they love me and are just happy to have me home safe.

Being out cold for almost five days, the stress on my system and lack of nutrition is obvious. I look like a shadow of myself. My cheeks are sunken, I have dark circles under my eyes and even my hair is brittle, compared to its normal full and glossy self. Whatever those guys gave me, has wreaked havoc on my system and it's going to take a long time for my body to recover.

Exhaustion doesn't even begin to cover how I'm feeling. I've had messages from Shaun and Sam telling me not to worry about my shifts at the bar, that I can take as long as I need. Zoe and Sophie just keep ringing and crying.

But I'm not ready to see anyone yet. What nobody knows about, apart from Jake, who witnessed them during my unconscious days, are the nightmares. The insecurities that have crept into my mind, imagining what could have happened.

No one can take away that feeling of helplessness. The memory of feeling and hearing the world around you, but not being able to do anything. It was like being dead, but alive. I'm not ready to speak to anyone about it yet. I won't admit out loud that the reason my recovery is taking so long and I'm still so ill is because I never fully rest. I lay awake at night, terrified to go to sleep and terrified where my mind will wander.

I just need time.

✳✳✳

It's been almost two weeks since that day. I've avoided everyone. They get it, as I asked Jake to let them know I needed space, and I would get in touch when I was ready. But now, as time is passing by, I'm becoming restless and major cabin fever is creeping in. Nothing is helping to settle my mind.

Looking out the window from my bed, where I've been sitting watching some random Netflix boxset on my laptop, I notice the weather outside looks stormy and unsettled. One of my favorite things to do when I'm feeling out of sorts is to run in the rain. There's something calming about the feeling of the water on your skin. The raw feeling of nature, like your emotions.

I decide it's exactly what I need to clear my head, throw on my running gear and trainers, and pull my hair back into a ponytail. Luckily, Mom and Dad chose today to go back to work, so I have no one to answer to. I know they'd put up a huge protest at me going out on my own, so soon after what happened.

I put my headphones in and quickly leave the house. Setting a rock playlist going, my feet instinctively hit the pavement in a rhythm. I've no idea where I'm going, all I know is I want to run. Run until I'm too tired to think anymore.

I sprint along the sidewalks and make my way over Brooklyn Bridge, feeling euphoric from the running high I haven't felt in a long time. The further I go the harder my body wants to push. I've never run this far ever, but I don't care. I make my way into Manhattan and then I push even harder.

At some point the weather worsens and the rain starts pounding against the roads, drenching me to the bone. As it's still the height of summer, it's red hot, so the water is refreshing and a welcome relief.

I eventually find myself at Central Park. I must have been running for a couple of hours, but it feels like I've only been going a few minutes. Slowing my pace, I meander round the park, relishing in how quiet and peaceful it is, despite it being the middle of the afternoon at the busiest time of year.

When I reach the one place I always come to when I need to think, I sit on the ground to rest, looking up at the statue of Peter Pan, the boy who never grew up.

Wouldn't it be great to be a child without any worries or huge decisions to make?

Without thinking, my fingers send a message from my cell to Jake. [I need you. At my favorite place.]

I don't overthink, I just do. And then wait.

It was never really a question of if he would come. Deep down I knew he would. So, it doesn't come as a surprise, when a while later, I hear his voice in the distance, shouting my name. I don't turn even though I hear him. I'm not ready to see him yet. The fact he still knows where I would be after all this time sends fireworks through my body.

He stalks over, yanking me up from the ground and presses his body to mine, wrapping his arms tightly around me.

"What are you doing? You're going to make yourself even sicker."

I don't get a chance to answer as he grabs my hand and drags me away. Before long I find myself in the passenger seat of his car.

The heat our bodies are giving out, against the cool of the rain, makes the windows steam. Jake doesn't do anything to rectify it, he's in no rush to go anywhere. It acts as a barrier between us and the rest of the world. I turn towards him, my breath coming out in little pants. I'm not sure whether it's from the rush to his car, or his close proximity.

When I manage to find my voice, I say, "Thanks for coming to get me. How did you know where I was?"

He doesn't humor me. "Like you need to ask that."

We sit in silence staring out the front window of the car.

The tension building is unbearable and when I can't stand it anymore, I break it by saying, "Michael and I broke up. Officially. That's why I was so irresponsible the night of the festival. I know it's not an excuse, but I was just feeling … I don't know, like I needed to be free. I needed to let go of everything. I may have let a bit too much of my reasoning go."

"Zoe and Sophie told me when we were at the hospital," he replies, still looking at the windscreen.

"I'm so sorry I put you through that." I mean it and put everything I can into those words, hoping he understands.

"It's ok. I was angrier it happened to you, than I was actually at you."

"Really? Thank you though. For everything. I don't know what would have happened if you hadn't been there. Then for everything you did afterwards …"

It comes out of nowhere. He's cupping my face with both hands, forcing me to face him, as he rubs my cheeks softly with his thumbs.

"I broke up with Amanda the week after 4th of July. That's why I was so distant and that's what I wanted to tell you the night I invited you to see the band, but you had other things you wanted to talk about. I haven't had a chance to tell you since …"

He searches my eyes with his, for something, anything. There's nothing more to say. Every reason that we had to fight what's between us is gone. So, I don't.

I climb over the center console of his car, straddling his lap with my thighs. He looks taken aback, but soon recovers, grabbing hold of my thighs and rubbing his hands up and down them. Tilting his head back against the headrest he lets out a sigh. For once not frustration. Relief.

The sight of him looking content makes me needy and I lick my lips in anticipation. Not wanting to wait for him to start something, I begin peppering kisses along his jaw. Small kisses soon turn into more as I suck down, nipping gently.

Jake groans and his hips buck up into mine. I can feel how turned on he is and pull back, finding myself looking into those beautiful brown eyes. His hands tangle into my hair, and he brings my face towards his.

Finally, our lips crash together.

The first couple of kisses are clumsy, our want for each other overwhelming everything. But when he slides his tongue into my mouth, I'm in heaven and my heart pounds in my chest like it did six years ago. Only for him.

All I can focus on is being with Jake and feeling everything that we've denied ourselves all this time. For that snippet of time while I'm in his car and sheltered from reality, with the rain hammering down, I lose myself in Jake and his kisses. Nothing else matters, for now.

***

After our hot and heavy make-out session, Jake dropped me home. It's much later than I originally intended to be out, and I can see my parents are back, meaning I'm in for the third degree. They won't be happy I've left the house without letting them know where I was going, or that I was running so soon after being ill.

I brace myself for the onslaught as I walk through the front door, but as I move through the house all I get is silence. I know they're in, as the lights are on. Eventually, I find them sitting at the kitchen table waiting quietly, with a glass of wine each.

"Nice of you to let us know where you were," says Mom sternly, shaking her head.

"I'm sorry, I didn't thi-"

"That we would worry, when you're still recovering, after being plied with a date rape drug that could have killed you?" I watch as she grasps her wine glass tightly. I'm surprised it doesn't shatter in her hand with the strength she's using to grip it.

"I just needed to get out," I say. I hope they understand, but they're not going to let me get away lightly.

"That doesn't justify not letting us know where you were. What were you thinking running so far when you've only just started to recover? Do you understand at all, how hard those drugs hit your system? Running like that could have dehydrated you beyond repair. You could have done yourself even more serious damage ..."

"I know. I don't think I need to apolo- wait how did you know how far I ran?" It clicks that I haven't told them anything, so how did they know where I went?

"Jake rang your father."

I look to him and he nods his confirmation, staying silent. His disappointment in me is evident.

"Of course. So, Jake is suddenly the favorite? Can I just remind you both that a few weeks ago you were warning me off him?" It's unreasonable of me to get angry, when I was the one in the wrong, but I hate double standards, especially when it comes to Jake.

"Calm down, Abby. All I'm saying is it's funny Jake managed to call and let us know you were safe, when you, our own daughter, neglected to do so." She raises her glass and takes a large drink of wine.

"I forgot, ok. When are you guys going to give me some breathing space? I'm ok. I was lucky, nothing happened and I'm fine."

It feels like days of frustration from being mollycoddled by them are pouring out, but they need to hear it. What happened doesn't change that I'm an adult and capable of living my own life and making my own decisions.

I continue, "I need to start living my life again, which I can't do if you guys are constantly breathing down my neck. I never had to tell you where I was before, so why should I now?"

"I think you owe us a bit more respect than that, Abigail," Dad finally speaks up. "We get a call late at night, informing us you're in the hospital, having been drugged, and we're meant to just bounce back to normal? We're meant to be happy and pretend like nothing happened? We're your parents, we worry, that's how it works."

It's been years since we've had an argument like this, and it doesn't feel great.

"I know. Do you think I don't get it?"

A wave of emotion washes over me, and my shoulders start to shake uncontrollably. Before I know what's happening, I'm collapsed on the floor sobbing.

I haven't cried since the morning I woke up in Jake's bed, which is probably a bad thing. I've pushed everything to the back of my mind. Today I tried to run away from the feelings that were starting to surface but look where that's got me. Here with my parents, consumed by the raw emotions of what happened. What could have happened.

Luckily, they're the only people in the world, besides Jake and the girls, who I would let see me like this. They rush from their seats, both collapsing down beside me.

We sit there on the floor, for what feels like hours, my parents holding me as I let everything out. I don't think I'm just crying over what happened at the festival. I'm crying from the emotions of returning to Brooklyn, splitting up with Michael, being around Jake and my friends again.

I'm crying over the choices I'm still not ready to make.

Thirty

I t takes a couple of days after my breakdown for my parents to come around to the idea of me going back to work at Riffs. Eventually they give in when they understand how crazy it's driving me, being at home alone all day.

It's been over a week since I've spoken to anyone and walking into the bar, I feel anxious, not knowing what their reaction will be. I'm certain Sophie and Zoe will be there waiting for me. It wouldn't be them if they weren't. They know this is the one place I can't avoid them or screen their calls.

I step through the door and two pairs of arms fly around me. I feel like I'm being suffocated by my two best friends.

"Guys, I can't breathe," I barely manage to say.

"Good. You deserve it after scaring the shit out of us like that," says Zoe.

"Please don't ever ignore us for that long again," says Sophie, looking at me sadly. "We thought you hated us and were never going to talk to us again after what happened."

They both have tears in their eyes, and I take a deep breath. I'm not going to be able to avoid this conversation.

"I don't hate you," I say. "And I don't blame you. You weren't the ones that put that stuff in my drink. You also weren't the ones that put that drink in my mouth. I had a choice, and I made a bad one, one that I won't make again. I'm sorry if I scared you and I'm sorry for ignoring you. I was feeling ashamed and needed some time to get my head around what happened." It feels good to let them know how I've been feeling.

"We understand," they say at the same time, nodding their heads in acceptance of my words.

I smile. "How about we make a pact?" They look expectantly. "A pact to act our age and not put ourselves in compromising situations like that again. What do you say?"

"Definitely," replies Sophie immediately.

Zoe looks away, her face full of regret. "I never understood why you guys were always getting on my case for getting wasted. I never really understood why it was such a big deal. Seeing you like that, Abby, so helpless ... I get it now. Anything could have happened, especially if Jake hadn't been there and acted so quickly. I promise, no more getting trashed with random guys."

"Good." Relieved, I shepherd the girls to a table and give them another smile, one that confirms the conversation is done with. It's time to move on. "So, besides all that drama, catch me up to speed?"

"There's not much to catch up on. We've all been quiet since what happened. You scared us all into being boring," laughs Zoe, fumbling with her hands. She's still nervous and scared I'm going to blame her for what happened. Like me, she just needs time.

"Well then, maybe I need to catch you guys up to speed."

I spend the next ten minutes briefly telling them how Jake looked after me while I was out cold. They both sing his praises, commenting on how much he's changed. Part of me wants to keep what happened with him outside the park a secret. But I know that's the last thing my friends would do and it's unfair to hold the details back from them.

"... there was a slight turn in events," I say.

Zoe raises an eyebrow in amusement. "Like a Jake related turn in events?"

"Yes. Did you guys know he and Amanda broke up?"

"He told us at the hospital when we were waiting for news from the doctor. He was tearing his hair out at the fact he might never get the chance to tell you." As Zoe speaks Sophie nods, confirming her story.

"We kissed ..."

"Took you long enough," Zoe smirks. "Now all you have to do is fuck and maybe you won't be so uptight all the time."

Normally I'd bite back, but I love that she's being normal with me again, so I don't.

Sophie chuckles and asks, "How was it?"

"Familiar ..." I reply.

"How was it really?"

"Life changing. If my head wasn't screwed before over what to do, it is now."

"Will you stay?" Sophie looks at me with hopeful eyes. I don't have it in me to give her an outright no, because I'm not really sure of the answer.

"I don't know. It seems silly to throw away everything I've worked so hard for just for one kiss. We've not even spoken since. It could have just been a one off?"

"No way," interrupts Zoe. "That guy is completely in love with you and has been since we were seventeen. When are you going to get that into your head?"

"I still don't get why we broke up in the first place though. Why all those wasted years if he's always felt the same about me?"

"Maybe there are some things you just don't need to know. Can you not just accept that despite what's happened, after all these years, Jake is still here and still in love with you?" Sophie's the romantic out of us all, so it's typical she would answer with this.

"I'm not sure."

I can see they're both frustrated at my answer. To them it seems like I'm being irrational. But I've suffered six years of heartache with no answer why. I don't think I can forget all that because of one kiss.

Jake didn't just break my heart, he obliterated it.

When we kissed, it was the first time it felt like it could start beating for someone again. I could let him in, let him mend the wounds he made, but if I did and he walked away ... If he broke my heart again, there would be no coming back from it.

✶✶✶

6 years earlier

It's been five days since I've heard from him. Five days since his mom kicked me out of the house. It's the longest time we've spent without speaking in the whole time we've known each other. To say it hurts is an understatement.

I don't need much, just to know he's safe and okay. Sometimes my mind goes on a rollercoaster, wondering where he is, if something has happened to him. Anything to explain the silence. Deep down I know that isn't the explanation for why he hasn't contacted me. If something had happened to him, someone in our group would know for sure and would have told me.

Instead, I have radio silence, and it hurts. Nothing can dull the ache in my chest, or the churning feeling in my gut that something isn't right, that something bad is about to happen. As if he's reading my mind, my cell lights up on my desk, next to the homework I've been attempting for the past four hours.

I take deep breaths in and out, looking at his name on the screen. A feeling of dread crawls over me, making my skin break out in goosebumps. Every part of me screams not to open the message, shouts that ignorance is bliss and to give myself a few more hours pretending everything is fine. But I know I can't do that. I need to know what's wrong.

With every ounce of strength, I have, I open the message.

Jake [We need to talk]

Me [Ok]

Jake [I'm outside]

I hate how readily available I am for him. For all I know these past five days he's been running around with whoever he likes. Doing things we haven't done, while I've been here moping and waiting for him.

Even though I want to message back that I'm unavailable, make him think I'm busy without him, I can't because I need to know what is going on. So, I walk down the stairs slowly, feeling slightly numb. It's a little bit like that feeling when your parents tell you they have bad news. Everything goes into slow motion.

I feel hopeful that at least I'm going to get some answers, rather than constantly wondering what is going on. As I walk out the door, he's standing at the bottom of the steps that lead up to my house. He looks up as he hears the door click shut behind me, with a sad expression on his face. It's then that I know this isn't going to be good.

Walking down slowly, the only thing that could make this situation worse would be for me to fall on my ass. I watch him shove his hands into his jean pockets, looking down at the ground, stubbing it angrily with his toe.

I'm the one to break the awkward silence. "So ..."

"Sorry I've not been in touch. Things have been difficult since the other night. It's taken time to get things straight." His tone is off, and his voice doesn't sound familiar. I try not to focus on it.

"Right." I nod as if I know what he's talking about. Really, I have no clue where this conversation is going. All I can feel is that little knot of dread.

"I don't want to drag this out any longer than I have to. So, I guess I'll just say what I came here to ..."

I've not been able to meet his eyes since I came out the door, but I look up now, hoping that if I catch his eye for even a second, I'll be able to change his mind. Change what deep down, I know is about to come out of his mouth.

He won't look at me. He looks over my shoulder, distant.

As he speaks his voice is arrogant and cold. "I can't do this anymore, Abby. I'm sorry, it's just not gonna work out. I'm ending whatever this is."

271

Tears sting my eyes. I don't want them to fall and shed the last bit of dignity I have. I don't want him to see how much I care, how much I love him, when everything he said was clearly a lie.

"Was it me? Did I do something wrong?" I ask, shakily.

I don't expect the answer I get and the harshness of it shatters my heart into a thousand pieces.

"Nah you didn't do anything. I guess you're just not The One for me. I met someone else and we've been seeing each other these past few days. She's given me things you wouldn't, you know what I mean. So yeah, that's it, I'd better get going, I have practice with the guys. Thanks, Abby, it's been fun."

He doesn't say anything else, doesn't touch me, doesn't even look at me. All he does is walk away without a backward glance. I watch the guy I gave my heart to, the one that knew all my innermost thoughts and fears, the one who I was willing to give every part of me to, walk away to another girl. All because she could give him what he wanted faster, carefree and without any strings attached.

My chest tightens and I'm struggling to catch my breath, as the reality of everything he said sets in. Crumbling down onto the steps, I sit there for what feels like hours, silently crying and shaking, watching where Jake walked away. But it wasn't Jake who came today, it was a cold stranger that spoke to me and discarded my heart so easily.

It's dark and freezing when my mom comes rushing out, down the steps, frantically asking what's wrong and shouting that I'm going to make myself sick. If I thought I'd broken before, I was wrong, because then I really do. Every emotion I've held in comes pouring out as I sob in her arms. I don't know how to make it stop.

She says that everything will be alright, and it will get better.

But I don't know if it will, because Jake has broken my heart, ripped it out and shattered it into tiny pieces. I don't know if I'll ever be able to put it back together again.

Thirty-One

My first shift back at the bar is hard going, even though I know Shaun has gotten extra staff in to break me in steadily. After the long run I took a few days ago, I feel broken and the exertion of being on my feet again for so long is exhausting. The toll the drugs have taken on my body is hard to accept. It's difficult to get my head around how something so small, could have the lasting effect it has and do the damage it's done.

Even though it's tiring, it's nice to be around my friends again and I regret avoiding them for so long. Once the initial awkwardness is out of the way and they're reassured that I'm not a complete wreck, they begin to treat me like normal. That normality and positivity is what I need to bring me around. I want to get on with my life, my lesson has been learnt.

Shaun and Sam spend most of the shift cracking jokes and staying close by my side. I keep telling them I'm fine and they don't need to watch over me like I might break, but they refuse to budge. My shift is close to ending and I'm relieved when Shaun gives me a break from the front of house, giving me the task of restocking the bar before it gets busy.

I'm struggling to reach some of the stock on a higher shelf, huffing and puffing unattractively, when a voice from behind me asks, "Need a hand?"

I instantly recognize Jake's voice, but it doesn't change the fact he's scared the shit out of me, sneaking into the stock room without making his presence known. Before my body has a chance to catch up with my brain, I instinctively flip around, elbowing him hard in the gut. Bending over in agony, he coughs and splutters in pain.

"Oh my god! Jake, are you ok?"

He offers a pained grunt, unable to speak. I wait for him to catch his breath back.

"Thanks for that," he mumbles eventually. When he tries to stand up straight, he winces.

"Well, seriously. What on earth? Who sneaks up like that on someone, alone in a storeroom? What did you expect?" I say.

"I thought you heard me come in," he says, sheepishly, realizing his error.

"Obviously not, or I would have turned around and at least said hi. You know, like most normal people do."

I place my hands on my hips and throw him a stern look. He's lucky I didn't have the pepper spray Dad gave me to hand.

"Now that we've cleared up that you can look after yourself, do you need a hand?" he asks.

"I could do." I smile sweetly. Really, I'm exhausted and if I can get out of doing this last task by batting my eyelashes a little then I will.

Looking up at the shelves above me, he asks, "Which ones do you need down?"

I begin pointing to the different beers I need off the shelves, telling him exactly how many to put in the crate I've set on the floor. I wind up taking full advantage by getting him to help with the rest of the stock, despite it being within easy reach. I hope he hasn't noticed that he's doing my job for me, as I sit on the floor, admiring his muscles flexing beneath his t-shirt, each time he reaches for handfuls of bottles.

"I may as well apply for a job here." I can hear the humor in his voice without looking at his face.

Busted. I offer another sweet smile and flutter of my eyelashes when he turns to look at me. "You were doing such a good job. It seemed a shame to interrupt you."

"Yeah. Right."

I'm treated to a deep, throaty chuckle and it dawns on me this is the first time I've really heard him laugh since I've been back in Brooklyn. It feels so normal. There's no bickering, no hateful looks towards each other. We're just two people together, laughing and enjoying each other's company.

The kiss in the car changed more than I anticipated, and for the better. Any past issues that were getting in the way of us having a normal relationship have disappeared. For him at least.

The silence from my pondering hasn't gone unnoticed. "You ok?" he asks, uncertainly.

"I was just thinking. It's the first time I've heard you laugh ... since I've been back, I mean."

He smiles solemnly. "It's been a rocky road, hasn't it?"

"That's one way of putting it."

I go to stand, and Jake offers his hand, helping me up off the ground. My hand tingles when it meets with his and I take in a sharp breath. Jake notices as his eyes focus on me, full of intent. He tugs firmly, so

I'm flush with his chest and the contact with his body causes mine to heat up everywhere.

"I can't stop thinking about that kiss," he says and trails his nose lightly across my skin which burns everywhere he touches.

I lick my bottom lip involuntarily and my chest rises and falls, hard. The longer I stand in Jake's arms, the more my body responds. I don't get chance to reply to his words, as his mouth meets with mine and all coherent thoughts disappear.

At first, he's hesitant, not knowing how I'll react to him kissing me, but I love that he's taking what he wants. Lucky for him, I have no control, and even if I did, I wouldn't stop. The kiss deepens and I feel him pushing into me, demanding more.

We walk backwards and he presses me up against the storeroom door, caging me in and kissing me more forcefully, as he slowly trails his hands under my top. I'm incapable of doing anything but kiss him back with the same passion he's giving me. My body has become a useless, writhing mess and I'm open to anything he wants to do to me. I would say yes to everything.

His hands wander everywhere, tracing over all the sensitive parts of my skin, brushing briefly over my breasts and then making their way down to my pants. His kisses have moved to my neck and as he nips and sucks at the overly sensitive skin, electricity shoots through me. I circle my hips against his, feeling how hard he is and needing the friction between my legs, to soothe the ache.

"Jake ..." I moan.

He responds by thrusting his hips into mine, grinding against me over and over as he covers my mouth with his, kissing me deeper than he ever has in a bid to keep me quiet. From this alone I could come apart completely, but he has other plans. He begins fumbling with the button on my jeans and I respond, doing the same to his. I'm desperate to feel him inside me.

Any reservations I might have about the fact we're about to have sex for the first time up against a storeroom door go flying out the window. We could be in the middle of the bar for all I care.

"I want you inside me, now," I say, into his ear.

This only encourages him, as he kisses me desperately, trying not to break contact as he struggles to remove the few layers of clothing that stand between us. Just as his hand begins to dip into my pants and I hold my breath, preparing for the first time Jake will touch me like this, there's a hammering at the door.

"Ignore it," I say, urging him to keep going.

I can see in his eyes the battle between wanting to fuck me and the reality that he was about to do so against a door, in his best friends' bar.

The hammering comes again, but this time more persistently and Shaun shouts through the wood, "Jake, you better not be screwing Abby in my storeroom. Not cool, bro."

I let out a frustrated sigh, knowing he's got him, nothing will happen now. I look up at Jake and he gives me a disappointed frown. The moment is gone, but maybe it's for the best. Do I really want my first time with him to be in a dingy, damp storeroom against a door?

He places a few affectionate kisses on my lips, and I can feel my heart rate settling back to normal. Reluctantly he pulls away and when I've adjusted my clothing, I go back to finishing the job I originally came in for.

Turning the handle to leave the storeroom, he looks back and says in a low voice, "I'm done waiting, Abby. I've waited six years. Next time, nobody will stop me fucking you."

He leaves with a smirk on his lips, and I stand gawping at his back as he walks away.

What have I gotten myself into?

Thirty-Two

Everything should be on my mind. What direction I'm going to take at the end of summer with my career. Whether I'm going to leave everything that has become important to me. My friends, my parents, the city I've fallen in love with again after all these years.

There's plenty on my plate, with work from dad and shifts at the bar filling the gaps in between. But only one thing consumes my mind. Jake. I am royally screwed.

Everything that had seemed important suddenly doesn't. Everyone keeps commenting how happy and content I seem. That I'm more relaxed. I've even managed to go for a few girls' nights with Sophie and Zoe without commenting on how much they're drinking. Zoe asked over and over if I was ok, stating I wasn't being normal.

The irony is, the one thing, or should I say person, who caused me the most stress over all these years, has been the one to cure all my worries, fretting and sleepless nights. That's the scariest thing of all.

It's terrifying, the thought of handing my heart on a plate to Jake again, when he broke it so badly the first time. It seems crazy that he's the one to fix it. It feels like there's more on the line this time and there would be no coming back from this. Fool me twice, shame on me.

"Earth to, Abby, you there?" Zoe snaps her fingers in front of my face with an amused smile.

"Sorry. I zoned out there."

"Let me guess, Jake on the brain?"

I frown. "That obvious?"

"Well, he seems to be the only thing your brain can deal with at the moment. It wasn't a hard guess," she chuckles.

Falling back on my bed, I groan. "I'm done for."

"Seriously? I can't watch you do this to yourself. Up," she demands. She snaps her fingers in my face for the second time in a few minutes.

"When did you get so authoritative?"

"Someone has to. You obviously checked out when Jake decided to start sticking his tongue down your throat again."

I wrinkle my nose in disgust. "Gross. How do you make everything sound so nasty?"

"It's a talent," she sings.

I roll my eyes and laugh. "So, you were saying?"

"Wait! For this we need wine."

She walks over to my dresser where there are two glasses ready, and fills them to the brim, then turns back, handing me one.

"For the first time in years, you seem happy. Yes, you got burned in the past, but we all have been in one way or another. That's life, Abs, it's not perfect, and at times it's pretty damn painful." She looks at me with a grimace. There's something she's not saying, but before I have a chance to ask what, she continues, "Surely, it's better to get on the rollercoaster, as scary as it is, and experience the highs and lows, rather than stand watching."

"I think I get what you're saying?" I'm actually totally confused. She has a habit of giving these random, life affirming speeches, none of which I've ever been able to make any sense.

"You don't. If you did, you'd be with Jake right now. Yes, he hurt you, but we were all young and didn't know what we were doing. What matters is that we're here now, and despite everything, this time round he's fighting for you."

My mind zeros in on the words *despite everything*. "Is there something you're trying to say that I don't know about?"

She shakes her head. "It's not my story to tell. You know who you need to ask if you want answers to that question. Please, for once, Abby, just be. You spent years pissing about, pretending you were happy with this picture-perfect life, when really you tapped out and played it safe. It's time to get back in the game. Yes, you might lose, but you also can't win if you're not playing."

I take a large gulp of my drink and look her straight in the eyes, contemplating what she's saying. "You've become deep in your old age, oh wise one."

That gets me a punch in the arm. "Seriously, shut up!"

"Ow! That hurt." Really hurt. The girl can pack a mean punch when she wants to.

"That'll teach you for trying to put me down when I was offering you some sound advice," she sniffs. It dawns on me she's spent some time thinking about what she was going to say, and I may have hurt her feelings a little by turning it into a joke.

"I'm sorry and you're right. So, what do I do?"

"You drink your wine and put on the sexiest outfit you own then get yourself to this party with me. Don't give Jake any other option but to ravage you all night long."

Trying not to laugh and risk offending her again, I repeat with a straight face, "Ravage?"

She does that annoying eyebrow wiggle at me. "Just wait. Long awaited sex is the best kind of sex."

"How would you know? When have you ever waited long enough for sex to be long awaited?"

Instead of an answer, I get a pillow to the face and we fall back on the bed laughing harder than we have for years.

✺✺✺

A couple of hours later we make our way to the party that Jake and his band are throwing at their place. I haven't been back since he looked after me when I was drugged, but I didn't take in much of my surroundings then. It was all a haze.

When we reach their house, I take in the surroundings, thinking it's typical Jake. It's an old building that's been converted into trendy, shared living. To most this is the dream, maybe not quite so much for Jake, as he was raised surrounded by money. For him, it must be refreshing to not be living under his family's roof with their pretentious ways.

Zoe makes her way quickly up the steps to the front door, and as we're running late, Sophie is already inside waiting. Looking back over her shoulder, she says, "Party time," and blows a kiss, before opening the front door, causing music to spill out into the night.

The house is literally pumping and there are bodies everywhere, crashing together as laughter fills the air. There's a small stage set up in the large, open plan living area. A crowd has congregated cheering loudly as Jake's band is finishing setting up. We made it just in time and they begin playing as we find a place to stand.

When the music starts, everyone becomes lost in one song after another. Each one is hypnotizing, reaching a part of every person in the room, demanding their attention. There's no questioning how they got a deal with my dad's label.

"Good, aren't they?" says Sophie into my ear, handing me a bottle of beer.

"Yeah," I reply. It's all I can manage as I'm mesmerized watching them from a distance, knowing Jake still hasn't spotted me. "They get better every time I see them."

"They got the deal you know ..." She watches for my reaction out of the corner of her eye.

"What did you say?" I take a long drink of my beer and turn my attention towards her fully, so I can take in what she says.

"They got the record deal. They signed it today. I guess they wanted to keep it quiet until it was official. Sam told me before they went on."

I don't get a chance to dwell on what this means for Jake and me. For the future. The current song they're playing ends and my attention is stolen when Sam says into the mic, "This one's for Abby."

He points directly at me with a wink and I watch Jake's eyes follow the direction he's pointing in, finding me. His whole expression relaxes, as if he wasn't sure I'd come, even though I promised I would. The song starts and my feet move forward through the crowd, so I can see them better. My eyes don't leave Jake's for a second, as he plays the guitar effortlessly without looking away from me.

Those few minutes of the song feel like an eternity, and nothing else in the room matters. It sounds cliché, but I'm entranced by the guy standing in the background. The one who often gets overlooked, never demands attention, but brings the music to life by strumming out melodies that vibrate through your bloodstream and resonate in your soul.

By the end of the song, I'm completely useless, lost in everything Jake. So much so, I'm barely aware they've stopped playing, until he moves towards me with the crowd cheering in the background. I stand blinking, trying to gather my bearings, but don't get much of a chance as I catch his expression.

He approaches me like he's stalking his prey. God, I hope that's what he's doing. Every part of me is throbbing and my body aches to have him inside me. Six years of foreplay is a long time and I'm not willing to wait any longer.

He grabs the beer in my hands and places it down, I'm not sure where. Then he grabs my hand firmly, pulling me through the crowd in a hurry. We receive knowing glances from most of our friends as we pass them by without acknowledging them. He guides me out of the main room and along the hallway. I stumble as I struggle to keep up with him.

He catches me by the waist, leans in and murmurs, "Steady, Abby. I can't fuck you if you're injured."

My heart almost stops. After all this time he's confirmed it's going to happen. With that promise, I'll be damned if anything is going to get in our way.

Taking the stairs two at a time, I catch Zoe's eye briefly through the spindles of the bannister. She thrusts her hips backwards and forwards and begins to make a blowjob motion with her mouth. I shake my head embarrassed, but all she does is laugh.

When we reach the top of the stairs, Jake can't contain himself any longer. It takes me by surprise when his hands are all over my body, but it doesn't take me long to catch up. I moan into his mouth, as his hands make their way under my top, grasping my breasts over the thin material of my bra before they make their way around the back, battling with the clasp.

I pull away panting and give him a stern look. "Jake. Our first time is not going to be a show for the rest of the party."

He steps back laughing, and mumbles something to do with getting carried away, before opening the door and dragging me into his room.

The door slams shut and as he presses me back up against it, I feel him turn the lock. It's like we never left the storeroom at the bar, but this time, we both know there will be no interruptions. He's relentless as he starts to consume my body with his mouth and I'm a puddle on the floor. I can't do anything but groan in satisfaction. Hell, I can barely keep myself standing upright.

He chuckles as he nuzzles his face in between my breasts. "You ok there?"

I manage to form a coherent sentence and croak out, "I need you inside me. Fucking me. Now."

I've never been particularly forward when it comes to sex, but there's a side to me that Jake brings out. One I didn't know I had.

Pulling away, he stares down at me with a dark look in his eyes. "I think this is the first time I've enjoyed your snarky attitude." I let out a yelp when he slaps my ass and lifts me in the air and my legs wrap around his waist.

Carrying me, while kissing me deeply, his lips never leave mine. When we reach the bed, he reluctantly pulls away dropping me down gently. I whimper at the feeling of being separated from him, even just for a few seconds, but I'm immediately distracted as he begins removing his clothes. I can feel my mouth watering as he lifts his t-shirt over his head. As his arms rise upwards, his body flexes and I'm rewarded with the sight of his defined abs and strong chest.

"When did that happen?" I murmur. It comes out louder than intended, and he raises an eyebrow in question. "Shhhh, I'm just appreciating the view. Carry on." With that, I flop back on the bed like the cat that got the cream.

I'm rewarded when he slowly unbuttons his pants and steps out of them. My eyes almost pop out at the sight of his black boxers tented by his erection. With sex and Jake on the brain comes a lack of filter over my mouth, and I say, "I don't remember it being that big."

"Seriously, Abby?" He pulls me forward and tugs my top quickly over my head then makes quick work of my pants. "I suggest you shut up, or I'm going to have to spank you."

"I don't think that would shut me up."

He doesn't attempt to silence me with words again. He devours my mouth instead and all I can focus on is how amazing this feels after all this time. I've had moments of longing, when I've allowed myself to imagine what it would be like to have him, but none of those dreams have ever lived up to this reality.

Taking advantage of my silence, he reaches around my back and unclasps my bra. He palms my breasts at a mind-numbing pace that has me squirming underneath him. He only pulls away to drag my underwear down my legs, and then I'm naked in front of him for the first time.

As my brain catches up, part of me panics feeling slightly insecure, but then I remember that the years have been kind to my body. I'm better now than I was as a teenager. I have a woman's body and with that, comes a confidence you only get with age and experience.

He growls with satisfaction at what he sees in front of him, and then he's found a condom and is rolling it on quickly. Neither of us want foreplay. It's been too long a journey and anything other than the final act would be a waste of time. We both know what we want and it's not like it's needed. I've never been more ready for anyone in my life.

I take hold of him, wanting to feel what he's like in my small hands. "Get this straight," I say. "I do not want gentle. I want you to fuck me like you've imagined it every day for the past six years."

"You have no idea what you're letting yourself in for," he smirks.

"Try me."

With that last challenge, he thrusts inside me all the way. I cry out in ecstasy, as he begins a relentless pace that tips me over the edge quicker and more intensely than anyone ever has.

It's not perfectly romantic. It's messy and complicated, but that's exactly what Jake and I have always been. After all this time, it's our own kind of perfect.

Thirty-Three

T he next morning, I wake up with a slightly fuzzy head, feeling disorientated. It also feels like I'm in bed with a furnace. Opening one eye slightly, it all comes flooding back as I take in my surroundings. Rather than a hangover, my fuzzy head is due to the multiple rounds of mind-blowing sex I had with the guy lying next to me. Jake. He's also the source of my overheating. He's sprawled across the bed with his leg and arm draped over me, possessively pulling me underneath him, as if he's scared to let me go.

I know the feeling. After all this time, it feels like a dream that I'm here lying next to him, with his naked body pressed against mine. In fact, a dream is an understatement, I've died and gone to heaven.

The sun streams through his bedroom window, casting soft morning shadows across his back which is covered in a giant scarab beetle tattoo. I finally got my answer about tattoos in unseen places. I can't stop my eyes tracing a journey all over, drinking in the sight before me. I could happily spend every morning for the rest of my life like this. I don't know how long I lay there, watching Jake sleep, or so I think …

"Are you done staring at me? I know I'm a sight to behold, but even I have a limit for how long someone can watch me sleeping." He opens one eye, with a cheeky smile on his face.

"Sorry. It's taken a while to get my head around being here, with you. You know, like this." I don't want to feel shy around him, but this is all so new. At least being honest, he knows how I'm feeling.

"Worth the wait?"

"More than you know." He gives me a warm smile, not breaking eye contact until his gaze begins to wander downwards, over the full length of my body. I hadn't noticed I wasn't covered by a sheet, probably due to the hot water bottle lying next to me.

Normally I'd rush to cover myself up. In fact, normally I'd be up early, making sure any hint of morning breath and non-perfection were gone, ready for when Michael woke up. That's how he liked me, perfect. Things aren't like that with Jake. Neither of us are perfect, our relationship has always been anything but. To force this moment and make it picture perfect would make it something we're not.

That's why everything feels more real, because it's so raw. The feelings, everything, are intense. Neither of us has any control over this thing that is happening and that's what's so scary. I guess sometimes scary isn't always a bad thing.

"Penny for your thoughts," says Jake snapping me back to reality.

I'm distracted by the hungry look in his eyes. "Again?"

"What can I say, we've got years of catching up to do."

I let out an uncharacteristically girly giggle, as he pulls me on top of him so are bodies are completely flush with each other. Kissing him deeply, I begin trailing my lips down his neck, then slowly make my way down his chest.

When I reach his stomach and the trail of hair leading lower, I look up through my eyelashes innocently and say, "I guess we better get started then."

✷✷✷

We spend the rest of the morning in bed, until we both admit defeat without any food. Like the true New Yorkers, we are, we order breakfast in, because in New York you can get anything delivered to your door.

Ten tons of waffles, bacon and syrup, and a gallon of coffee later, I finally manage to drag myself out of Jake's bed and home to shower. I promise to see him at some point later. Before I even reach the corner of his block, my cell vibrates in my pocket.

When I open it, it's a message from Jake. [Too long apart already.]

Being the lovesick female, I am, I'm still unable, hours later, to wipe the smile off my face that he put there.

I'm sitting at the breakfast bar in my parents' kitchen, editing some photos for the record label, when my cell begins ringing with a call from an unknown foreign number. I know it's one of the calls I've been dreading for weeks. Of course, it would come today, the night after Jake and I have finally made it clear to each other what we want.

I answer reluctantly. "Hello, this is Abby speaking."

"Hi, Abby," says a familiar, South African voice, that I know to be Sooz, the head of PR for the company I interviewed with in Cape Town. "Do you have time to speak?"

"Hi, Sooz, of course I have time. Firstly, can I apologize for taking so long to get back? The decision has been a lot harder to make than I thought."

"No need to apologize, we understand. Making a permanent move around the world is a big decision and we know how many offers you have on your plate. However, I'm calling because our situation has changed. Unfortunately, the pressure is on for us to fill the position you applied for sooner than expected. With that in mind, our deadline has been cut to the end of the week, and in case you decided to turn down the offer, we will need an answer from you by midday tomorrow."

"Tomorrow?" I gulp in shock.

"I know it's short notice, but our hands are tied and there's nothing we can do. Don't make the decision lightly, Abby. I know it's a big one, but you need to give me a call no later than midday tomorrow, otherwise I will be forced to fill the position with someone else, regardless of what your answer is."

"I understand. Thank you. I'll be back in touch shortly."

We hang up and I drop my head to the counter with a bang.

"Everything ok, sweetheart?" my mom asks.

I look up to find both my parents standing in front of the bar, with concern on their faces.

"I suppose I could say yes, but also no?"

"Expand ..."

"The South Africa job has pushed the deadline for my decision earlier. Like midday tomorrow earlier."

"Ahhh ..." Dad sighs knowingly. "Have you made a decision then?"

"No way near. And the decision has gotten harder."

"Jake?" asks Mom skeptically. I know neither of them are going to like the answer.

"That obvious?"

"Baby, there's only one person that could bring out that ridiculously happy smile you've had on your face this week," she says sadly.

"So, are you together?" Dad asks.

"I guess we are. I'm not really sure?" I think it's a given after everything we've said and done, but we've yet to have that 'official' conversation and I've learnt to never jump to conclusions, even if something seems obvious.

"Right," he replies coldly. Of the two of them, he's the one I thought might be more open to the idea of us, as he works with Jake and knows him better.

"Is something wrong?"

"I wouldn't say wrong. I'm just worried."

"About?"

He hesitates before answering. "You know Jake's band signed the record deal yesterday?"

"Sophie mentioned it last night, but I never really got a chance to chat with Jake about it." My cheeks flush knowing why. I hope neither of them notice or this is going to be even more awkward.

"It's big, Abby. Really big. Mainstream big. It would mean being on the road most of the time. Tours, groupies, interviews. Maybe now wouldn't be the best time to start something up again?"

"Because you think he wouldn't be able to keep his dick in his pants?"

"Abby," Mom says sternly.

"No, that's not it. I don't doubt how Jake feels about you, or you him. We know how he's felt all along, and if things hadn't been the way they were back then, I guess he never would have let you go."

"Why does everyone keep saying that?" I grumble to myself, making a mental note this is one conversation we still need to have.

He holds his hands up and says, "Jake will need to explain that to you. But the decisions made back then, have placed you both on different paths in your lives ..." He pauses for a second, thinking about what he's saying. "What I'm trying to say is you're both at a point in your lives where you're about to achieve your dreams. Everything is yours for the taking, but can you really give it your all, if you're constantly thinking and worrying about each other? Wanting to be with each other and not being able to?"

What he's saying is true even if I don't want it to be, meekly I say, "So you're basically trying to tell me we'll hold each other back?"

"Yes, that. Or, if one of you gave up your dream for the other, would you regret it and resent each other in the end? Would it be better to wait? If this is meant to be you will find your way back to each other. But he's walked away once, right now, can you wholeheartedly say you trust him not to do it again?" His expression is somber, and I know he hates being the one to have this conversation with me.

After six long years, last night was perfect, it was a glimpse of what our lives could be like and I want to scream in frustration. It's not fair. We want each other, need each other, but the way fate keeps intervening, it feels like we're just not meant to be.

"We've just found our way back to each other, after everyone telling me to give him a second chance. Telling me he'd changed. Now you're telling me to give up on us?"

"I'm only thinking of the both of you, honey."

"I need to go for a walk." I stand up and begin walking out of the house.

"We've only got your best interests at heart, baby," Mom shouts after me.

When I get outside, I pull out my cell, dialing Zoe immediately. "Can we meet?"

Thirty-Four

"What are you going to do?" Sophie has tears in her eyes, not happy that our summer bubble is about to pop.

"I really don't know." I place my head in my hands, wanting to check out for a while. This whole situation sucks.

"You don't have long to decide," says Zoe, as if she's being helpful.

I look up and roll my eyes. "You know, I really love it when you both state the obvious."

Zoe narrows hers at me in response. "You don't need to be, bitchy, we're here to help remember. Would you like us to leave?"

"I'm sorry. It's just my time has literally run out and I feel like my hand is being forced." I don't feel ready to make such a big decision, not yet. I've only just started to make sense of one area of my life and now straight away I'm expected to jump in and solve another. Life can be harsh sometimes.

"Really, you need to do what's best for the both of you." I don't want to point out to Sophie, always the romantic, that really, I shouldn't let Jake influence this decision, especially when we've just had sex.

"I get that, I do. But we've just found our way back to each other. It seems ironic that our careers are suddenly taking us in completely opposite directions."

"What's the one thing that Jake has always wanted? I mean besides you?" ask Zoe.

"To make it big in music."

"Do you think he'd follow you, if you chased your dreams? Or even stay here and be with you if that's what you wanted, rather than following his career?"

"Potentially ..." I think he would, but the fact he walked away the first time makes me not so sure.

"Could you watch him do that?" she asks.

I get where she's going with this, although I don't want to answer because I know what it means.

I reply, "No. It would kill me watching him give up everything he's worked for. Especially when we're only just starting out and we don't even know whether we'd work together as a couple."

"It kills me to ask this, but if you weren't together, would you be able to stay here, knowing Jake will be coming home on occasions. That you'll see each other but not be able to be together?"

I shake my head. "No, it would hurt too much." Even thinking about being in that situation, after the night we shared, is physically painful. I could never stand on the outside, wondering what it would feel like to really be with him and have all of him. Not now I finally know.

Zoe says sadly, "I think you've got your answer."

My eyes widen in shock. "You're telling me to go?"

She sighs, "I'm not telling you to do anything. Neither of us are because of course we don't want you to leave again. But sometimes you have to not be selfish if it's what's best for the person you love."

"If you took the South Africa job, what would happen with the job in Australia?" asks Sophie.

"I would just have to let them down. The position doesn't start for another couple of months, which would be too long to be here and reminded of him constantly."

"Well then, I agree with Zoe. You have your answer." Tears are running down Sophie's face. "I'm going to miss you so much."

"At least it's a new place to party?" I'm not sure whether I'm trying to convince them or myself.

"This definitely calls for drinks." Zoe stands up, ready to head to the bar. "I'm guessing you're going to tell him tonight?"

"Yeah ... I also need to figure out the time difference so I can ring them back and confirm the job." The words coming out of my mouth feel alien, it feels like I'm in a parallel universe. Every part of me aches to jump back twenty-four hours and relive those perfect hours with Jake.

"You're going to need something to numb the pain. My best heartbreak numbing cocktail is coming up." Zoe's a woman who means business when she stalks off to the bar. It's not ideal, but it's her own way of coping. She'd never show how much she's hurting, she's too cool for that.

We're several rounds of drinks in, congregated in a large group laughing and joking when Jake arrives with Zach by his side. I feel uncomfortable as I smile up at him when he stands behind me, it hurts knowing what I'm about to put him through. He doesn't pick up on the vibes I'm giving off though, because he lifts me from my seat effortlessly and sits back down with me in his lap. He turns my face, drawing me in for a long, slow kiss that leaves me breathless and tingling everywhere. I close my eyes and let out a deep breath. He's not making what I'm about to do any easier.

"You taste amazing," he says quietly so the rest of the group can't hear, "but not as good as you tasted this morning. I could have you like that every day for the rest of my life and be the happiest man alive."

I look down at the table. My chest tightens, and my eyes burn as tears brim at the surface. I reach for my drink, taking a big gulp to force down the emotions threatening to burst out of me.

Sophie and Zoe shoot glances in our direction, but I look away quickly so as not to make it obvious to Jake, in front of the group, that something is wrong. Leaning back into him, I allow myself a little more time of me and him before it feels like the world will come crashing down around us.

The bubble we spend the next couple of hours in is a welcome distraction. But, as the evening moves on, I can't avoid the conversation any longer. At the same moment I decide it's time to talk, he leans in to kiss me. I awkwardly shrug him off and my heart tugs painfully at the hurt expression he gives me.

He whispers, "Is something wrong?"

"Can we talk somewhere a bit quieter?" I ask, trying not to give too much away with the tone of my voice.

"Erm, yeah sure?" He looks confused but follows my lead.

"Be back soon," I mutter to Zoe and Sophie. They nod, while Sam, Zach and Shaun don't hide the uncertainty on their faces.

I lead us out of the bar and further up the block away from the bars, where it's quieter and there aren't as many people around to hear our conversation. All the way, I avoid any contact with Jake. He notices because he shoves his hands into his jean pockets awkwardly.

"Is everything ok?" he asks. His voice falters and I can tell that he doesn't really want to ask the question, afraid of what the answer will be. It's like we've been transported back six years and our roles have been reversed. I struggle not to laugh at the irony of it all.

"Not really," I reply honestly.

"I guess a lot can change in twelve hours." His voice is bitter.

"Don't be like that, Jake," I plead. I shouldn't though, not when I know what I'm about to do.

"Like what, Abby? Pissed? Wanting answers as to why, after a night and morning together, you're suddenly doing a 180. Did I do something?" He steps towards me, and his face looks so vulnerable that I want to scream at how unfair the universe is being.

I step back. I know if I let him touch me, I'll crumble and lose the courage to do what needs to be done. "Why didn't you tell me the band signed a deal?"

He rubs his hand over his face. "That's what this is about?"

"Why didn't you tell me, Jake?"

"I don't know. It didn't seem important. I just wanted us to have some time together, see where this would go."

"No. You knew that if you told me, it would have changed things. That maybe I wouldn't have gone down the path I did with you last night."

"Come on, Abby. It wouldn't have changed things at all."

"Yes, it would, Jake. I can't be with you now. Not when you have something so big going on in your life."

He laughs, as if I'm being ridiculous. "Why not?"

"I don't want to hold you back. You've wanted this since high school. You need to focus, and it will be too much if I'm always there in the background."

"We can make it work. I don't want to give up on us. I won't, Abs."

"You did the first time, and you will again." I practically choke this part out, knowing it's opening all the old wounds we've worked to heal.

"I won't, I promise. Things are different this time." I want to believe him, but I can't.

"I've chosen the job in South Africa."

"We will still make it work. We can," he says desperately.

"No, we can't. It's too much too soon." Tears stream down my face. I don't even try to hide them.

He looks at me helplessly and says, "How will we know unless we try?"

"If we can't survive high school, how the hell can we survive the real world?"

My heart feels like it's tearing in two, I pray to God that he backs down and gives up, because I'm not sure how much fight I have left before I give in and drag him back into my arms.

"When did you become so negative? I can't believe you're just gonna give up when we can finally be together?"

I pause. "What do you mean?" He's being cryptic again. It's as if there's part of our story I'm missing. A part that would make sense of everything. It's no good though if he won't give it to me.

He looks away and says, "Forget it, it's not important."

301

"This is what I mean, Jake. You close off. Why did we break up the first time? Everyone keeps saying I don't know the real reason. Well tell me. Change my mind."

I'm practically begging at this point. Maybe if he gives me this, it will solidify what we have, make it seem like it could survive an ocean and all the other crap that life might throw at us. But without the truth how could I ever trust him? How can he be all in like he says he is, if he's not willing to give every part of himself, flaws and all, to our relationship. For me to be able to trust him, he has to trust me. If we can't come full circle together, what's the point?

The pain in his eyes in unbearable when he says, "I can't, Abby. I just can't. It changes everything."

"Then I'm sorry, but I'm not changing my mind."

He looks lost and his shoulders drop in defeat, thanks to the heartbreak that's engulfing us. I'm certain I can see tears beginning to the surface in his eyes. This is the real, Jake, not the cold, distant one that broke up with me all those years ago.

"Why are you doing this?" he asks.

"We're at the most important parts of our lives. What we've been working for all along. We can't just give it up on a whim. So, what ... we've fucked and suddenly that means everything? It's not enough right now, especially not to make it work long distance. It will be too much, and it will tear us both in half. Between our career and wanting to be with each other. If either of us gave up our dreams, we'd eventually end up resenting the other." I'm almost echoing my dad's words, it's the only way to get through this. I stop and take a deep breath.

"I'm not sure if you're trying to convince me or yourself."

"Both," I reply, "do you think this is easy?" Tears continue pouring down my face, as the adrenaline subsides and the reality of what I'm doing kicks in. "Last night was amazing. You know I'd be lying if I said it wasn't. That doesn't mean that it's right. I guess we've just got our timing wrong … again. Maybe it's a sign it's just not meant to be."

He rubs the back of his neck and asks, "When do you leave for South Africa?"

"In a few days. They wanted my answer immediately, so I think they want me there as soon as possible."

"This is really it? You're really doing this? Giving up on us and fucking off to the other side of the world?" The bitterness in his voice and sudden hate he has towards me is so strong it makes me feel sick.

"Jake … you were the one that gave up on us without a real explanation. And you're wondering why I'm giving up?"

"Because it's all about you and your feelings …"

"I've already told you, I'm doing this for the both of us, so we can pursue our dreams."

He throws his hands up and says loudly, "Bullshit, you're scared."

"Do you blame me?"

"Look, we're going around in circles and you've made up your mind. How about, Abby, you forget last night happened? That way your conscience is clear when you tell people you're leaving."

He doesn't give me a chance to reply. He shoves past without looking me in the eye and storms off along the sidewalk.

I'm tempted to call out to him, as waves of pain pass over me, but it would be pointless. I've said what needed to be said. Even if he doesn't believe me, I've done it for the best. For both of us. It doesn't make

303

the gut wrenching, heartbreaking feelings hitting me any easier.

So, six years later, I watch Jake's figure disappear into the distance for a second time, praying that I haven't made the biggest mistake of my life.

Epilogue

Jake

Loud hammering yanks me from my pit of self-pity, but there's no need to respond as the door flies open and Sam storms in.

"Was there any point in knocking?" I snap.

"Stop acting like a little bitch. What are you still doing here?"

"Excuse me?"

He rolls his eyes. "Come on man, you're not really that clueless ..."

I hold up my hands. "Guilty as charged."

He tugs on his crazy blond hair, making it stick out more than normal. "I swear between the two of you, it's no wonder you keep dancing in circles around each other. She's leaving ... today!"

"What's your point? Abby made it clear she didn't want anything to do with me." I flop back onto the bed and pick up my guitar, like I don't give a shit. But I'm distracted by her perfume, her scent lingering on the sheets.

"And you're just going to leave it at that? You're not going to fight for her?"

"Sam, she made it clear she wants nothing to do with me. She's given up."

"Bullshit! That girl has been in love with you since high school and you know it. We all do. If I'd have known you were going to give up so easily, I would have fought for her myself ... I've never stopped thinking about how it would feel to slip m–"

My anger flares and I fly off the bed towards him, grabbing him by the scruff of the neck and slamming him against the wall so hard the pictures hanging on the wall shake.

"That's more like it." He grins in my face. "Now stop fucking about, get some shoes on and let's go get your girl."

✗✗✗

Sam's car barely screeches to a halt outside Abby's home when I'm out and running up the steps. I bang my fist against the front door, praying somebody is in. When the door opens, I sigh in relief at the sight of John West. My face falls though when I see his expression.

"She's gone," he says.

I look at my watch confused. "No ... Sam said she wasn't leaving until this afternoon."

"She set off early to make sure she didn't get stuck in traffic."

Of course, super organized Abby. One of her most positive traits is now, to me, her biggest flaw. Why for once couldn't she have left at the normal time?

"What time's her flight?" I ask. "I could still make it."

John shakes his head. "I don't think that's a good idea, son." I flinch at his use of the word. No one in my life has ever used such a term of endearment. It feels wrong.

"Why? Don't you understand? I can tell her what she needs to hear, I'm ready." I know I sound frantic, but I can't keep wasting time like this if I stand a chance of catching her before she steps on that plane.

"Wait here, I won't be a moment." I watch in disbelief as he steps back into the house.

I haven't got a clue what he's playing at. If he wasn't technically my boss and the band's career didn't rest in his hands, I'd walk away and finish this myself. But I can't. He doesn't make me wait long, and slips back out quietly, glancing over his shoulder as if to check nobody is watching.

"Here," he says and hands over a wad of papers.

"What are the—" I stop in my tracks when my eyes settle on images. Hundreds of images of the band, from the day in Riffs when Abby photographed us for the label. *Wow!* I say to myself.

I can't take my eyes off them. They're perfect. Somehow, she's managed to capture the perfect lighting, perfect angle. She's caught the emotion on our faces as we perform at just the right second.

"Brilliant, isn't she ..." he says. His voice isn't happy and proud, it's sad. "Don't follow her."

I look up from the photos. "Why not?"

"You know why. It's not the right time."

"We could make it work."

He shrugs. "Maybe. But what if you couldn't? What if everything you'd both worked for, fell apart on a whim?" What he's saying sounds familiar. It's virtually the same thing Abby said to me when she ended things. "Don't hold her back, Jake. Don't hold yourself back."

"I love her."

"I don't doubt that. But sometimes love isn't enough. You and Abby both have growing to do, as people. You have so much to offer the world. You walked away from her years ago for the exact same reason, so it shouldn't be so difficult now ..."

I don't know how, but he knows the truth, I can feel it. He places a hand on my shoulder and squeezes gently.

"I'll see you at the label to sign the contracts for the West Coast tour on Friday. I know you'll make the right decision."

I watch as he shuts the door – and that's it, end of discussion. Abby's images are still in my hands. I want to tear them up in frustration. I turn and walk slowly down the steps.

Sam meets me at the bottom, his brows furrowed together. "What happened?"

"She's gone."

"Then let's go after her!"

I shake my head. "No."

Abby's right. Her dad is right. Now, isn't the time for us to be together. Too much is on the line and too much remains unsaid. There's still pain and animosity that neither of us can fully understand. We have so much growing to do as individuals on completely different paths, to discover who we really are.

"Then what are you going to do?" asks Sam.

"Don't worry, I have a plan."

We'll get our happily ever after – eventually. Not now, but somewhere in the future. I meant it all those years ago when I told her I loved her.

Abby West is *it* for me. She's my always.

308

Acknowledgements

I will keep this brief. First, a huge thank you to Peter. The late nights, temper tantrums and tears have all been worth it and we got there in the end. This book may not have graced the world without your understanding of Word ... who knew it was so complicated uploading a document?

Next, I would like to say thank you to my girls who have been so patient at times where mummy has been 'working'. They have inspired me to keep going and chase my dreams in the hope one day I will be an example to them to do the same.

Thank you to Sarah, my proofing goddess. What a tiring and painful job on top of everything you already do. You did it selflessly and never complained. I think we managed between us all to make it pass.

Lastly, and most importantly, to whom this book is dedicated, Babs. You were the first to ever lay eyes on my work and your expertise and patience have made it what it is today. I never dreamed you would even enjoy it, so thank you for believing it was worth putting out there and encouraging me to keep going.

And then to you. Thank you for reading and giving this book a chance. Without you it would not matter. And I promise there is a sequel.

Always Us

How do you mend a broken heart? If anyone has the answer let me know.

It's been two years since I chose to turn my back on the one that got away. I thought I was doing the best for both of us. Instead, I'm fighting to forget what it felt like being in his arms.

Now it's another summer, and this time, I'm surrounded by Rock Gods on Jake's European tour. It's the life most would dream of, but things are never that straight forward and a chance meeting with a stranger leaves me feeling torn.

Just when I think things can't get any worse, I'm faced with one of the biggest decisions I'll ever have to make.

They say the heart wants what it wants, but my heart wants two people at the same time.

Printed in Great Britain
by Amazon